It is up to the Emperors of London to protect the throne—without risking their hearts...

Governess Eve Merton would have fallen into serious trouble on her walk home if a handsome stranger had not stopped to help her. But when Mr. Vernon gives her a lift on his horse, he makes no secret of his attraction. As a well brought-up young lady, Eve does her best not to notice, but when he sets about courting her, she knows she's in trouble. For she has a secret: she is the daughter of a deposed king, which means not only is she without a dowry, but also that her life is in danger...

Little does Eve know that Mr. Vernon has secrets of his own. In truth, his name is Julius, Lord Winterton, and he's well aware that Eve is the offspring of the Old Pretender. In order to save his sister, must convince Eve to wed—though he wants nothing to do with . But as the two grow closer and an attempt is made on Eve's life, may realize that fighting his heart's true desire is a battle most gladly surrendered...

Books by Lynne Connolly

Emperors of London
Rogue In Red Velvet
Temptation Has Green Eyes
Danger Wears White
Reckless In Pink
Veiled In Blue

Published by Kensington Publishing Corporation

Veiled In Blue
An Emperors of London Novel

Lynne Connolly

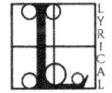

LYRICAL PRESS
Kensington Publishing Corp.
www.kensingtonbooks.com

First Electronic Edition: October 2016
eISBN-13: 1978-1-61650-574-5
eISBN-10: -61650-574-5

First Print Edition: October 2016
ISBN-13: 978-1-60183-570-3
ISBN-10: 1-60183-570-1

Printed in the United States of America

*To Kathryn Falk, friend and mentor. I have found delight in your company,
so I hope you find some delight in this.*

Author's Foreword

Before 1753, marriages were irregular and difficult to prove. That, and the story of a previous King of England, Edward IV, brought me to this idea, that the Old Pretender, the son of James II, had a clandestine marriage and a family unknown to history. His official marriage resulted in two sons, before his wife left him to live in a convent, and his history of melancholia, probably a severe form of depression, led his advisors and friends to look for distractions for him.

Thus I came upon Maria. In my version, The Old Pretender went back to her after the failure of his marriage. They were bound to have children. These books are their stories, but also the stories of the Emperors of London, a powerful, wealthy family similar to the Howards or the Cavendishes.

This is a "what if" story that grew more plausible as I researched it!

Chapter 1

Julius picked up the buffer and passed it over his perfectly polished nails before glancing at his valet. "I'll eat in an hour. Tell the innkeeper to serve the meal here." He put the pad next to the paring knife, absently noting their perfect alignment.

"Pardon, *monseigneur*?"

Julius patiently repeated the information in French. Whatever had possessed him to employ a French valet?

The dapper man bowed and smiled. "*Oui*, my lord." At least he'd learned that much, although Julius preferred his servants to address him simply as "sir."

Someone scratched at the door, and Lamaire went to answer it.

He returned with two letters, which he handed to Julius, carefully avoiding personal contact. Julius took them with a nod. He picked up the knife from the dressing table and broke the seal on the first one. It was from his mother.

Winterton,

Your father and I are expecting your presence shortly, and we trust your visit to your cousin will take no longer than a week or two. This is merely to inform you that your sister and your daughter arrived at the house today and are well. This time I must insist that Helena remain with me. You have not employed a companion for her on a regular basis, as you promised to do. Neither have you remarried. I cannot allow my daughter to live with you if you are unable to offer her the protection she deserves.

I have also invited some other of our acquaintances, and I am sure you will wish to meet them. Lady McComyn, Lady Murtagh, Lady Burton, and several others will be there with their families.

Yours, etc.

Julius swore viciously. Red rage filled his heart and burned in his veins. Damn the woman. By hook or crook, his mother wanted him married again, and she would hold his sister Helena to ransom until he selected one of the candidates of her choice.

Now she had Helena. Helena had been a bone of contention between his mother and him for many years. The duchess desired Helena to become her unpaid companion, the helpmeet for her old age. Julius was equally determined that his sister would have the life she wanted and the husband she deserved. Life with his mother did not bear thinking about.

But the duchess had won a march on him. The women listed in the letter were her particular allies, and their daughters would be firmly under their thumbs. His mother sought to control him through his wife. But if he was to rescue Helena, he would have to go to the Abbey and face her. Otherwise the duchess would never let her go. She would have him married before the end of the summer. In chains for life.

"My lord?" Lamaire stood by him, an enquiring expression on his sharp features.

Restlessly, Julius rose from his chair and took the other letter to the window, gazing out at the bustling inn yard below.

A young woman crossed the inn yard, her clothes simple and a cloth-covered basket on one arm. She progressed until she passed through the great arch that led out of the yard. She bore herself gracefully as she turned her head to smile at a man standing by the door to the taproom, her hips swaying slightly, her bearing almost regal. Julius smiled. The man doffed his hat to her. That meant she wasn't a doxy, but a respectable female with some business at the inn.

She progressed until she passed through the great arch that led out of the yard. Watching someone else, someone who had nothing to do with him conducting a life, calmed him and helped him to set his infuriating mother out of his mind, at least for now.

The young woman could even be his quarry. His spy, a servant he used to employ who was now working at this very inn, had told him the young woman occasionally came into town to shop on market day. The notion of a woman travelling without an attendant mildly surprised him, but since she presumably had no idea of her importance in the wider world, she would probably think nothing of it. He'd ordered his man to stop for the night here. It wasn't up to the usual standard he insisted on, the rooms cramped and the noise from the taproom too loud, but it would serve. In any case, luck might be with him, and that pretty dark-haired wench could be the one he was looking for. She was dressed respectably, though not fashionably, in a warm cloak with a dull-green-colored gown underneath, ankle length so as not to gather mud. Her basket was covered with a clean cloth, but in appearance, she could be a country wife rather than the granddaughter of a king, albeit a disgraced one.

Julius wrenched his thoughts back to the second letter. The outer part was scarred and creased. It had come a long way to find him. He broke the seal. This was from his brother Augustus.

My dear Julius.

What we suspected is, indeed, the case. Good luck in the hunt.

I trust this finds you well. I will be with you in England before the end of the month, if the weather stays fine.

Yours, etc.

Augustus.

The cryptic communication accompanied a letter he had in his pocket. He pulled it out now and read it again. This was entirely in the code Julius used with his brother, but he had transcribed it.

Here is the information you were looking for. I discovered this letter in the ruins of a house, and I have hopes of finding more. This copy is damaged by fire, so we only have two further names.

Julius had made it his mission to seek out and make safe all the legitimate children of the Old Pretender. They were not, as many supposed, the Young Pretender and his brother, Cardinal Henry Stuart, but the children of an earlier, secret marriage. The son of the last Stuart King of Britain had undergone a clandestine marriage to Maria Rubio, and after his short-lived official marriage, had returned to Maria.

They were political explosions waiting to happen.

Maria had given her children away at birth, either to secure their safety or to keep them hidden or both. She had chosen British tourists to Rome, of which there were legion, and Julius had had the devil of a job tracking them down. Now he had clues to the identity of one more.

Augustus had copied the relevant parts of the letter. It contained names they already knew plus two others. The one Julius was tracing here was from a man who was an academic at Oxford but had married and accepted a modest living in Appleton, Somerset, a few miles away from the inn Julius stood in. He glanced out of the window again. The woman had gone.

Ten miles from the village, Julius's cousin Alex had taken a house, so that his wife could undergo her confinement in peace. Julius's plan was to visit Alex, congratulate him on the birth of his son, and then travel on to his family home, to collect his sister and his daughter. During his visit, he could check the existence of the reverend and his family, ensure the child was cared for, and that nobody knew about her real identity.

But the sight of the woman unnerved him. Who else might be watching for her? And wouldn't a visit from a real life duke's heir cause some comment and cause the very fuss he was anxious to avoid?

Julius changed his plans. He would become Mr. Nobody of Nowhere for a week or two. He would still visit Alex, but he would not reveal his identity to the villagers. The child was a girl, Miss Eve Merton, purportedly the daughter of the Reverend and Mrs. Merton of Appleton. The thrill of the chase stirred inside him. He had a job to do, and by God he would do it before he walked into his mother's trap.

He snapped out his orders in French. "Pack a saddlebag with everything I will need for the next day or two."

"My lord?" Now Lamaire sounded confused, as well he might be.

Julius tipped back his head, closed his eyes, and drew air into his lungs, plans rapidly ordering themselves in his mind. "Go downstairs and hire me a horse. In the morning, use one of my coats and leave as if you are me. Go to my cousin's house. I will give you a note for him."

His last valet wouldn't have turned a hair, but Julius had spent years inuring him to his requests. Now, thanks to the man finding a wife and leaving his service, Julius had to start all over again. "I do not want anyone to know that I have left. I will travel as a gentleman." He thought of something the valet would definitely understand. "It is a delicate matter concerning a lady. *Comprenez-vous?*"

Lamaire's expression cleared. "Ah, I understand! I am most discreet, *monseigneur*. But would you not prefer a dress coat, something to impress the lady of your choice?"

Julius shook his head. "I don't intend to announce my presence in the village."

Lamaire nodded and bowed, the trace of a smile on his lips. "As you say."

That would keep him quiet and on Julius's side, even if the explanation was not completely accurate. The Frenchman would assume that Julius wanted to hide his identity so the lady would not pursue him. Julius could see that by the sidelong glances the man shot him. He could not be further from the truth.

"Pack the brown coat. I will wear the green."

When Lamaire presented him with the emerald green brocade Julius shook his head and indicated the duller one, in plain English cloth.

"That one." When he held his hand out, lace floated over the back of his hand. An ordinary man would not have anything so fine. He proceeded to pull away the neat running stitches and remove the Brussels lace ruffle. Then he unwound his cravat, exchanging both for plainer garments. He would be travelling incognito.

Half an hour later, Julius was on his way. With a pistol in each pocket, a sword by his side, and saddlebags full of clothes and other necessary items, he felt relatively safe. He'd exchanged his wig for a simpler one and his gold-braided cocked hat for an undecorated example. Instead of his sapphire signet ring, he wore a simple worn one of gold. Few would recognize it, but it was enough to identify him if the worst happened and he was waylaid and murdered. A man in his position must always consider that eventuality. The succession could not be put in doubt.

The vile mood engendered by his mother's demands still simmered. Once on the road, he released it. With nobody in sight he let rip, cursing a blue streak. He kept it up for at least half a mile before he could think clearly again. Ever since he had left home to set up his own establishment, his mother had fought to control him. It would not happen now. Or ever.

Julius was no nearer discovering a way to thwart his mother's attempted control of his life, except for one wild thought when he'd first glanced up from her letter and seen the young woman crossing the inn yard. He was tempted to follow the old legend of the king who'd promised to marry the first woman he saw.

Dusk was falling, and he had to pay attention, or the nag he'd hired would stumble in a rut on this none-too-carefully maintained road.

A slumped figure appeared ahead, someone in a shapeless heap of dark clothes. Since the person was bent over, Julius couldn't discern who or what it was, but he went on his guard, transferring the reins to one hand. He shoved his free hand into his pocket and curved it around the comforting butt of his pistol. Footpads would often appeal to the kindness of travelers. An old trick, but not one Julius intended to fall for now. He tugged on the rein, urging his horse to give the individual a wide berth.

The person straightened and revealed itself as a woman holding a basket, probably the same female he'd seen crossing the inn yard— perhaps even his quarry. He relaxed his grip.

As he approached, she stopped again, and bent once more. When she stood up this time, she gripped the handle of her basket harder than necessary. She had gloved hands, a sign of a gentlewoman. No country wench, this, and no footpad either.

Her shoes, barely visible below her ankle-length skirts, were sturdy, the buckles catching the light of the setting sun. She faltered. She was limping.

Julius drew level with her. He slowed his horse, his chivalrous instincts balking at the notion of passing her.

She glanced around and then snapped her head back to watch the road. Her profile was lovely, her nose straight and true.

"Are you in trouble, ma'am?" he asked her. "May I be of assistance?"

"No, sir." Her voice shook, but no discernible country accent tinged it. "I will manage. I merely caught my foot in a rut. I will be perfectly well shortly."

Julius pulled up and dismounted. "I insist. I am of no danger to you."

Coming to a halt, she put up her chin to glare. "I assure you, sir. I am fine." She bit her lip. "I should warn you that I am armed and I know how to use my weapon."

Julius caught his breath. Despite the plain clothes and tight jaw, she was truly exquisite, one of the most beautiful women he had ever seen. The lines of her face were clean and clearly defined, her skin so pure it begged for his touch. Was he tumbling into a different kind of trap, perhaps? He was in peril of falling for his own fantasy.

Smiling, he drew his hand out of his pocket just far enough to show her that he was armed, too. When she shifted on the rough road, her shoes scraping against grit with an audible sound, he was sorry he had shown her.

He drew his hand from his pocket completely, leaving the pistol behind. "I beg your pardon, ma'am. As you can see, I have released my weapon. If you follow suit, I feel sure we shall be more comfortable."

If she bit her lip any harder, she'd draw blood. "Please to go on, sir," she said.

"I wouldn't dream of abandoning a young lady so unprotected."

He meant it. She was terrified of him, and she had good reason. Without a house in sight, they were alone together. It would be a matter of moments to overpower her.

Fortunately, Julius had no such intention, but he had no way of proving that to her. Normally he'd provide his card. Not in this case. He had no visiting cards, and if he started flaunting his wealth, his low profile would not last for long. Money didn't just talk; sometimes it screamed.

"How far do you have to go? Will the next village suit you?" If it did not, he would travel farther. "I will not leave you to be accosted by a real ruffian. Please, ma'am, let me help."

"Who are you, sir? What are you doing on this road? It hardly leads to anywhere important. If you are heading for Bath, I am afraid you have lost your way."

Smiling, Julius shook his head, rapidly inventing a history for himself. "I'm a man of business, and I am travelling to see Lord Ripley. I have some papers for him to sign."

"Oh." Her shoulders slumped when she breathed out. "Lady Ripley has just been brought to bed."

"You know them?" he said quickly.

"No, that is, I have met them once, but I cannot claim acquaintanceship. Lady Ripley's…illness precluded that." She sighed, her bosom swelling enticingly under her plain blue gown. "Your name, sir?"

"Julius Vernon." He would not stray too far from the truth in case he was found out. Hiding under a completely false name would make this enterprise too shady. He wanted this woman to trust him.

No recognition of the shortened version of his name shaded her eyes. She touched his hand briefly when he held it out to her. "Eve Merton. My father was the vicar here before his death."

"I'm sorry." Julius's sympathy came automatically, but inside he was crowing his triumph. His luck had held. His quarry had fallen into his hands. The stars were in alignment, and the gods favored him today.

She shook her head. "I'm over the first grief of his passing. He died five years ago."

He nodded. "Still, losing a parent is never easy. I'm delighted to make your acquaintance, Eve Merton. Can you ride astride?"

She gave him a derisory glance, her mouth turned down, her eyes scornful. "I can claim it as one of my skills."

He cupped his hands. "Then please take your seat, Eve Merton."

She placed her foot in his hands and allowed him to throw her into the saddle. Before she settled properly, he swung up behind her. She flinched, but said nothing. He would love to know what was going on in her mind. Did she know who she was? Whose daughter she was in truth?

* * * *

Apprehension clutched Eve's insides, tightening her throat. Would he prove honorable?

She had taken a rational decision, the only practical one in the circumstances, but she had not reckoned for him riding with her.

Had it not been for tripping on that wretched rut, she would have been home by now, but her foot pained her more than she had let herself dwell on. The hedgerows were of the annoying tight-knit kind with the brittle twigs, so she could not even cut a branch to help her progress. If not for that, she would have been home before nightfall.

Dusk was falling quickly. A female alone on a country road was ripe prey for footpads and highwaymen. If this man was a villain, so be it. Better one than a gang.

Mr. Vernon felt strong and protective. He had to curve his arms around her to control the reins, giving her an unaccustomed sense of being cared for. Normally she did the protecting.

He even smelled good, of soap and something subtle, like an aromatic wood. He used cologne. She found that deeply intriguing. She did not know any men who used perfume. In this district, any that dared would be labeled effeminate, but this man was far from that. Power remained leashed in him, but the easy way he moved and the sheer strength surrounding her demonstrated his essential masculinity.

"Are you staying with Lord Ripley?" she asked.

A pause followed before he laughed. "No indeed. I was hoping I could find somewhere to stay. Do you know of a respectable inn?"

"I do." The nearest stood opposite her house on the village green. "I can direct you to one, if you wish."

"I would appreciate it. I confess I'm not used to sleeping in the open."

"Oh!" She couldn't allow him to do that.

She felt churlish for not complimenting him on his excellent horsemanship, but she was on edge. His proximity was sending prickles along the length of her spine. She had to lean back, because she would unbalance them and mar his vision if she tried leaning away from him. At least, that was what she told herself when the horse stumbled and she was jolted back against him.

Had she imagined the hum of appreciation rumbling in his throat?

Oh, no, no. She would not succumb to such idiocy. She was far too old for that kind of foolishness, after all. Having attained the advanced age of seven-and-twenty, she should have been long past flirtation and foolish imaginings. Besides, her foot hurt, though she had to admit, not half so much as it had before.

She clutched the handle of her basket to stop herself reaching for his arms to test their strength. The urge to touch him grew unbearable. Before she could stop herself, Eve asked, "Do you own your own business, sir?"

He sucked in a breath, the sound loud in her ear. "In a small way. What made you ask?"

"You have no assistant with you. Men of business often travel with clerks."

"I have a special relationship with Lord Ripley," he said promptly. "The matter is fairly trivial, but he will wish to know of it." He huffed a laugh. "You are very perceptive, Miss Merton."

"Thank you," she said primly. "And you have an excellent way with a horse."

"Thus indicating that not all city men have the same facility. Neatly done." He shifted in the saddle.

That was when she felt it. She was not the only person affected by their unusual proximity. Knowing she would be walking home, Eve had left off her hoops and wore but a softly padded roll to give her skirt some fullness. Consequently, she felt it. Felt *him*.

A hard ridge, like a rod under his breeches, pressed against the curves of her bottom. Mr. Vernon was sporting an erection. A considerable one, by the feel of it. Eve had never, ever been so close to a man in a state of excitement, at least not knowingly.

She should be shocked, move away, or insist he put her down. He must know his body was misbehaving. What did that mean? She had no idea. Men responded with a physical immediacy foreign to women, or that was what Eve understood.

She did the only thing she could. She pretended not to notice. Holding her body rigid, not moving cost her a great deal of effort, but it was worth it.

Perhaps if she talked about something that might help him. Searching frantically in her mind for something to distract him, she fell on the one sure-fire subject—the weather. "They say this will be a fine summer."

"Do they? I am beginning to think it will be." The horizon glowed, the redness of the setting sun coloring the undersides of the clouds scattered over the rapidly darkening sky. "So tell me, Miss Merton, why are you walking alone at dusk? You're evidently a respectable woman. Surely you should have an attendant with you?"

She laughed. "The maid has better things to do than taking me to and from town. If I had not hurt my ankle, I would have been home hours ago."

"It can't be right," he said.

That was true. Her mother was always criticizing her for taking too many liberties with her person. "One day," she would say and then launch into a number of blood-curdling and totally imaginary situations.

Her body heated when she thought of this man laying her on the hard ground and taking her. Knowing she would probably never have a man in such a situation, Eve had treated such possibilities as harmless fantasies, but now they appeared all too real. She must not turn and press her mouth to his, as the fantasy Eve might.

He had firm, warm lips. They were most likely warm, though how could she know? She never would, and she would not try to find out. But if she had not imagined it, she would not be in this predicament, feeling a man's member hard against her and knowing what it meant. His body wanted hers. Perhaps he hadn't had a woman for some time, or she had given him thoughts he should not have. Then shame on her for thinking them.

Mr. Vernon slowed the horse and picked his way carefully along the uneven road in the growing gloom.

"I am not of marriageable age," she said. "I am of the age when I should be reading to old ladies."

"Is that what you were doing?" He gave no apology for his curiosity.

"As it happens, yes." She swung the empty basket. "There is a home for poor, respectable women in the town. I took some scones and read the newspaper to them. They like to discuss the latest *on-dits* and scandals." And go on and on and on about Eve finding a husband—as if that would ever happen. Eve's portion was so small as to be miniscule, not enough to attract any man. She had reconciled herself to the fact. Even Eve's mother did not create such a fuss, at least not on such a regular basis, but the ladies at the home thought their seniority conferred special privileges on them.

"Just like the fairy tale. And have you come across the big, bad wolf, I wonder?"

"Not until I started to walk home."

His chuckle vibrated against her in the most intimate way imaginable. She forced herself not to squirm and closed her eyes, forcing concentration.

"I have been called many things, but not that." He paused, guiding the horse around yet another rut. "Or maybe I have. But a man of my position has a reputation to consider."

"As a man of business? Are you financier or lawyer?"

"A little of both," he said, "But mostly concerned with land. I am not qualified in law, if that's what you mean."

He spoke to her as an equal. She found his attitude a pleasant change from the men who either took no notice of her at all or treated her like some kind of idiot who couldn't hold a sentient thought in her head for more than five minutes. She would far rather talk to him about anything but the embarrassing staff that reared between them.

"How much farther do we have to travel?" he said.

"Another two miles, perhaps, sir."

"I had travelled farther than I thought, then, when I came across you. I must have been lost in my own imaginings. It's a wonder I didn't stumble long before."

"You're paying attention now."

"I have more than myself to consider."

His words made her feel cared for, if only on a casual, temporary basis. Her anxiety subsided.

"Do you stay long in Somerset?"

"Longer than I had at first imagined." He spoke dryly, as if reluctant.

Her defensive instincts rose. "It is a lovely county, sir. Have you visited before?"

"I have. Yes, it is indeed lovely. Somerset boasts some glorious views. Bath is not far, is it?"

Much to her relief, he spoke about general things and let her tell him about Bath, the kind of people who could be seen in the pump room and the delicacies obtained there. "I have not seen everything Bath has to offer, despite living there for a time and living so close for most of my life."

"I have lived in London for some time, but I have not yet seen it all."

"Did you ride all the way here, sir?"

He paused. "Not all. I hired this horse locally. Travelling in a coach can become tedious."

Especially a stagecoach. They must have been invented to torture ordinary people. "Do you have to send the horse back?"

"Not immediately. I will use it to travel to Lord Ripley's house. I'm looking forward to my visit. He insisted I come, despite his wife's condition."

Had his voice softened when he talked about Lady Ripley? She was a lovely woman, it was true, and stylish with it. Her husband adored her.

"She had no idea what she was getting into when she became involved with an Emperor."

"An Emperor?"

"The Emperors of London," he said, amusement touching his voice.

She wished she could see him properly, because the other half of his tone sounded wry, almost jaded.

"Ah, yes. A nickname." She had heard it, but had not taken a great deal of interest in it. Nicknames were, in her opinion, a frivolity that only the rich could afford to spend time on.

"Their parents took an oath to name their children after emperors of the past," he said, drawling his words in a way she had not heard before.

Then it was as if he had snapped back to attention and his tones regained their crispness. "Lord Ripley's given name is Alexander."

"The greatest emperor of them all," she said.

"Perhaps. Do you have a classical education, Miss Merton?"

"No, sir. By profession I am a governess, so I do have a reasonable education. I was taught the rudiments of Latin, but I teach the feminine arts."

"Dancing, deportment and flirting?"

She took umbrage at his response, bridling. "Women must know more than the graceful arts if they are to live a fulfilling life."

"I couldn't agree more." He chuckled. "Are you surprised at my response?"

Her heart sank. He probably had a wife. "And your wife is of that ilk?"

"My wife is—" He paused, and the muscles in his arms stiffened. "My wife died six years ago."

"Oh, I'm so sorry!"

"Thank you." His voice was steady. "Now we are both sorry for the death of someone we did not know."

It took her a moment to untangle the sentiment. At first, she'd imagined—but that could not be what he intended to say. "It's always sad when we lose someone." She had the sensation of moving on uncertain ground, and resorted to the trite comment in order not to make a *faux pas*.

He answered with a grunt, and silence reigned for the last part of the journey. Even his erection had subsided, or he had managed to move it out of the way. She did not dare lean against him to discover the truth.

At last, they ascended the final gentle rise that gave them the view of the church tower.

"That's the village," she said.

He sighed, though whether from regret or hopeful anticipation she couldn't tell. Probably the latter. The horse was certainly tired, its head drooping and its gait slower than ever.

"Appleton." He drew a breath, as if to say something else, but must have changed his mind.

"It's a sleepy little place," she said.

"Have you ever been anywhere else? Apart from Bath?"

Some villagers had never even crossed the parish boundaries. "I've been to Wells. I haven't visited London, although I would like to. Perhaps I can get work there."

"Perhaps," he said, but he sounded guarded, as if he didn't think she could do it.

A spark of irritation flashed through her. "I'm a very good governess!"

"I'm sure you are," he answered, and this time his smooth tones sounded perfectly sure.

This annoyed her more than his doubt.

"Are you concealing your true feelings?"

"In my position, I have to do so from time to time."

That didn't exactly answer her question, but she would not press him further. He was a stranger, after all, although this ride into the village had made her better acquainted with his more personal assets.

Her own arousal had settled into a simmering want, a vague sense of emptiness that she still had a great deal to experience in life. She would probably not have that pleasure, or otherwise, since she was in a limbo of respectability that demanded marriage and without the financial wherewithal to attract a suitor.

Her situation left her as the perpetual spinster, of which England had a distressingly high number. She had accustomed herself to the notion, at least she told herself as much. Only in the dead of night did she allow herself to dream about finding a handsome, young, wealthy man who would adore her. In clear daylight, she knew how impossible that was.

They rode over the rise and down to the village. Closing her eyes, Eve allowed herself a few moments of imagined pleasure. She snatched them from life, but she had to admit that being cradled in the arms of a handsome man was not something she would object to if circumstances were different.

His warmth lulled her into a false sense of security, and it was a jolt when he spoke again.

"Is that the inn?"

When she opened her eyes, the glow of the building confronted her. "Yes, you should find a room there."

The inn blazed its welcome, torches shining brightly outside and lamps in the yard, as well as the lighting inside the main rooms. Upstairs a few lights flickered where guests must have been in their rooms.

"Thank you. Where do you live?"

"Oh, not far. I can manage from here, truly."

"I must escort you to your door. No, I would not hear of abandoning a respectable female to the night."

What would her mother say? However, short of leaping from the horse's back, Eve had little option but to direct him to the other side of the green.

In her house on her side of the green, the curtains were open. A light flickered in the window, but only one. "I live here," she said.

"Here?" He sounded surprised, his usual baritone rising.

The house was perfectly respectable, if a little on the small side, but it was far from a rough cottage. Brick built with a good slate roof, the place lacked only space. Her mother had pointed that out when Eve had returned home after her brief sojourn as governess in Bath.

It was almost fully night now. "I must have been mad to think I could get home before dark."

"You will not do that again." He spoke with certainty, as if he had some say over her movements.

He swung from the saddle and reached for her. The horse was too weary to take advantage of his lightened load and stood patiently while Mr. Vernon slid his hands around her waist and lifted her effortlessly to the ground. He did not release her immediately.

Eve held the empty basket like a shield, the only protection she had against more intimate contact.

He smiled down at her. He was half a foot taller than her, if not more. "Do you think you can take your own weight, or should I carry you to your door?"

"Sir!" Scandalized, she opened her eyes wider while heat rushed to her cheeks. The notion of all the residents of the green watching while he picked her up was unthinkable. Or almost. The small part remaining was her romantic self, the part she ruthlessly crushed. It lingered this time to whisper, *What if I let him?* in the dark recesses of her mind.

Showing nothing but polite gratitude, she thanked him kindly. "I daresay you will be away in a few days, so I doubt we will meet again. So allow me to thank you now. I am deeply grateful for your help, sir."

Now, looking directly at him, she sensed danger lurking in the clean-cut features. This man had a wild edge, well concealed but there. Intelligence gleamed in his eyes, together with the wry humor he had displayed during their journey. For one reckless moment, she thought he might tighten his hold, force her to drop the basket, and kiss her. His lips were full, eminently kissable. Not that she had much experience.

The light left his eyes as if he'd forced it away. "I will release you now, ma'am, so you may test your theory. I do intend for us to meet again. Would you have any objection if I called on you?"

"You cannot. My mother is a widow."

"I wish only to see how you are doing and if your ankle is well. Should you object to that?"

She did not. Why not allow herself another slight thrill, another memory? "No, sir. I am past the age of missishness. However you will be busy at Woolton, will you not?" With the owner, Lord Ripley.

"Not all the time." He glanced up. "How far is the house?"

"Another five miles by road. Two if you walk across the fields."

"I see. Then I shall stay here in the village. That way I am sure to see you sometimes, am I not?"

Treacherous hope rose in her breast, but Eve suppressed it. "Indeed you will. There is only one church. Even Lord Ripley and his lady attend, though I doubt we will see them this Sunday."

"No, indeed. His lordship may well be taken up with the new addition to the family." He paused.

By the light of the flickering candle in the window, she made out his clean, clear-cut face and the blue eyes glimmering with promise. His jaw showed signs of golden fuzz, so under the plain conventional wig, his hair must have been fair. She had never found herself drawn to fair men, but she would make an exception in this case. He was well formed, without fault, his hands strong and his shoulders broad.

"Have you finished looking?" He sounded amused rather than offended.

She dragged her attention from his feet back to his face. "I'm sorry. I was—"

"No matter. It's flattering when such a beautiful woman pays me some attention."

She stared up at him, but she could not deny his statement. She had a mirror. Not that her looks were anything but a curse.

Chapter 2

Julius stretched and groaned as the twinges from sleeping in a confined space made themselves apparent. Sunshine bathed the grubby ceiling of the room the landlord of this benighted place had allotted him, what passed for drapery at the windows not equal to the task of keeping out the light. He picked up his watch and flicked open the cover, listening to the chimes ring out half past seven. Early for him, probably half the morning gone according to most of the residents of the village.

Horses clopped past, people called to each other, scintillating chat like "Nice day," and "Will you be at the inn later?" The sounds were not too different from his bedroom in London. Except that his room there faced the back of the house, and here he couldn't hear any street vendors or the rattle of carriage wheels on cobbles. Oh, yes, and this room was the size of his powder room. He glanced around. If he'd had this old, worn furniture in his house, he'd order it chopped up for firewood.

Particularly this bed. When he'd ventured to investigate what lay under the prickly horsehair mattress, he'd found a crisscrossed pattern of ropes. For the first time in his life he'd slept on a rope bed. After he left this place, he would never sleep on one again.

He swung out of bed and removed the chair he had propped under the door. Since the entrance to his room had no lock, only a latch, he had considered the possibility of being murdered in his bed and decided on the single chair, which, having one leg shorter than the other three, was of little use for anything else.

Outside the door, he found a can of water. At least he could shave.

Lamaire had provided him with soap, razor, comb, and other necessities, including, he was amused to discover, a small silver-topped bottle filled with the cologne he customarily used. He appreciated the inclusion of the small luxury, even more that Lamaire had remembered not to put it in one of his crested, monogrammed bottles. No doubt, the dressing case containing the bottle and its fellows was on the way to Alex's house. As Julius should be, except he'd decided on this mad plan.

Sometimes a man had to get away. Julius's habit of travelling as Mr. Vernon would have given his mother conniptions, but she had no idea of his occasional excursions as a simple untitled gentleman. She would have no idea he even knew how to shave himself or dress himself for that matter. As far as Julius knew, his father had never shaved himself in the whole of his life.

He poured water in the small washing bowl on the chest of drawers, lathered some soap, and began the task, squinting into the small cracked mirror hanging above the basin.

Twenty minutes later, respectably dressed, he viewed his reflection and grinned. Nobody would give him a second glance if he walked past them in the street. In this village? He knew country life well enough to realize they would be interested in the stranger in their midst, so he had better go downstairs and order something to eat while letting small morsels of his history drop.

The rickety stairs heralded his presence more effectively than a trumpet blast, but only a few people glanced up when he entered the taproom and asked if they were serving food. Several people already occupied the place. He ignored two people who were obviously travelling on after eating. They would not care who he was, or he them. As long as they didn't recognize him, he had no interest in them. He doubted his own household would recognize him in this getup.

He enjoyed the meal—hot, well cooked, and fresh—and the solitude afforded him when he ate. The landlady brought out his food herself, and he took the opportunity to ask about Woolton Manor.

"Did you see it on your way past?"

"No, I have business with his lordship."

Her pale blue eyes rounded, and her grey-flecked eyebrows went up. "My, sir, are you a guest?"

"Merely one of his lordship's men of business."

The corners of her mouth turned down. "Ah. Well it's about eight miles away, if you ride. There's a footpath if you want to walk, and that's much shorter."

"I have a horse."

"Eating its head off, the ostler said," the woman remarked. She wriggled her shoulders, and her linen fichu slipped a little. She hitched it back up and offered Julius a four-toothed grin. "Should you want it today, sir?"

"Ah, no. I'll walk today. Do people from the household generally pass by this place?" If they did, his goose was cooked, because they'd know him for sure. Julius had never visited the manor before. Alex had chosen it because it was out of the way. He had brought Connie to this place for a secluded honeymoon, and apart from the occasional visit to town, they'd remained here ever since. Julius would shortly find out what the appeal of Woolton was, although he guessed it was less what than who. Alex had fallen head over heels for Connie, and Julius's previously wayward cousin had become a family man.

He prayed it would never happen to him. Julius enjoyed his life exactly as it was. If he married, he would do it with a clear head this time. Not in haste and not to a woman he barely knew. He wanted a sensible woman who would give him sons and help with his daughter. Nothing more.

He took another mouthful of devilled kidney, enjoying the spicy flavor.

After his repast, Julius left the inn to explore his surroundings. He strolled past the pretty church, fifteenth century from the shape of the windows and the tower, with its peaceful graveyard, the stones neatly regimented, although some had tilted to one side. It only gave them a picturesque air. Along the side of the church in the shelter of a dry stone wall a path led away from the village, presumably to Woolton.

The village was a prosperous one, the buildings clustered around the green solidly built and relatively modern. A few ramshackle cottages stood farther out, but Julius did not intend to explore them. He'd seen the inside of some of the cottages on his father's estate, and he had no wish to repeat it. However even they were in reasonable repair, the thatch thick and well trimmed and the windows shuttered.

A sense of freedom filled his soul. He was on holiday. He was Mr. Vernon of London, a working man with no family he had yet admitted to.

He kicked away from the tree and continued his walk. Except, of course, he had better keep to the truth if he was ever to tell Eve who and what she was. He should leave her alone, have a watch put on her in case his enemies caught up with her. During his walk he had seen nothing untoward, nothing that would suggest anyone else suspected anything. She was safer if she remained hidden. Having once experienced her haunting beauty, he had a severe disinclination to leave her alone.

As he strolled back toward the green, a carriage bowled past him, sending up a cloud of dust from the rain-parched road. Julius brushed himself down. By the time he reached the inn, the carriage was outside the house across on the other side, together with another. The Mertons must be having an at home day.

So why should he not call? It would be polite to enquire after her health. In all his perambulations, he had not forgotten Eve, merely tried to put her at the back of his mind. But the memory of her sweet body pressed against his proved persistent, and despite his better judgment, he acknowledged a longing to feel it again.

Julius strode around the perimeter of the green. Two sheep grazed peacefully there, keeping the grass down. A pond in the middle featured a few ducks swimming on the water and waddling around the edge. Behind the pond, a great tree grew, similar to the oak he was leaning against.

As he rounded the edge of the green, a brown duck waddled in his direction. With a wry grin, he showed the creature his empty hands. It carried on coming and then veered off and headed for the inn instead. It probably had a regular port of call there. Just like a London gossip, crowding him for tidbits.

Smiling, Julius strolled through the open gate and rapped smartly on the door. A servant opened it, and he delivered his message.

"Mr. Vernon, here to enquire after Miss Merton's health." He had no cards, not in that name, at any rate.

The maid glared at him before turning abruptly and striding into the shady depths of the house. A minute later, she returned. "If you'll come this way, sir." A woman of comfortable proportions, she seemed afflicted by a chill, as her sniff when she led him indoors proclaimed.

Since nobody had taken his hat or gloves, Julius stuffed his gloves in his pocket and removed his hat, holding it in one hand.

He entered a room already full. The modest space held, besides Miss Merton, an older lady, two gentlemen, and two other young ladies. The sun poured in through a window at the back of the house, which overlooked a charming private garden. Roses in the first flush of summer nodded their heads. The carefully tended bushes beyond surrounded a quaint bower with a seat made for courting.

A murky painting with a carved oak frame hung above the fireplace, depicting a country scene not too far removed from the one he recalled from his journey yesterday. The picture must once have been fresh and bright, but it was now smudged with soot and general household dirt, the thick impasto ingrained. Several vaguely repulsive china figures adorned the mantel itself, and the corner of the room boasted a set of shelves with yet more ornaments. Shepherds and harlequins were the least egregious of the figures.

Julius bowed, careful not to make it too elaborate.

Miss Merton's beauty struck him anew. Cleaned and neatly dressed, she was a star fallen amongst hogs—and he included himself in that description. Julius did not miss the warmth in her eyes before she lowered her gaze.

"Mama, this was the gentleman who was kind enough to help me yesterday," she said.

"Oh, sir!" The older lady flicked her fan open. The sticks were worn, but she flourished it well. "I am so grateful to you. My foolish daughter might have lain on the road all night were it not for you!"

What had Miss Merton said? What he had actually done was not something many mothers would approve of. He should probably have let her mount the horse and then walked by its side, but to hell with that.

Mrs. Merton introduced the other people present. Sir Henry Fulworth was the larger man, and Mr. King smaller and more fashionably dressed. The two gentlemen on the sofa had to move up to give Julius room. He perched on the edge and refused the delicate dish of tea offered to him by the older lady.

The gentleman next to him, who barely made concessions to admit Julius, and to be truthful, needed the space more than most, nodded civilly. "You are a stranger to Somerset, sir?"

Julius considered his answer. "Not entirely. It is such a lovely country, though I wonder why I haven't remained here longer." He gave Sir Henry his sweetest smile. "I'm a man of business from London to visit Lord Ripley. Considering his wife's confinement, I judged it best to come here instead of allowing matters to wait."

Sir Henry visibly relaxed. "I see. Then do you stay long?"

"As long as his lordship needs me."

The man on the other end of the sofa, Mr. King, was watching the exchange carefully but taking no part in the conversation.

"And you, sir?" Julius asked him.

"Like you, I am not a native of Somerset, but I moved here last year. It suits me. I have a mind to stay for a while."

That told Julius precisely nothing. The hair on the back of his neck prickled in undefined warning. "You are from London?"

"No, sir. I am from the north, originally. I am recently returned from Rome."

Julius's thoughts came to a screaming halt. Rome meant far more than a distant city. It was where Maria Rubio had given birth to her children. But no, it could not be. Many people visited Rome. Nevertheless, he would write a letter to London as soon as he returned to the inn and set enquiries in train.

Julius heaved a great sigh. "Rome is an enviable destination."

"It is above all things lovely. But I confess I am pleased to be home again."

While the men discussed local politics, Julius had a moment to address Miss Merton. "Have you fully recovered from your ordeal, ma'am?"

She met his gaze directly, her rich brown eyes revealing warmth. "Indeed I have, sir. As I told you, I had merely wrenched my ankle. If I had thought to rest by the side of the road, I probably would have recovered, but I was anxious to get home."

"Quite rightly. You should not be roaming abroad after dark."

"Indeed, sir, we have a great deal to thank you for," her mother put in. "I dread to think what might have happened to her had you not come along!"

The sharp gaze of Mr. King flicked from Sir Henry to the quiet conversation Julius was having with Miss Merton.

Mr. King had already annoyed Julius by his perceptiveness. He had the look of a man interested in everything going on around him, and his answers about his origins had been as vague as he could get away with. Mr. King was definitely following everything going on in the room, including the apparently innocuous discussion between Julius and Miss Merton.

He nodded to Mrs. Merton. "It was my pleasure to be of service, ma'am. I could hardly leave a gently nurtured young lady to the terrors of the night."

He glanced at Miss Merton when she made a noise that sounded deliciously like scoffing.

"Indeed I have much to thank you for, sir," she said, her dancing eyes belying her prim tone.

"I would be happy to oblige you any time," he answered in the same tone.

They were getting perilously close to flirting. Julius loved a woman who could flirt charmingly.

Fortune favored him toward the end of the half-hour, when he should have, by the rules of good behavior, taken his leave. Apparently convinced that although he worked for a living, Julius could behave like a gentleman, Sir Henry cleared his throat portentously before announcing, "If you are in the neighborhood for a time, Mr. Vernon, you might wish to consider attending my little evening's entertainment. I hold a gathering every year, and I would be pleased to send you an invitation."

Julius smiled. "It sounds utterly delightful, sir. If you are sure I won't put out your numbers?"

"No, sir, I am inviting half the county."

"I would be delighted, if I'm still in this part of the world."

Sir Henry nodded graciously and picked up his tea-dish, taking a refreshing slurp. He replaced it carefully in its saucer before he spoke again. "Maybe you can prevail on his lordship to accompany you."

So that was why Sir Henry had invited him. "Her ladyship has not been in the best of health, but I will certainly mention the affair to his lordship when I see him."

It was time to take his leave. Julius got to his feet, automatically shaking out his coat skirts, although they were not nearly as voluminous as the ones he usually preferred. Cuffs were still monstrous and decorated with rows of buttons. The ones on this coat were plain brass but well-polished. He wore plain linen ruffles at the ends of his sleeves instead of his usual fine lace, and his neckcloth was similarly unadorned with lace. He trusted it was still well tied, though. He was not entirely without pride in his appearance.

He bowed, first to the older lady and then to Miss Merton, holding himself back from his usual elegance. In any case, there was not enough space in this room. "Thank you so much for your hospitality. It was good to find you recovered, Miss Merton, although I have yet to see you walk enough to satisfy me you are completely over your ordeal."

As he'd hoped, she got to her feet immediately. "In that case, I will see you to the door, Mr. Vernon. You may observe my gait and satisfy yourself that I am completely recovered."

With the beady stare of Mr. King fixed on them, she took Julius's arm, and they left the room together.

Outside, in the small but neat hall, surprisingly servantless, he clapped his hat on his head. "I am still not entirely happy," he said. "If you are walking in the village anytime soon, I can assure myself of your health."

Her laughter was a totally enchanting gurgle, low in her throat. "I often take my mother's dog for a constitutional walk before dinner. He's an old spaniel, so I have to take my time."

He enjoyed her swift acceptance of his delicate invitation. Her lovely face lit up when he spoke to her, her appreciation of him flattering, although he could not accept he was the only result.

Walking across the green back to the inn, Julius tucked his hands behind his back and cursed himself for an arrant fool. He had fallen in lust once before in his life, and look how well that had turned out.

Why, then, had it happened again?

Perhaps the feeling would pass. His passion for Miss Merton was merely the novelty of meeting someone new, out of his purview, and of course because of her undoubted beauty.

Of course it was. It could hardly be anything else, could it?

* * * *

Julius walked to the manor a day after he had visited Miss Merton at home.

He strolled around the back of the pleasant building, where he found two people sitting on the terrace, enjoying the summer sun. At his approach, Alex leaped to his feet. Connie lifted her chin and smiled. She was dressed in a light silk gown, very informal, and Alex was in his shirtsleeves.

"You have turned delightfully rustic in your bucolic wilderness," Julius drawled, tipping his hat back.

"And you have turned positively dowdy," Alex said, but his statement didn't stop him striding down the shallow steps to give Julius his hands and then drag him into his arms for a back-slapping embrace.

Few people saw the bright, genuine smile Julius turned on him when they parted. He reserved it for his dearest friends. "I am truly happy for you," he said, and meant every word. Seeing his cousin so content in his marriage was worth every effort Julius had made to ensure that it happened.

Alex's perpetual expression of cynical endurance had completely gone. Julius had largely left him alone to make what he would of his marriage, and he had made much. He glanced at the woman still sitting in an easy chair on the terrace. Connie had always been beautiful. Now, in the wake of giving birth, an event she had despaired of ever happening, she was radiant.

When Connie made to get to her feet, Julius waved his hand and hurried up the stairs to ensure she did not. He embraced her warmly, but as a friend now. Connie had lived with Helena and him for a while, and Julius always stood her friend. At one point, he had considered asking her to become his wife, but Alex had stepped up to the mark. Alex loved her, while Julius was merely fond of her, but that had been a positive asset in his opinion. He wanted no more ungovernable passion in his life.

"You look wonderful, Connie. I sneaked to the back of the house because you are so well-guarded they might not have let me in."

Connie spluttered with laughter. "You know they would never refuse you, Julius. Do you like the house?"

"It's utterly delightful." He kept his attention on her. "So are you."

"Are you flirting with my wife?" Alex had mounted the stairs and stood behind him. In different circumstances, he could appear threatening, but Julius knew better.

"Absolutely." Julius straightened and turned around, still smiling. "Congratulations to you both. Are you planning to stay here awhile?"

Connie had had a hard time of her pregnancy, and childbirth had not been easy, either. That was why Alex had moved here, for the privacy they could claim, to give Connie a chance to rest.

"Until forever, if we can manage it." Alex raised a dark brow and sighed theatrically. "I fear that will not happen, though. After Connie is churched, we have to steel ourselves to receive guests. My father is waiting to meet his grandson. He stayed away because I asked him to."

"Your brothers?"

"Tiberius and Ivan are with my father. Unlike you, they are waiting for an invitation."

"I understood I was invited," he said.

"You were," Connie assured him quickly. "Any time we said, and we meant it. But you were due to arrive after the baby was born. Our son decided to wait until the last minute before making an appearance."

"Do I get to see the little princeling?" This child would surely be treated like a prince. His parents evidently were already in love with him. Julius remembered that feeling, the overwhelming, helpless love when seeing one's child for the first time. Caroline's birth had provided a moment of blinding revelation for Julius, one that had changed his life forever.

"He's napping after his feeding," Alex said, and by the way he glanced at his wife and avoided Julius's gaze indicated she was taking a hand, or rather, a breast, in their son's nourishment. From the way she smiled at her husband, he was still her world. "You can see him later." Alex swept Julius with a comprehensive study, head to foot and back again. "Why on earth are you dressed that way, Julius?"

Julius raised a brow. "Guess."

Although Alex and Connie were dressed in a casual way, they easily outdid Julius for stylishness and costliness of dress. Connie's flowered silk might be a comfortable gown meant to accommodate her body after the birth, but it was exquisite fabric fashionably made. Julius's brown coat and plain breeches were none of those things.

Alex's smile faded. "More Stuart children?"

"One more. Very close," he said shortly.

He glanced around as a footman approached, an expression of determination on his features. "Is this man bothering you, my lord?"

Alex laughed. "No. Leave us alone, if you please." He glanced at Julius. "Unless you require anything?"

Julius shook his head and indicated the pot on the table. "If the tea is drinkable, I'll take some of that. Nothing else, thank you."

"Bring a fresh pot, if you please," Connie said to the man, who bowed and moved away.

Alex waved to the garden chairs, and Julius took his place close to the couple. "Did my man Lamaire arrive?" Julius asked then.

"He did. He was deeply confused, but I have retained him for you."

"Did you say retained or detained?" Julius asked, grinning.

Connie laughed. "We nearly had to do the latter. However, we soothed him. He thought he was in dereliction of his duty to let you go off alone. He's set about refurbishing everything you sent with him. You won't find a speck of dirt on anything."

"It relieves me immensely to hear it. I do require more clothes."

"Why the sudden change of plan, Julius? Why not come here as yourself?"

Julius sighed. "It occurred to me that if I arrived in full glory, so to speak, I would draw attention to the fact that I am here. The Dankworths watch me, and so, I'm sure, do the Stuarts. I could be drawing them to the child. If the woman I have discovered were unsuspected, I would have left her be, but I wanted to check for myself. I only received the information from Augustus last week."

"Why did you not tell me?" Alex demanded. "I could have dealt with the matter."

They paused when the footman returned with not only a fresh pot of tea but a plate of delicate pastries for them to enjoy. Connie thanked her and waved the man away, saying she would serve their guest.

"I would not dream of discommoding you at a time like this," Julius said. "I meant to visit you anyway, but on my way to the Abbey. When I received Augustus's letter, I decided to pause at the village and ensure all was well. Matters have turned out differently. There is a man I suspect may be a spy." He took a grateful sip of tea before he spoke again. "Do you know the village?"

"I made enquiries, and I've attended the village church, so I know a few people by sight, but not much more," Alex said. "Who are you interested in?"

"Sir Henry, for a start," Julius said, watching his cousin. Alex might have an air of lazy lassitude, but he missed nothing.

"A country squire. Assiduous and locally influential. Has a good income, and is very content with his lot. He's hanging out for a wife, if only to stop his mother's perpetual nagging."

Julius nodded. "Mr. King."

Alex's gaze sharpened. "A newcomer. Very observant, but speaks only when he needs to. He says he's travelled extensively, but now he wants to settle down. Also hanging out for a wife. I believe his income to be sufficient."

"He says he's visited Rome."

"The devil!" Alex said with feeling.

Julius shrugged. "Many people have. That may mean nothing, but still, I'd like to be positive that Miss Merton is safe before I leave the district."

"Miss Merton!" Connie exclaimed. "She is the one? You believe her to be a Stuart?"

With a wry smile, Julius nodded. "I more than believe it. Augustus discovered a new document in Rome. Most of it was destroyed, but the Mertons featured on it. It listed some of the other children, too. Now I've seen her, I don't have any doubts."

"What do you intend?"

Julius hesitated. Before he'd met her he'd have said he planned to leave her in peace, but in all conscience he could not claim that now. So what did he want?

His body knew. He heated every time he was close to her. But his mind—he would not let his basic urges dictate his decisions ever again. He did not answer Alex, but spread his hands. "I will decide when I know more."

Alex exchanged a glance with his wife that Julius decided not to pursue. "I am living at the Crown in Appleton." He snorted. "If you can call it living. It's adequate. I do not want anyone to recognize me, not yet. I take it you have not done much in the way of social events locally?"

"Not at all," Alex said. "We've used Connie's health shamelessly as a shield." He clasped her hand warmly in his.

"Alex was far too anxious," Connie said, turning a laughing face to first her husband and then Julius. "I was fine. A little sickly, it's true, but rest and a careful diet took care of that."

Alex shook his head. "The birth was agony. They wouldn't let me anywhere near her."

"To fret around me while I did my work?" Connie laughed. "No."

"I know. I recall the day Caroline was born. I went to my wife when she howled for me, but they protested vigorously until I threatened them with force." The birth had come as a deep shock to his wife, who had expected nothing like the experience she'd undergone. How she could have remained ignorant of the realities of giving birth had mystified Julius, but further shocks had remained in store for them both.

He turned his mind away from the memory of what had happened after the baby's birth. He had no wish to dwell on it, especially on such a happy occasion and with two of his best friends.

Connie and Alex looked to be as deeply in love as ever. Julius was happy for them and felt no jealousy when he saw them together, any more than when he saw the other Emperors with the people they had found to love. He told himself that more frequently these days, although he didn't doubt a wife would make his life easier from a practical point of view.

Inevitably, his thoughts drifted back to Eve. Would she—no, he could not even think it. He had to give himself more time.

"We will not be doing that again," Alex said firmly.

Connie merely laughed, but her exchange of glances with Julius told a completely different story. She wanted more children, and if Julius knew her at all, he would not wager on her not getting her way.

"That is entirely your concern," he said, thus forestalling any discussion until after he had left. "I have been invited to attend a soiree at Sir Henry Fulworth's house. Am I likely to meet anyone there?"

"I would hope so," Connie said, "or the soiree will be a complete failure."

Julius rolled his eyes. "You are perfectly aware of my meaning. Anyone who might recognize me."

"So you'll put up with indifferent service at an inn and not seeing Caroline for a while?" Alex said.

"She and Helena are with my parents. They will be safe enough for a week or two." Although Julius had his worries in that quarter, he would not concern his cousin with them at the moment. Once he would not have hesitated, but Alex had his own worries now. "I need to ensure this person is safe."

"I could do that for you."

Julius finished his tea. "I will take care of her safety before I leave."

And give himself time to recover from his inconvenient tendre for her. Mere infatuation wore off on its own. He should know. By the time he left, he should be clear-headed once more.

In any case, she had two suitors. Although he suspected one, he could not in all conscience stand between her and Sir Henry. His personal dislike of the baronet should not matter in this instance. *Should not.* He repeated the words firmly in his mind, but it made no difference. He still wanted her, still held feelings he could not deny or quell. She had wit and intelligence. She should not waste it on the pompous Sir Henry. Julius was torn, but he would overcome his doubts. He must, because Eve did not belong in his world.

And he did not belong in hers. How could he even consider it?

He glanced at Alex to find his cousin regarding him from below half-closed lids. The sleepy expression did not fool Julius for even a second. Alex was watching him with the kind of careful speculation that had made him a deadly opponent on the card table and in the fencing studio. He missed nothing.

"What?" Julius demanded irritably.

"If you should find yourself in need of shelter, you will come here," Alex said, making what might have been a question into a statement. He stretched his legs out. A bee bumbled its way along the terrace, finally finding its way back into the garden. It seemed to hold a fascination for Alex, but he had the habit of fixing his attention on something else when he was thinking. "It sounds as if you might be playing a dangerous game." He turned his regard back to Julius, and now there was nothing lazy about his eyes. "You are on your own, not even a servant to help you. Send word if anything happens. If you find yourself in any danger, come here at once. Bring whomever you need to."

Recognizing a stone wall when he saw it, Julius nodded. Alex would not take a denial, nor would he turn his back on his cousin, even if Julius asked him to. "As you wish. I promise I will come if I need to." Although the last thing he wanted to do was bring trouble to Alex at this time.

"Good."

Julius picked up a small cake and popped it in his mouth, chewing appreciatively. The landlady of the inn knew how to cook a good breakfast, but the rest of her offerings were less successful.

Alex scraped back his chair and got to his feet. "Now, may I introduce you to our son before you leave?"

An hour later, Julius was on his way, a plain parcel in his hands. He would never forget his poor valet's face when he insisted the garments be wrapped as tightly as possible in brown paper. He was still smiling when he walked back into the inn.

Chapter 3

"Oh look," Mrs. Merton said. "There's that man, Mr. Vernon. And he's carrying something. I wonder what it could be?"

"Mama, it's none of our business." Eve refused to gawp out of the window. While she guessed who "that man" must be, she would not succumb to the kind of curiosity the rest of the village indulged in. She wasn't so high-minded she thought gossip was above her, but she considered people had a right to go about their business without others speculating about them.

This time, a curl of curiosity crept up, despite her good intentions. "What is he carrying?"

Her mother turned around, her eyes sparkling. "I knew you were interested in him!"

"Mama, he is new to the village. That is all. My interest is merely academic." Carefully, she stuck her needle into the fabric, taking more care than necessary, so she did not have to look at her triumphant parent.

"Nonsense. You have three suitors, my dear. You should be pleased with yourself."

Why did her mother persist in such nonsense? In three years, Eve would reach thirty, well past marriageable age. "I have no portion, Mama. None. What man will take me without that? And what security could I hope for?" They might flirt, but they might never come up to the mark.

Six years ago, on her father's death and the lowering discovery that he had lived beyond his means for a number of years, Eve had set her mind away from marriage. "Sir Henry enjoys flirting. That is all. Mr. King is merely ingratiating himself with local society. Mr. Vernon is moving on in a few weeks. None will make me an offer, Mama. Why should they?"

"Sir Henry wants a mother for his children. He is comfortably off and may make provision for you himself. Mr. King is well-circumstanced. Of all three, Mr. Vernon appears the least endowed, but we do not know for sure." Mrs. Merton shrugged. "He could be one of those wealthy Cits we're always reading about. I am not so particular, and I know you are not. You could be a good wife to any one of them."

Eve refused to get her hopes up. She would not yearn for something beyond her reach. That had been her whole purpose in seeking a post as a governess. She refused to let life pass her by, and she would do what she had to. "Nevertheless, they will marry other ladies, Mama. Their company enlivens the day, but I will not consider any of them as serious until one actually makes good. Not that I expect any of them to do so," she added hastily, when her mother's expression lightened.

"My dear, what you lack in fortune, you make up for in beauty. A beautiful woman may go far."

Eve sighed. Why was she having this discussion yet again? She glanced outside at the sunny day. "I will not be holding my breath," she said.

She liked all of them, in different ways. Sir Henry's steadiness and his position in local society must always appeal to a young woman with an uncertain future, and Mr. King had purchased a not inconsiderable establishment a few miles away. Mr. Vernon—he was merely being polite and perhaps amusing himself while his lordship kept him kicking his heels.

Her mother took a deep breath and clasped her hands. "Then you should," she said. "What if he knows of your true origins?"

Eve's stomach sank. "Not that again, Mama. I am Eve Merton."

"You are Eve Stuart," her mother said. She indicated the engraving on the wall that hid the secrets.

Or the fairy tale that had enlivened her childhood. All her life, her parents had referred to her as special. Eve had at first assumed that was because she was an only child, but after her father's death, her mother had shown her the papers.

The staggering fact that she was the granddaughter of a deposed king had amazed Eve while it stretched her credulity to its absolute limits. For a while, she had spent her nights dreaming of the time when she would go to Rome and reclaim her heritage. A happy fantasy, but she never fooled herself that there was any truth in the story.

Then she had examined the papers. From then on, Eve accepted that the stories had some truth. But what did it matter? After all, nobody could imagine such a thing. A secret princess, hidden in a sleepy village just waiting for her prince? She hardly thought so. Where her mother was a dreamer, Eve was a pragmatist. Someone had to be, especially when her father had left them so ill-circumstanced.

"I am Eve Merton," she repeated now. "Mama, I wish you would just burn those papers and leave be."

As a child, Eve had been glad of the stories her mother told her at bedtime, about princes and beggar maids, beauties hidden in kitchen ashes, but now? It was past time to put childish things away. Although she had come to accept her heritage, she had not spun dreams and imaginings around it, as her mother had. What point would there be? So she was a king's granddaughter. Plenty of people were, and not all of them reaped the benefits. Plenty got into deep water, though. If her biological father had wanted her, he would have sent for her, but all the evidence pointed to the fact that he couldn't care less.

She sprang to her feet. "I will take Muffy for a walk," she said. "The exercise will be good for him."

If Mr. Vernon had reappeared, perhaps she would meet him, as she had said she would. She had little faith in the casual question, but was heartened by his visit. Perhaps he would appear. Anything was better than sitting in this room listening to her mother's rambling.

Her mother's old spaniel tended to keep his perambulations to the house and garden, but as a result he was growing somewhat stout. A brisk walk on this lovely day would suit them both.

Mrs. Merton glanced out of the window again. "No one would want to be cooped up on such a lovely day. In fact, I believe I will dead-head a few rose bushes. It is a fine day, far too good to waste."

Relieved her mother had not continued with her lecture, Eve hurried away to find Muffy and his lead. Ten minutes later, armed with an ageing spaniel, a broad-brimmed straw hat, and a pair of gloves, Eve sallied forth on to the village green.

A familiar figure stood in the shade of the big oak tree near the inn. Her heart took a leap, banging hard against her chest, but the distance between them gave Eve a chance to regain some of her calm. Eve headed toward the church at the other end of the green, setting a brisk pace. It took him little time to catch up with her. He tipped his hat. "A fine day, Miss Merton. And a fine-looking dog."

She laughed. "Muffy belongs to my mother. He's an old boy, but he has all the enthusiasm of a puppy. When he is not sleeping, that is."

Muffy wagged his tail vigorously as if he knew she was talking about him. Laughing, Mr. Vernon bent and patted him. Muffy reacted with shameful abandon. Placing his paws on Mr. Vernon's knees, he rose so Mr. Vernon could give him the tribute he deserved.

Eve couldn't resist smiling. Nothing daunted, Mr. Vernon ruffled the spaniel's ears, in a way that always turned Muffy into a slavish follower.

"Do you have experience with spaniels, sir?"

"I like dogs." He glanced at her. "My daughter has often begged me for one, but I told her to wait. She has reached her sixth birthday, so I suppose I must consider it now. Would you recommend a spaniel?"

He must miss his daughter. "They're good natured and lively. Muffy sleeps a lot these days, but when they're puppies, they're always busy. And they shed."

Easing Muffy's paws off his legs, Mr. Vernon brushed at his breeches as he stood. His lips held a wry smile. "As I see. He works hard at that, doesn't he?"

She laughed. "He does indeed." Muffy had left his presence on not a few pieces of furniture. "My mother tends to take the path of least resistance and favors brown as her color of choice for upholstery."

"Although not her gowns."

"No, indeed." Her mother had a penchant for green, a color that appeared nowhere in Muffy's fur. Consequently, her clothes became bedaubed with strands of brown fur, especially in the spring and autumn, when Muffy concentrated on shedding the coat of one season and gaining another. Each coat was becoming streaked with grey, like her mother's own hair. Eve's dark, glossy hair had not shown signs of grey yet. How would she feel when it happened? Relieved, probably. Maybe then, her mother would stop pushing her at people. Men in particular.

Tugging at Muffy's lead, she moved on. Mr. Vernon fell into step by her side. "You will be leaving Appleton soon, will you not, sir?"

"I may have to stay a little longer than I planned."

She glanced at him and met his clear gaze. He had the most remarkable blue eyes. They seemed to pierce through her soul. She shook her head, her response too fanciful for her liking. It had shaken her far too much.

"I thought you said your business was trivial."

"It is, but his lordship is disinclined to conduct business. I've brought a few papers for him to sign, and he wants to read them through. Or so he says."

"You went to the Manor?"

"Indeed." He opened a gate for her when she made for the footpath that led around the outside of the village. She always took Muffy this way, but she had not previously considered how private part of it was. She would hurry through. Not that she didn't trust Mr. Vernon. After all, he had brought her home safely, despite the effect she'd had on his body. He had behaved like a gentleman, although he could have dismounted and tumbled her in the nearest hedgerow.

She would not have objected.

It had taken her several sleepless nights before she could accept that simple truth. She had wanted him to do something. She still did, and that was utterly foolish of her.

They strolled along the shady lane, the dog frolicking by her side. When he dragged at the lead in his effort to reach the nearest hedgerow, she switched the hand she held him with. That brought her closer to Mr. Vernon. His warmth infused her, and when she stumbled, he caught her.

He did not release her immediately, but waited until she looked at him. This time his eyes were grave, lost in looking at her. "You are most lovely, you know," he said softly.

"I know." Why should she dissemble? "It's a curse for someone in my position."

A smile touched his eyes but did not curve his mouth.

Pulling away, she began to walk once more.

He remained with her. "You should celebrate it," he said softly. "You give people a great deal of pleasure."

"I do nothing to achieve that. It isn't something I have worked for."

"Sometimes they are the finest moments in life. When everything falls into place and creates something beautiful."

He stopped, and reached for the dog's lead, turning her towards him. Fascinated by those piercing eyes, Eve remained still. With the leather wrapped firmly around his wrist, Mr. Vernon gave one sharp tug. Muffy sat.

She turned her attention to the animal. "How on earth did you do that?"

"Dogs appreciate a firm hand." He tilted her chin, turning her face up to his. He met her gaze. "I want to kiss you. I've wanted to do so since I first saw you."

"Mr.—"

He touched her lips with one finger. "My name is Julius. It would give me great pleasure to hear it from you."

As enthralled as the dog, she murmured, "Julius."

His voice lowered to an intimate tone. His breath heated her cheek when he spoke. "That sounds as perfect as I knew it would. You are not merely beautiful, Eve, you are fascinating. I would not have let any woman travel that road alone at that time of day, but you—I would have given you that nag I'd hired and walked on myself, if you had wished.

You could have asked anything of me. Anything," he repeated, his voice even softer. His eyelids drooped as he fixed his gaze on her mouth. "You want it too. Hold still, then, while I fulfill both our wishes."

He parted his lips. She felt his breath on her cheek, but she did not move away. He pressed his lips to hers. She sighed, unable to resist him.

When he drew away, he was smiling. "Open for me, my sweet," he murmured, and kissed her again.

He looped his free arm around her waist, drawing her close until she felt it again, that hard shaft of forbidden sin. The intimate contact sent thrills of excitement through her.

At first, she rationalized her need. What did a few kisses matter? They were in a sheltered part of the path, and they would hear anyone approaching, thanks to the loose stones festooning the hard-packed earth beneath their feet. He'd chosen the part where the path curved to take in the farthest part of the churchyard, giving them relative privacy.

He tilted his head, sealing them more securely together, and licked into her mouth. She had no idea when she had parted her lips. She had certainly not intended to. He released a small groan, the sound reverberating down her throat and into her center. Stubble on his chin abraded her skin, and she moved, the better to experience the foreign sensation. His passion encompassed her while he took all he wanted and she gave it to him.

No passive recipient, she. Eve considered herself past the first flush of youth, but now she felt like a green girl, newly left the schoolroom, instead of a respectable governess, the daughter of an impoverished country vicar.

He stroked her back. Although she was fully dressed, she imagined she could feel his touch, his hand spread over her skin to claim it for his own. When he licked the roof of her mouth, flicked the tip of his tongue along the seam in the middle, it became her turn to moan, a soft sound that made him inhale sharply and increase the depth and the fervor of his embrace.

He finished the kiss, withdrawing slowly, parting from her with a slowness indicating reluctance, but he did not release her. He studied her, his eyes taking in the contours of her face. Then he caught his breath and kissed her again, as if drawn to the embrace despite his better judgment.

As she most certainly was. Lost in him she returned his kiss, cupping her hand over his cheek, the rough abrasion adding to the sensations rioting through her. His beard shadow did not show as other men's did, being fair, but it was as potently masculine as any she had ever seen. Never touched, nor had the burr ever had such an effect on her before.

His lips on hers, his skin under her hand delivered waves of sensation that rippled over her skin, enlivening her and bringing all her senses to a peak. He murmured something against her lips and kissed her again. This man knew exactly what he was doing, which was more than Eve did.

She stretched up, arching her neck, her back hollowing in her efforts to get closer to him. An urge filled her, one she was not used to, to press her body against his, head to foot, to drink in as much of him as she could. He tightened his hand on her back and curled the other around the back of her neck, gently caressing her bare skin, his fingers thrusting into her hair to cup the back of her head under her linen cap. He had her exactly where he wanted her. Eve couldn't have been happier about it.

Reckless thoughts invaded her mind. Why should she not let him go as far as he wished? If she had hung out for a lover, she could not have found a more worthy candidate. He was leaving soon, likely never to return, and from his kisses he would know what to do and how to do it, which was more than she did. She could take him, and nobody would be the wiser.

She lost herself in him. Sinking into his arms, letting him lead her to places she had never visited before was deceptively easy. Seductively easy. He caressed her softly, tenderly, but their passion increased every time his lips returned to hers, and her willingness to accept him grew more eager.

With a gasp, she pulled away and shoved her hands against his chest.

He opened his eyes, his mouth still curled in a smile, reddened with their kisses. "Calm yourself, sweetheart," he murmured, but he let her go, releasing her gradually, giving her time to regain her balance and her sense of where she was.

Her first thought was for Muffy. Sometime during their embrace, he'd released the dog. The spaniel could be anywhere. But when she looked down, there he was, lying with his head resting on his paws, fast asleep.

"I kept my foot on his lead," Julius said. "He seemed content." He took her hand. He could well be applying the word to her.

His warmth seeped through her, inviting her to return to the shelter of his arms.

Seductive was exactly the right word. "What were we thinking?" she demanded, when she should have asked the question of herself much earlier.

"I was thinking that you are lovely and you fit perfectly in my arms." He smiled. "I wouldn't have compromised you."

He said the last softly, but she wasn't sure what he meant.

His lips curved. "I wouldn't have gone any further than I did. Truly, I didn't intend to take you this far. Only a kiss, I thought, but you are too lovely for just one kiss."

She swallowed. "I didn't mean to encourage you." This would not be the first time a man had accused her of leading him on, although that time she'd been innocent of any such intention.

Julius frowned. "None of this was your fault. The only way you caused it was by being here. I will keep you safe, Eve, I swear it."

She glanced down at their joined hands, where he'd increased the pressure slightly. He was not drawing her back, though.

"I should not. We have not known each other long. We have met only a few times…" Panic swept in when she realized how far he had taken her with but a few kisses. She fought to keep her breathing steady.

"I know. But you draw me, sweet Eve. I want to know you better, if you will permit it."

"You're going back to London soon."

He nodded. "Not for a while. And are you fixed permanently here, in Appleton?"

She was not. "I'm a respectable woman, sir. I may not possess a great fortune, but I cannot consider any other way of life."

"I know you cannot. If this friendship progresses the way I want it to, it will lead to the expected outcome."

Marriage. When he said it, the prospect did not sound so distant. That could not be right. She couldn't expect marriage. Except this man wasn't a landed gentleman, and he wasn't in the first flush of youth. Both points made him more eligible for her, not less. He could please himself where he married. He had a daughter, a motherless child, and he had a prosperous business. Either that or he was a charlatan of the first order. "You would consider that?"

He nodded, tugging on her hand so he drew her back to him. "Of course. I would welcome an intelligent woman to help me in my life's task. That you are unutterably lovely and intelligent make this an even more delicious prospect. Should you object if I set to courting you?"

Eve could hardly believe she was accepting his proposal. "I should say no. We have met but three times, counting today."

What would he say if she told him she was a princess, the granddaughter of an anointed king?

She knew immediately. He would her mad, and he would reject her. If she believed her mother, that would mark her as a madwoman for sure.

He gazed at her, warmth in his eyes, so she knew he was getting great pleasure from her appearance. Since she had hardly dressed up to take this walk with Muffy, that was saying something. "I can move quickly when the mood takes me."

She'd wager he could. He was a successful businessman. That, and his air of command told her more than the scant information about himself that she knew. He was decisive, strong, and bone-meltingly handsome. Not that the last had anything to do with the situation, except she loved to look at him. She would find it no hardship to see his face on the pillow beside her every morning.

Her body heated anew, though they were only linked by their hands.

Muffy stirred, and Eve took the opportunity to look away, lest she appear a lovesick fool. She would have bent and picked up the lead, except he did it first. The dog trotted happily by his side, the plumes of fur wreathing his legs bouncing perkily with every step.

"He'll never do that for me," she said. "He pulls at the lead all the time."

"He just needs to know who is master," Julius said, glancing down at the dog.

He didn't release her hand or offer his arm for her to take in a more formal manner, but linked his fingers with hers and swung their arms gently as they continued with their walk. "I thought my daughter too young for a dog before, but taking responsibility for another creature might help her."

"Oh?" That didn't sound encouraging.

Neither did Julius's gentle sigh, scarcely a breath, but his expression changed, his mouth flattening. "She's growing up fast. I would like her to remember her mother, but that is impossible. My wife died just after Caroline was born." He flicked a glance at her.

"I'm so sorry."

"Thank you." He studiously kept his attention on the path before them. "We manage, my daughter and I." His expression lightened, his eyes sparkling. "She's a lively child, and her intelligence is better than I have seen in others. Of course she's lovely." He was smiling when, finally, he turned his attention back to her.

"You must miss her while you're on this errand."

He nodded. "Yes, I do. Who knows what she will do while I'm away? She's staying with my parents, under the supervision of my sister."

She smiled, easy now his mood had shifted. "You have sisters?"

"I have two sisters and one brother. Helena is closer to me in age than Lucinda. Usually she makes her home with me."

"And your brother?"

"He's abroad. A scholar." His smile broadened.

"You are fortunate to have the means to indulge him."

"Oh, he supports himself. He is not without means."

Whatever that was supposed to convey. Was Julius wealthier than she had supposed him? The notion made Eve uncomfortable. She would appreciate a comfortable life, but not one so far different to the one she knew.

She didn't need to know everything about him now. She could wait. Perhaps their closer acquaintance would end in failure. She refused to get her hopes up and let her dreams run away with her. Despite the way he had aroused her, she would not succumb. He had but asked for her permission to see more of her and assured her his intentions were honorable, should they decide to take their acquaintance further. Nothing else.

Easy to say now, when he was but holding her hand.

He paused, lifted her hand to his lips, and brushed her palm with them. "If you do not pursue our friendship, I will understand." He smiled at her, his old confidence returning like a shield to protect his deeper emotions from becoming exposed. "That is, I will understand, but I will not give up."

His audacious remark made her laugh. "I take it that doesn't mean you wish to abduct me? One reads the accounts in the papers and trembles with fear. Although I must make a confession to you."

He raised a brow in query.

"I do not have a dowry, sir." Better he knew now, even if he had not guessed it. "Not a jot. There is no dowry, no provision for me, save what my mother has preserved." Gentlemen married for gain, not for love. Despite what he said, the cold, hard fact remained between them.

"I'm sorry to hear that, but for your sake rather than any other reason." He retained her hand and walked on, giving Eve a ridiculous sense of togetherness. With his hand touching hers, she felt better, more than she was in an odd way. She could not think like this, could not.

A woman without any source of income was a vulnerable creature. He should understand her position. She could not allow him to continue with her if he had any doubts.

With Julius, Muffy behaved like a well-trained gun dog, trotting by his side and sitting when they paused, as they had just now.

"My father engaged in several unwise speculations. When he lost money, he would find another hare-brained scheme. We had no idea he had spent everything until after his death." Her father had been as much of a dreamer as her mother, but his dreaming had been more dangerous.

His hand tightened around hers. "He was feckless. So you have nothing?"

"An annuity opened in my mother's name by her father. It is our sole source of income now."

"Your father was the vicar here?" he asked.

"Yes."

"I'm so sorry." Abruptly he halted and turned to face her. "That must have been difficult for you."

"Yes." She could not deny it. She had gone from a comfortably circumstanced young woman to a pauper in the space of a month. His concerned gaze told her he really cared. He wasn't merely expressing sympathy because it was expected of him.

"The house is yours?"

She nodded.

"I'm glad to hear that. Miss Merton—Eve. I would very much like to see you again. Like this. I feel we have learned a great deal about each other in one short walk." His words sounded formal, but the burning gaze he fixed on her was not.

She heated under his appraisal, wanted nothing more than to please him. She would have to take care. For a woman in her position, the sentiment was dangerous.

They had reached the place where they either looped around the church and returned to the village or took the path to the Manor. People could come upon them here. Gently, she freed her hand, and he nodded as if he understood.

He left her outside her front gate and lifted her hand to his lips. "I will claim the first dance at Sir Henry's ball. Be ready for me, my lady."

She liked being his lady. Liked it too much. If they had too many moments as private as this, she would make herself too vulnerable to him. She must be careful not to spend time in private with him. Not only for propriety's sake, but for her own peace of mind.

Chapter 4

Julius only accepted the invitation to dinner at the vicarage when he heard that Eve was attending. After that one reckless moment by the church, he had behaved impeccably, although he had made it subtly clear that he was interested in Eve.

He had seen her at church, and during the week he accompanied her on her walks with Muffy. He dared not indulge himself again. He'd found her kiss and the heat of her body against his overwhelming, too much of a temptation to repeat. His declared intention was to remain close to her while he waited for a reply from his enquiries to London, but the more time he spent with her, the more she attracted him and the more he wanted her.

He walked around the green to the vicarage on a fine summer afternoon that was gently mellowing toward evening. The house was a reasonably substantial building next to the church, superior to the smaller establishment where Eve and her mother currently lived. Built and much improved by the last incumbent, or so the gossipy landlady at the Crown had informed him. It appeared that the Reverend Mr. Merton had been too profligate for his own good. And more importantly, that of his wife and child.

A neatly attired maid took his hat and gloves and ushered him into the parlor.

The Reverend Simpson, his wife, and daughter waited to greet him. Julius blinked when Miss Simpson curtseyed, his view of her bosom more suited to a ballroom than to a sedate dinner engagement. Blond and pretty, Miss Simpson was the eldest child of the Reverend, her two siblings being still in the schoolroom. Julius assessed her to be no more than seventeen.

She flourished her fan and bade him sit next to her. The gracious drawing room was a stark contrast to the little parlor across the green. This was furnished in a more modern style, the parquet floor highly polished and the upholstery matching.

"La, sir, you must have seen much of the world. Is London so very exciting?"

"It depends what you consider exciting," he said cautiously.

"Balls, and the theater, and the opera, and the pleasure gardens. Not to mention the shopping! I have been at Father this past age to allow me a season there, but he has only promised Bath." She pouted.

"In a year or two, we will consider the visit," her mother said.

Mrs. Simpson was a comfortable woman with the same pale blond hair as her daughter and a flamboyant, not to say individual, style. Her burgundy gown contrasted vividly with the turquoise petticoat, but her daughter was not to be outdone by such a bold statement. While her gown of the palest pink was of a suitable color for one her age, it was cut daringly low, and adorned with a great many brooches and pins. A row of lace bows marched down the front of her stomacher. She was overdressed for court, much less a country vicarage. She should have been left in the schoolroom to mature for another twelve months and a suitable governess found who could give her polish.

"I believe the Mertons were here before," Julius said, not wishing to talk about life in London for fear he might give something away.

Miss Simpson made a face. "Miss Merton was much indulged by her father, or so I heard, although I was a babe in arms when she made her come-out. However, there she is, still single. She quite fancied herself the belle of the district when she lived here. She was of course much reduced in circumstances, but gossip had it that she was none too particular about her friends."

"Really?" Julius's acquaintances might have taken the hint when they heard the frozen tone of that one word, but Miss Simpson took no notice.

"A man such as you, sir, aware of the traps of the world, must realize what dangers a woman faces when presented with a handsome man." Her fanning grew more vigorous.

"Must I? Miss Merton has never behaved with anything but the greatest propriety." And may the gods spare cutting his tongue out for speaking such lies. However, Julius had vastly enjoyed her relatively mild impropriety, and he did not intend to share his delight with anyone else.

"She is playing fast and loose with Sir Henry. Surely you have noticed?"

Had this child not noticed Julius's own interest in Miss Merton, or was she willfully blind? The truth hit Julius as the little madam moved closer to him, giving him an unwanted view of her immature breasts. He raised his attention to her face. "Miss Merton is a woman of great sense, far too much to flirt with a man who is already at her feet. Most men are, you know, but it isn't merely a matter of her looks. She has intelligence and grace."

Miss Simpson smiled archly. "She is not alone in that."

Was she suggesting that she had similar qualities? Miss Simpson could be a pretty miss, like some of the others here tonight, but she needed more appropriate clothes and style, and she should definitely not wear face paint at her age. While paint had its place, and Julius had employed the art himself on occasion, it appeared grotesque on the face of a seventeen-year-old, particularly the more artificial look utilized by older ladies of his acquaintance.

He would dearly love to give her parents a piece of his mind, but of course he would not.

She tilted her head and flicked her eyelids closed and then open in a strange parody of flirtatiousness. Julius swallowed his sharp comment. He had not shown such restraint for a long time, and he was fully aware why he did it. He didn't want to make affairs difficult for Eve. This young lady had power over Eve, of a slightly superior standing, and parents willing to indulge her.

To his immense relief, the bell clanged, and in a moment Eve and her mother came in. Julius had eyes only for Eve. Her burgundy-colored gown was adorned with a deep hem of summer flowers that Julius strongly suspected Eve had done herself, since he'd come across no commercial pattern like it, and her plain ivory petticoat had been turned, but was a restful relief to the finery of Miss Simpson and her mama.

His smile was genuine when he made his bow. Meeting Eve's eyes for a bare moment, he noted the slight arch of her brow when she glanced at Miss Simpson and was hard put not to burst into laughter. Their understanding was becoming far too profound for him to remain dignified in public, and he looked forward to her no doubt perceptive comments about the young woman when he accompanied her on her walk.

Sir Henry Fulworth and Mr. King arrived shortly after, and they went into dinner. Julius was far too wily a hand to allow himself to be maneuvered into taking Miss Simpson in. That honor belonged to Sir Henry, who showed himself adept at suppressing the young woman's over-bright conversation. She could do a lot worse than Sir Henry, who despite his staidness showed a deal of common sense.

Mr. King watched. He might just be an observer by nature, but Julius wondered about that. He took the bull by the horns. "You must tell us about your travels, Mr. King. You told me that you had visited Rome. Did you enjoy the Eternal City?"

Mr. King sent him a smile as he helped himself to creamed asparagus and offered it to Mrs. Simpson. That had given him time to marshal his thoughts, damn him. "Indeed, sir, although the odors are those of any large city in Europe."

"I am accustomed to London. I cannot imagine anything more... pungent." He would not go into details at the dining table. The food showed a tendency to over-elaboration, but was palatable. He would have preferred the lamb a little rarer, the pork better cooked, and a few less rich sauces, but that might just be his personal taste. "Of course it depends on the part of the city one wishes to go."

"I cannot say I have ventured into the more noisome parts of London," Mr. King said. "Only the squares and the parks, in general."

"Which squares would that be?" Julius asked. The Dankworths lived in St. James's Square. Would King mention it?

But King did not answer him directly. "Most of my business is conducted in the City. The Cocoa-Tree, for example."

Julius seized on the snippet with savage delight. At last, something he could use. "Where the Jacobites congregate?"

King paused, lifting a forkful of food to his mouth. When he had finished eating and taken a sip of wine, he answered Julius. "And not a few Tories from the countryside."

Jacobite ones, certainly. "I see. What is your line of business, sir?"

"Oh, this and that." Mr. King met Julius's gaze directly, his eyes sparkling with barely concealed anger. "I could ask you the same."

"Property," Julius said smoothly. "That is my business."

Their eyes dueled in a moment of pure animosity before Mr. King turned his attention to Eve and toasted her, lifting his glass slightly before putting it to his lips. "You are, as always, exquisite, ma'am. I wish I knew your mantua-maker."

Eve laughed, a ripple of pure merriment. "Her name is Eve Merton, sir, as well you know."

"You should have the services of the best dressmaker in London."

At least they could agree on that.

Being so close to Eve and yet unable to talk to her properly proved frustrating to Julius. So much that at the end of the evening, he offered to escort Eve and her mother back to their home across the green. Mr. King had said nothing Julius could positively act on, and he seethed with annoyance.

"You do not like Mr. King, do you, sir?" Eve asked him. She had her gloved hand tucked into his arm. It felt perfect there.

"No, I do not. I do not trust the man. He is far too cautious about the information he imparts. He says he comes from the north, but his accent is southern."

"He has been here for six months, but I feel I know you better than I know him."

All Julius's ill-temper dissipated at the sound of her voice and the pressure of her hand on his arm. Her touch soothed him. "I have been trying to understand you. Perhaps he is too busy learning to fit in the neighborhood." And being a close-mouthed bastard.

But Eve preferred him. She had chosen him as her escort instead of Sir Henry's carriage or Mr. King's. That made Julius inordinately, foolishly proud.

Tactfully, Mrs. Merton quickened her pace, moving ahead of them.

Julius lowered his voice. "I can blame neither of the gentlemen. You are temptation itself, Eve. Your parents named you well."

She sighed. "I had hoped you would not mention that. My parents named me because I was the first daughter. Had there been a brother for me, I have no doubt his name would have been Adam."

"And the next daughter? Would she have become Lilith?"

They were moving under the shelter of one of the large oak trees that adorned the village green. Acting swiftly, Julius spun her around and claimed a kiss. Far too brief, but it served to take the edge off his frustration and desire for her. She flushed rosily, but when he steered her back, she walked to her house sedately enough and waited until he had bowed over her mother's hand and her own.

Every time he saw her, he wanted her more. He had tried so hard to rein in his feelings and made an effort not to act decisively on it, but already he knew that when he left Appleton, he would not be leaving Eve behind.

It remained to be seen whether she would be there in spirit, in his heart, or in person.

Chapter 5

Sir Henry held his ball the Thursday after the dinner at the vicarage.

He owned a tidy country house, about the same size as the Dower House in the grounds of Julius's father's country home. Perhaps six or seven bedrooms, Julius assessed, as he rode up the drive to the main doors.

He was relieved to find a groom waiting. Stabling his own horse didn't feature in his usual plans for a ball. For that matter, neither did arriving on horseback.

He'd retained the services of the nag he'd hired at the Appleton inn, livelier than the horse he'd previously used. He would still vastly prefer one of his own. The carriages he owned were becoming fond memories. Accustomed to being waited on, he'd nevertheless taken care to ensure he could look after himself if he needed to, and now he was glad of it. His father couldn't even shave himself. When his valet had fallen ill, his father had grown a beard until the man had recovered rather than undertake the task or employ someone he didn't know to do it.

Sir Henry lived five miles from the village, and Julius had enjoyed the ride past green fields and flourishing hedgerows. Life was so much simpler like this. He could live this way for some time, in bucolic ease—except for the rope bed and the raucous sounds in the taproom of an evening. Julius handed the reins and a half-crown to the groom, who seemed pleased with the gratuity. The boy led the nag away.

Of course he could not live like this much longer, but the illusion had been pleasant while it lasted. He had work to do, and he must never forget he was here doing it and not for his own amusement.

His rustic paradise would not have been half as enjoyable without Eve. He visited her house regularly, chafing at the demands of society which meant he could not see her privately again.

His impressions had only been confirmed, the more he got to know her. Eve was beautiful, intelligent, and gracious. She would make a charming countess. Those stray thoughts alarmed him more than he would admit to himself, but they kept happening.

He longed to hold her, to kiss her, to feel the delicate, soft skin of her breast in his palm. At night he dreamed of it. He shifted, his erection making itself uncomfortably apparent. Damnation, when had he become a randy boy again? Even thinking of her had him rampantly ready for her. He waited, thinking of other things—anything—until it subsided. The thought of her in the hands of the Jacobites did the trick.

At the sound of a fiddler scraping a tune, he smiled, although his senses screeched when the musician did the same thing.

He entered the hall to the scent of his childhood—cloves mixed with oranges. He'd helped his nurse stud whole oranges with the spice to freshen the air in the rooms of Edensor Abbey. His memories spun back to those times, before strife had riven his life, before ambition and worldliness had entered his perfect childhood world and torn it apart.

Shaking off the reminiscent mood, he took in his surroundings. He saw plain floorboards, highly polished, worn in places where the foot traffic was heaviest, portraits of stiff-necked people in their Sunday best. Fresh flowers in vases decorated the hall in its holiday mood.

The carved, twisted balusters were smooth with age and polishing. As he ascended them to the floor above, every tread creaked. He was obliged to duck his head as he turned on the landing to avoid a particularly insistent beam, but he carried on without further surprises and followed the sound of the music. A fiddler was scraping away in a room at the end of the narrow corridor, where the double doors lay invitingly open.

Although dusk was only just falling, the candles in the chandelier overhead were already lit. The room was of moderate size and heaving to its full capacity, the people not dancing in the central area standing around the edges gossiping. The smell of camphor was heavy in the air, and as the dancers swirled and turned, the waves of the aroma made him blink to clear his watering eyes. The clothes would have been stored that way, to preserve them, only brought out on festive occasions like this.

Obviously someone else had been similarly affected, because more than one window stood open, the casements letting in the pleasant evening breeze, the candles attracting the occasional insect. No doubt the odor would disappear in an hour or so. Or he would become accustomed to it. Either would suit him. The light cast a soft glow over the couples engaging in a minuet, their steps measured, slower and less fluent than he was used to.

Country balls often took place earlier than those in town because the participants could have some way to go when they were finished. This was no exception, and by the indecently early hour of eight o'clock the ball was in full swing. People were dancing, some more vigorously than others. Others stood around gossiping. The clothes were less extravagant than those worn by Julius's peers, the jewels not as grand, and fewer candles blazed in the chandeliers. Nevertheless, this sight struck Julius as familiar. The talk that happened in these gatherings was not always trivial, and the participants not all set on enjoying themselves. Business would be conducted here, as everywhere else, of all kinds. Arrangements for clandestine affairs, agreements to invest in a ship or a mine, and political alliances were all made in places like this. The gathering drew him, as they always did. Power resided here, even though it was of a local, not national, nature.

Once the camphor smell receded, a mingled aroma of perfumes and burning wax, together with the faint promise of supper, came to him. He smiled and glanced around for people he knew. He was in his element.

"Good evening, sir." Mr. King approached him, snuffbox in hand. "Would you take a pinch?"

Julius shook his head. "I don't count snuff amongst my vices, but I thank you for the civility."

Mr. King tucked his box into his coat pocket. His clothes were fashioned in the latest style, unlike those worn by most of the people present, including Julius. He was careful to retain a few garments that did not pander to fashion in case he found himself in places like this. Mr. King evidently did not consider such small subterfuges necessary, a matter of interest to Julius, who studied the small indications that could add up to a greater whole. "We have several things in common, sir. I venture to assume we are the only people in this room tonight who have an intimate knowledge of London, for instance."

He gazed at Julius directly, his dark eyes challenging.

A feminine voice came from his right. "Mr. Vernon?"

With relief, Julius turned to face the lady who addressed him, but he did not miss the tightening of Mr. King's mouth and the way his nostrils flared, and he widened his eyes. That slight change in expression disturbed Julius. Mr. King had just realized something, and Julius feared he knew what it was.

Whatever had he done, using his real name? True, Vernon was not a particularly unusual name, but anyone knowing it could presume he had a connection with the Vernons. His obsession with not lying had dragged him into a situation he did not appreciate.

His incognito journeys depended on his ability to remain unrecognized. But with Eve he had not been able to lie about his name, and that was proving a mistake. When she fixed him with those clear eyes, he could do nothing but smile like a fool and tell her whatever she wanted to know. If she ever asked him if he was the Earl of Winterton, he would be hard put to deny it.

Julius gave a faint smile. "I daresay, but our experiences must be very different. Did you not spend most of your time in the north?"

The hesitation told Julius much. The man had to pause to invent something plausible. "I have visited London frequently. Our experiences may not be so unlike," the man persisted. "We may have mutual acquaintances. Are you familiar with the Marquess of Strenshall, for instance?"

The name sent a warning jolt through Julius. He frowned. "I can't claim an intimate acquaintance." He could get no closer without telling a lie, and he wanted to avoid doing that. The marquess was his uncle, so "acquaintanceship" was putting their relationship a little too mildly.

Was the marquess, who had fingers in a number of pies, merely a name Mr. King liked to trot out to impress people? He would test that theory. "You move in exalted circles, sir."

Mr. King waved his hand carelessly and laughed. "As you must, also. He is a mere business acquaintance, but a valued one, wouldn't you agree?"

The man was testing Julius for sure, trying to push him into an outright lie. "I would indeed, sir. He and his family have considerable resources and influence. I believe his brother-in-law and his nephew are more active in the business world."

"Mr. Beaumont?" Mr. King curled his lip. "He married above his station. We should all be so lucky." He glanced around the room. "But I must not keep you. Many people will be waiting to speak to you. Especially when they know all your secrets." He tapped the side of his nose. "The Vernons are a distinguished family, are they not?"

He knew. Cold dread invaded Julius, and he felt he was walking into the jaws of an iron trap.

He would not retreat. He could not, if he wanted to keep Eve safe. He flattened his mouth in an unusual public display of distaste. He glanced at Mr. King, who was watching him closely. "There are many Vernons in the world."

King bowed. "Of course. I did not intend to impugn you or accuse you of dishonesty. Forgive me."

"There's nothing to forgive," Julius assured him, although he didn't mean it. King knew who he was, or at the least, which family he belonged to.

"Do you remain in Appleton long?" King asked.

"Longer than I initially thought."

King watched him carefully, but Julius was well accustomed to having attention fixed on him, and he revealed nothing, not the twitch of an eyebrow. He allowed his mouth to curve slightly. "Lord Ripley is taken up with the new addition to his family, and he has little time for business."

"Ah." Mr. King echoed the smile, but Julius saw no warmth in his eyes.

Dancers took to the floor and faced each other. The young women beamed, their eyes shining, and the men facing them returned their enthusiasm. When they danced, they did it wholeheartedly. None of society's grace and reticence pervaded their movements. Julius smiled too, their enthusiasm becoming contagious.

The floor bounced in time to their energetic leaps and hops. They were more or less in time, probably performing this and the others on a regular basis.

He felt Eve's presence close to him, not needing to look to know she was by.

"You're smiling," she said.

Her voice warmed him. "So I am," he said without turning around. "How did you know?"

"I saw you," she said. "A proper smile when you turned away from Mr. King."

He glanced over his shoulder. Mr. King had moved on and was out of earshot. "Are you implying something?"

"No, of course not."

He enjoyed the saucy smile she bestowed on him. As a matter of fact, he enjoyed everything about her. She wore a simple gown in a plain color, but the azure blue suited her, and she bore it, as she did everything she put on, with a sense of rightness, of belonging. He recognized a sense of style when he saw it. Faced with all the luxuries London had to offer, would she retain it? He wanted to find out, felt he would not rest until he knew.

When he was with Eve he could think. His feelings for her were so unlike those he'd experienced with Caroline that he had quite made up his mind to have her. Not love, but deep liking and a physical arousal he would be a fool to deny.

"You are, madam, and you could be right. Should I consider Mr. King a serious rival for your hand?"

She blinked, eyes wide, and only then did he realize what he had just said or implied. "My hand?"

He gentled his voice. "Can you doubt it?"

She jerked her chin to one side and then the other, uncharacteristically awkward. "Sir, you forget yourself. Or where we are. Flirtation is one thing, but intent is quite another. I should remind you of my circumstances."

"I forget nothing." He held still, watching her. A longing to touch her seized him, making him stiffen his muscles in the fight not to pull her into his arms in a shocking display of intimacy. "Why should I hide that I find you attractive?"

"I'm sorry sir, but…" A blush of adorable confusion mantled her cheeks.

He gentled his voice. "Surely you've heard that before."

She sighed, and appeared genuinely confused. "I don't like it…"

"What?" Despite his much-vaunted control, the word emerged too sharply. "Has someone hurt you in the past?"

"No." She glanced around.

Julius hated her discomfort. He searched for a way to alleviate it.

The fiddler stopped playing, and the dancers applauded. The man bowed but then tucked his instrument under his chin once more.

"Would you care to dance?" he asked her. A country dance would afford her a chance to retain her composure. Eve was charmingly open, unlike anyone he had met in a ballroom before. Most young ladies making their debuts in society had learned the correct behavior from the cradle. Consequently, their actions were similar, their behavior acceptable and within what society expected. In short, tedious.

With a bright smile, she placed her hand in his when he held it out. He turned it so her palm was resting on the back of his hand, but the brief intimate palm-to-palm contact pleased him and warmed his heart. His small flirtatious gesture made her flush adorably.

Taking note of the formation, Julius took his place in the set. He bowed to Eve and began the first figure.

Dancing in this way proved more difficult than he had imagined. Julius danced with grace and elegance, a skill instilled in him almost since he could first walk. Changing those habits forced him to think more than usual. While he could not actually stumble, he did remember not to place his feet too precisely and occasionally to land on the flat of his foot after he had hopped in time to the music. Country dancing was much more energetic than the elegant minuets that started balls in society, and on the whole, Julius preferred them, but this time, no. For once he appreciated the vigorous style, as Eve's body responded to the leaping and hopping. He had every excuse to look at her, too.

What was he becoming? The kind of bumpkin who got surreptitious thrills from watching young ladies' bosoms bounce? Dear God, he was despicable. He had best complete his mission before he became the kind of person he ordinarily despised—the leering, laughing type who made every ball a menace to women. Except he was only interested in one woman. One he could not call his own. Yet.

She drew him, urged him to behave in deeply inappropriate ways, like kissing her the other day. Even the memory of the warmth of her lips under his threatened to overcome his resistance. For two pence—less— he'd drag her out from the room to somewhere more private and ravish her the way his body raged at him to do.

Eve Merton was dangerous. She remained totally unaware of the effect she had on the men around her. If he told her everyone in the room watched her, the way she moved and smiled, she would not believe him. At least she was aware of her own beauty, but with looks so dazzling, she would have to be foolish if she were not, and she was far from that.

When they changed partners in the dance, Julius paid strict attention to the lady he was now paired with, refusing to glance at Eve. The occasional glimpse of azure distracted him, but he would not show this new partner discourtesy or give in to temptation. Each warred with his desire to watch Eve, to keep her safe and enjoy the sight of her.

When he turned and met his next partner, he watched the onlookers. Mr. King stood by a side table, positioned so he could watch Eve, which he did with discourteous avidity. He was in conversation with a woman Julius didn't recognize, an older lady with fine but out of date clothes, her hoop the wide oblong of ten years ago. There was nothing so derided as ten-year-old fashions.

He linked arms with lady facing him and whirled her around. She giggled. Julius could never abide gigglers, but he met plenty. Impatiently, he gritted his teeth, curving his lips in a deliberate smile of social enjoyment. She flushed and smiled back. As they turned once more, he heard, "La, sir, I declare you are the most athletic of dancers!"

Julius ground his teeth, but kept the smile. "A pleasure, madam," he said.

He needed every bit of his social training tonight.

However, his next three partners proved more pleasant, dancing well and exchanging polite nothings as well as any society lady. The floor bowed in an alarming way in the corner of the room, but that was not the only reason he was glad to make his way back to her.

Julius and Eve finished the dance together. When they had politely applauded the musician, Julius led Eve off the floor in the direction of the open windows. Eve flicked her fan open and wafted it before her face. "Thank you, sir. You should pay some attention to Miss Simpson, you know."

Sir Henry arrived and claimed a dance from Eve, so Julius had little choice. Good manners dictated that he spoke to Miss Simpson. Tonight, she was sulking, a pout pursing her lips. Her gown was too old for her, too low-cut, too boldly patterned and badly fitting to Julius's critical eyes. He offered to escort her into supper rather than endure a dance with her.

The supper room was smaller than the one set aside for dancing. The dark red walls and the heavy sideboard standing along one wall gave it the appearance of being a dining room in the normal course of events. Small collapsible tables were set along the other walls and under the windows. Several people already sat at them, plates of delicacies before them.

Was he fated to escort this young woman all night? "Are your parents here? I have not yet thanked your father for his sermon on Sunday," Julius said mendaciously. In fact the vicar had droned on about the prodigal son, making no points Julius had not heard many times before in different churches. He could, however, thank the vicar for his brevity, for the sermon had lasted barely half an hour. Before now he'd sat through two hours or more of haranguing and condemnation of worldly ways before watching the cleric waddle his way down the pulpit steps to stand before the altar. One gentleman, one he knew was a six bottle a day man, had even had the temerity to order the congregation to moderate their excesses.

At least he could leave Miss Simpson in the vicar's care, which he did, with alacrity. At first disappointed not to see Eve there, Julius began to wonder where she could be. This house was not large, and the host must have limited reception rooms suitable for such a gathering. Where was she?

Chapter 6

Eve had considered the ball an enjoyable affair, and her success in avoiding Sir Henry made her experience better.

Until she came face to face with the man who had made her heart beat faster. The knowledge lay in Julius's blue eyes, his gaze devouring her in a way that sent a light shiver drifting over her skin. She lifted her fan and used the action to swallow her nervousness and speak to him like a sensible person.

But then he asked her to dance, and she felt compelled to do so. She wanted to, but she longed for so much more, enough to shame her in the midst of these people she knew so well. Surely they could see right to her soul, which was a foolish sensation, but as she went through the familiar steps, they felt strange because of the man she was dancing with. He did not stand out from any of the other participants, hopping and leaping as enthusiastically, but his movements seemed more fluid somehow. Typical she should know this as well as everything else.

One of her acquaintances, a gentleman from the next village along, winked broadly at her, and when they met for their part in the dance, murmured, "You have an admirer!"

Eve made a face at him. She'd known Ian for a good many years and they never stood on ceremony. "I have admirers. They don't come up to scratch, and who could blame them?"

Ian sighed. "If not for Mary, I'd have married you in a heartbeat."

Oh, yes, and Mary had brought a comfortable competence with her. But she could not blame Ian. His parents had arranged the contract, and it had turned into a love match, so she could only be glad for them. Men of any substance needed to make such alliances, not to wed someone from merely liking them.

Even Julius would disappear. For all his fervor, he was probably amusing himself with her, whiling away a tedious visit to the country with a flirtation. When the dance ended, he led her off the floor. She was forced to spread her fan once more to cover her nervous swallow. She had to get away from him, if only to control her pounding heart, so she offered to introduce him to Miss Simpson.

He accepted politely, but with little enthusiasm, and then Sir Henry intervened and led Eve away. "I know you will not mind me speaking frankly," he murmured as they made their way to the next room, "But I thought you were becoming too particular with a certain gentleman. If I had not asked you to accompany me, you might have accepted another dance from him, and of course that would never do."

"Of course," she murmured. Not that she necessarily agreed, but she had learned not to argue too much with the squire. He would discuss his point until everyone except him was tired of the topic and wondered why they had ever brought it to his notice. If she argued back this time, she would appear guilty.

The kisses she'd shared with Julius had marked her soul, burned deep, though she had tried to deny it, to wipe them from her memory. Every night as she drifted off to sleep, she felt the pressure of his lips, his body hot against hers, and yearning filled her.

It heated her now, shortened her breath until she was forced to use her fan in earnest. She tried to laugh her response away to Sir Henry. "The nights are agreeably warm, sir, don't you think?"

"Indeed I do. Would you like a glass of chilled white wine? I ordered extra ice for this occasion. I knew the weather would grow warm." As if he'd ordered it himself, he beamed at her. "My little celebrations are rarely marked by rain."

Eve could think of at least three times she and her mother had made their way home in a downpour, but she wisely kept her counsel. "I have always enjoyed my visits here."

He led her to the table bearing the wine and a bowl of punch. Sir Henry believed in a powerful punch, increasing the potency of at least two of the five ingredients. Wary of the deceptively fruity drink, she accepted a glass of wine instead.

Sir Henry helped himself to punch and continued to regale her with topics that must interest her, since they interested him. Anyone would think he was considerably older than she, when the difference between them was a mere seven years. His gravitas would have adorned a man of more mature years, as would his comfortable rotundity. But he was kind and considered himself the principal man in the district, despite the advent of the baron at the Manor, a baron who would, in the fullness of time, inherit an earldom.

A sense of devilry invaded her, crept in uninvited. "What a pity Lord Ripley was unable to attend tonight."

Sir Henry shrugged, his tobacco-brown coat moving with his shoulders. That coat had seen a lot of evenings like this, and it knew how he moved. "One cannot blame him. He is besotted by his wife. He could have easily left her with her attendants tonight. Of course the man is to be commended for his care of his wife and heir, but—" His wry expression showed what he thought of a man ruled by his wife. "Mr. Vernon promised to convey my warmest wishes. It might yet bring him out of his house."

Sir Henry would be easy to rule. The notion came unbidden, and at once Eve was ashamed of herself for thinking so.

"Madam, I would have a private word with you before the evening is out. I have something particular to ask you."

She blinked. Surely he didn't mean…

When she gave him her full attention, she recognized the warmth and the self-satisfaction. Finally, after years of remaining single, was Sir Henry contemplating taking a wife? Her, to be precise? His mother had prevailed, at last. Or perhaps Julius's interest in her had given him the impetus to pursue his intentions.

He moved closer and smiled. Yes, he meant it. He would propose tonight. She could not refuse him on the grounds of waiting for a nebulous response from Mr. Vernon, and she refused to play one man off against the other. She would have to accept.

Dread filled her heart. She didn't want to become a wife to a man who considered his spouse his duty. Never to see the world, to quench for good and all the restless spirit stirring inside her. To kill that dream put a stone in her stomach. If she married Sir Henry, her dreams would die. His kingdom was this district, a concentrated twenty-mile area he had no desire to leave. The occasional jaunt to Bath would be her only excitement. That was why she had tried so desperately to make a life for herself as a governess—until she had come up against the reality of struggling through life on a tiny annuity.

But how could she refuse him? What other prospect did she have? She might dream of Julius, but he would be moving on very soon and most likely forgetting her. She had known Sir Henry most of her life. On paper he was the better prospect, if he was, as she suspected, finally coming up to scratch. Forcing a bright smile to her lips, she said, "I'm flattered, sir."

Once the baronet had made up his mind, he never changed it, a quality he frequently boasted of.

Panic rattled around her head. She would be thirty all too soon, and she had never achieved half the things she wanted to. Before the trap closed around her, she craved an adventure, something stupidly rash, but she must quell that desire and face reality.

As if she'd wished a bad fairy to appear, a smooth voice came from behind her. "Well met again, Miss Merton, Sir Henry. I thought I should inform you Lord Ripley has appeared in your main reception room."

An odd expression crossed the baronet's features, as if he were sorry and delighted at the same time. To have such an exalted character grace his rooms must fill him with pleasure, even if it meant he was not the highest ranked person present.

He bowed to her. "Should you like me to introduce you to his lordship?" he said.

A shadow seemed to darken the entrance to the room as his lordship entered. After a swift glance at Julius, who of course he knew, he crossed to them and bowed, while Julius made the introductions.

He stood tall, a dark shadow over his chin. He must have dark hair, but he was as devilishly handsome as Julius. A smile played around his mouth when he flicked another glance at his man of business.

Julius made short work of the introductions, making sure he led with her.

Lord Ripley bent over her hand, so close his breath touched it, although his mouth did not. "I'm delighted to meet you once more, ma'am. Sir Henry's mother introduced me to your mama in the other room and directed me here so I could greet my host."

His words were smooth, but they did not move her as Julius's did. He was dressed much finer than Julius, in a crimson velvet coat and waistcoat embroidered with spring flowers and bees. The buttons on his coat and waistcoat glittered, their cut steel brilliance reflecting every speck of light the candles emitted. His neckcloth was tied in an apparently casual style, crisp with starch, and he wore an elaborate society wig, its snowy perfection casting all others, including Julius's, into the shade.

She withdrew her hand as soon as she could and dropped a curtsey, thankful her education had covered matters like how low to go for a peer compared to a king. Not she would ever meet a king, and she was glad of that, too.

As if drawn, she glanced up at Julius. He was watching Lord Ripley, his face completely blank, but when he turned his attention to her, animation returned. A smile hovered at the corners of his mouth, and his eyes sparkled. "Shall we leave his lordship to get acquainted with our kind host?" He shot a sharp glance at Lord Ripley, not at all subservient, and then offered his support.

After a doubtful look at the pair, Eve placed her fingers on his arm and let Julius lead her away.

She leaned closer so she could speak to him alone. "Thank goodness you are not a popinjay!"

Julius swallowed, and his eyes opened wider. "Do you think Lord Ripley one such?"

"Oh, undoubtedly. I have rarely seen anyone so fine. I have always disliked people who pay too much attention to their appearance."

"And you have seen many of these?" Frost edged his voice.

She had gone too far. "I saw many such fine creatures in Bath when I worked there. I don't doubt that his lordship has many fine qualities. However, his appearance would daunt me far too much for me to speak to him in the same way I speak to you."

Julius cleared his throat. "I see. I have seen finer in my time. Lord Ripley is accounted a somewhat careless dresser in the ton, but his wife has brought him up to the mark."

"I have no time to waste on fine lace and costly silks. None at all." She ignored the jealousy that had sparked in her heart. "I possess perfectly adequate garments, and that is all a woman needs."

"You have never yearned for a fashionable gown?" He seemed amused now, a smile turning up the corners of his mouth.

"What good is there in yearning? I never wish for what I will not have." To be more precise, she tried very hard not to.

Julius patted her hand. "I would like to see you in costly silks. It is a shame to keep your beauty shrouded."

She was so taken with the compliment that she forgave him. She had once dreamed of such glories being hers, but had long since set her mind against it. She could not have them, so she would not wish for them.

The room had become crowded, especially around the table where hot viands were currently being served. She had not heard the announcement of supper, but while she had been talking, the fiddler had changed from dance music to quieter airs, indicating an interlude.

"Are you hungry? Would you care to eat?"

She shook her head. "Sir Henry always insists on plenty of food served, but I'm not in need of any." At the name, her mood returned, and gloom descended on her like a cloud.

A frown appeared between his brows. "Are you perfectly well?"

"Of course. I have merely…heard some news." But her voice dipped tellingly at the end, despite her efforts to appear cheerful. She suspected she would not have fooled him even if she had succeeded.

"Come with me." He quickened his pace, but still managed to pass through the crowd as if there was nobody in their way.

They went out of the room, through the larger room which now contained groups of people conversing quietly and along the hall. He opened a door on the left and ushered her into a small, unremarkable parlor.

He closed the door. "You are overset," he said. "What has happened?"

"Nothing."

When she tried to withdraw her hand, he covered it with his, and linked their fingers. His other arm went about her shoulders and it was all she could do not to curl against him and lean her head on his shoulder.

That she ended doing it anyway was more because of him than of her. Insistent but steady urging had her where she wanted to be, so she didn't resist much. "Sir, anyone could come in!"

"They're all busy," he said. "I'm more concerned about you."

She would have lifted her head, but he curved his hand around her cheek, gently urging her to remain there. She was too weary not to. This was the place she had longed to be for weeks, but had not dared to allow it. Now she was here, she could resist no more.

Of course he kissed her, but he only gave her one soft, sweet kiss on her lips before he drew away. "I see trouble in your eyes," he said. "I would like to think you would confide in me, but you don't know me properly, do you?" He smiled softly and touched his lips to her forehead. "That is a situation I would like to remedy. As long as no one offered you an insult, in which case I will rise instantly to your defense."

"No, of course they did not. Entirely the opposite." Sir Henry would obviously not consider his request insulting. She sighed. "I believe I am about to receive a flattering offer, as the saying goes. Tonight."

He raised a brow. His eyebrows were brown, a shade darker than the beard stubble she had noticed before, which was nowhere in evidence tonight. Unable to prevent the action, she snuggled closer into him. He wore a coat of dark blue embellished with black braid tonight, one she had not seen before, and a waistcoat of cream twill. Very smart, she'd thought him before she saw Lord Ripley's finery. Indeed, she still thought so.

"I had not intended to rush into this, but rather than lose my chance, I will do so," he murmured.

His hint did not affect her half as much as Sir Henry's. The delicacy of his words gave her a chance to stop him before he was truly done, to pass off his words as a joke, which, for all she knew, they could be. "It's Sir Henry. He said he wanted to speak to me when he had the time. It can be nothing but a proposal."

"Did he, by God?" Julius said, somewhat louder than before. He cupped her cheek. "And will you accept him?"

"I have little choice." She closed her eyes to force back the weak tears that threatened to fall. "He has shown an interest in me for years, but I cannot wish for it."

When she opened them, his frown was back. "Go on."

"Everyone in Appleton and beyond would consider me highly fortunate to receive such an offer. He is comfortably off, and the district looks up to him. His offer will delight my mother, and she will see it as our salvation."

"But do you want to accept?"

She bit her lip before replying, "No." The sting of the bite gave her something else to concentrate on, fighting back the tears that threatened to fall. "But I must. My mother needs security, and Sir Henry can certainly provide that. I know his mother has impressed on him the necessity of a speedy union, and once mine hears of his intentions, the deed will be done. My word will mean little. How can I abandon my duty in such a way, they will say? I went to Bath to try to forge a different life for myself, but it did not work. I was too young, too attractive for a governess, they said, although I did my best to appear a dowd."

"I see. Did Sir Henry say anything else? Have you committed yourself to him in any way?" His hand remained steady and his gaze purposeful.

Eve could rely on this man, his expression said. She could confide in him. Since she had no special friend and certainly nobody else she could talk to so freely, she would speak to Julius. He would be gone soon enough. Then she would go to her doom, head high, and make the most of what she had.

This could be her adventure, this man. While she would not insult her future husband by indulging herself in an affair, Eve could still talk to Julius, kiss him, and pretend she was a free agent. That she had some measure of control over her life and what she did with it. In truth, few people had that luxury.

Julius kissed her. When she opened her mouth under the pressure of his, he took the opportunity to thrust his tongue into her mouth, greedily searching out the places he had tasted before. His hold on her tightened, and his breath scored her cheek. With a small moan, she curved her hand around the back of his neck, under the queue of his formal wig. His real hair tickled the edge of her hand.

Julius sucked in a breath and increased the fervor of his embrace, holding her securely. In a daring move, she spread her hand over his waistcoat. His heart thumped in a steady rhythm under her palm. The reminder of the hard, strong body under the fine clothes heated her blood, and she returned his embrace, tasting him, sweeping her tongue into his mouth.

He sucked it gently in welcome and stroked her, deepening the kiss until their mouths were melded together. He drew her in until he became her reality, his seduction far more dangerous than all-out assault. She wanted him so much she would have given him anything at that moment and begged him to take it. Her sense of rightness, of what was acceptable, melted away as if it had never existed. When he touched the upper slopes of her breasts, she ached for more, but he only caressed her and then slid his hand around the back of her neck.

Breaking the kiss with a gentle parting of lips, he gazed at her. "You're irresistible," he murmured, his breath mingling with hers. "Dangerous."

How could she be dangerous to him? He could take what he wanted and leave, with nobody any the wiser. She would have to live with the consequences. Oh, but she wanted to. She drew him back. Power shimmered through her when he succumbed with a soft groan, flicking his tongue against her lips so she opened to him immediately.

She was so lost in him, the gentle click did not register in her mind at first. Not until a scandalized shriek rent the air.

"Miss Merton!"

Shock speared through her, but when she tried to jerk away, Julius held her close. He finished the kiss and murmured, "Trust me," against her lips before he withdrew, keeping his arm around her.

He held her steady, before he turned his head. Two people stood in the open doorway, with a few more crowding behind them. Sir Henry and Miss Simpson, her hand over her mouth, her eyes wide with horror. Or rather, feigned horror. She had taken Eve in dislike and never failed to put her down and attempt to humiliate her, particularly in public. Finally she had succeeded.

While different excuses raced through her head, only for her to dismiss them in short order, Eve froze, staring back at her disgrace. Behind Sir Henry, Mr. King watched and then moved as someone else shoved his way through. Just when she thought she was as low as she could get, the guest of honor arrived to witness her downfall.

The only solution Eve could think of was to leave Appleton immediately and find a position as a governess any way she could. Even then her reputation could follow her. Perhaps in London she might find someone who had not heard or didn't care about her predicament.

Nausea rose to threaten her. She could hardly hear anything for the buzzing in her ears.

Julius slid his arm away from her shoulders, but took her hand firmly in his. "I am not accustomed to having so many witnesses to my private moments," he said. "I had no intention of drawing attention tonight, but the deed is done. I'm delighted to inform you Miss Merton has accepted my offer. She has given me her hand in marriage."

Murmurs grew, spreading back along the spectators like the tide going out. The news would be all around the village by morning.

Julius's calm announcement stunned Eve speechless. She stood next to him, frozen. Lord Ripley watched them, the corner of his mouth curved slightly up and a glint in his dark eyes. He looked amused. Everyone else appeared as shocked as Eve, mouths open, low murmurs filling the air.

Then they surged forward to congratulate the couple. Julius lifted Eve's hand to his lips before releasing it to allow her to take the hands of the others.

Her mother entered the room as if catapulted into it, her cheeks flushed, her eyes rounded. "You never gave me any notion! This is all very sudden, my dear."

Because she had no idea until five minutes ago.

"I fixed my attention on her the moment I saw her," Julius said, gazing at her as if he really meant it, his eyes soft, a slight smile quirking the corners of his mouth. "When I realized she was as yet single, I couldn't believe my good fortune. If I had not spoken, I fear she would have been lost to me. I'm afraid my exhilaration on her acceptance led me to the scene you interrupted a few moments ago, but I can assure you, ma'am, my intentions are honorable. I will visit you in the morning and furnish you with all the information you require."

His assurance did calm Mrs. Merton, who swallowed and nodded. The color returned to her cheeks. Almost as if she'd spoken, Eve could discern her reasoning. Her mother was unprepared for the life of poverty into which she had been unceremoniously thrust. Although Mr. Vernon was not the man she would have chosen, he was undoubtedly a man of substance. Eve's mother could well find herself better off than before. She would probably expect to live with them.

What was she thinking? Eve could scarcely bear the congratulations of the guests, but Julius remained standing by the sofa, so she had to stay too and listen to the people she had grown up with congratulate her with varying degrees of sincerity. Agony tore her apart. How would she feel if this had truly happened, if this had not been a foolish attempt to excuse a discretion? Caught in a kiss, no more, they could have brushed past this, surely. The village would have gossiped for a fortnight and then forgotten it. Well, maybe not forgotten, but at least another topic would have arisen to take its place. It might even have been enough to give Sir Henry second thoughts.

Her thoughts raced, but by her side Julius behaved like a man delighted with his fate, not one appalled or trapped. Was he such a good liar? He'd come to this village on business and whiled away an hour or two with her. Eve knew her looks could turn heads and had done her best to appear less attractive, but she was no fool. Only a fool, looking in the mirror each morning, would fail to notice her classically proportioned features. But good looks were not enough for a lifelong commitment. He barely knew her.

At last the people filed out. All the time Lord Ripley had leaned against the wall, watching them with that devilish smile in silent amusement, as if this was all a great joke.

He moved finally and closed the door. "So, Julius," he said softly. "Fallen at last, have you?"

Julius shrugged, meeting his lordship's gaze with a cold, blue one of his own. "You could say that. What else could a gentleman do?"

A new emotion stirred in Eve, but she watched the two men, trying to find her bearings.

"Gentlemen should never have found themselves in such a position." Lord Ripley crossed the room to a chair, dragging it up and taking a seat, after flicking the skirts of his coat contemptuously aside. "Gentlemen wouldn't take a woman into a room, an unlocked room, at a crowded ball."

Julius leaned back, and folded his arms. "You would know all about that, would you, Alex? I seem to recall that you courted your wife in more inauspicious circumstances."

Alex? Julius?

Instead of taking offence, as she'd expected, his lordship burst into laughter. "Touché. But you, Julius, what happened?"

"Eve happened," Julius said, as if it were the most natural thing in the world for him to do this.

Eve would have thought he would have tried to reconcile his lordship, mollify him instead of answering like with like, riposting as if he had every right to do so. Julius leaned back against the heavy sofa. "I can't regret it."

Ripley lifted a dark eyebrow sardonically. "In deference to the lady, I'll say no more, but you should consider this time."

"I have." Julius seemed to be enjoying himself, seemingly completely at ease. "If the lady should dislike the situation, then she may cry off. I had considered this course of action before I brought her in here. Do you think a lady of Eve's rare qualities deserved to be immured in the countryside, married to the likes of Sir Henry?"

Lord Ripley glanced at her. His gaze lingered on her for a bare moment before he returned his attention to Julius. "If that is what she wants, we have no right to gainsay her."

Julius turned his head to regard Eve, his eyes soft. "Do you? Be assured everything you say in this room will remain between us."

"You didn't have to say that," she said. "I trust you."

"Yes I did. I could wait no longer, especially when you informed me that Sir Henry was about to offer for you." He grinned when Lord Ripley gasped. "Well may you think so. I could not bear the thought of such a glorious creature immuring herself in the country with a bucolic squire."

Was that all he wanted? Had he not offered because he wanted her?

Ripley gave a sharp bark of laughter. "Ha! You don't say! Sir Henry appears to me to be a man well satisfied with the world and his place in it. From my brief acquaintance with him, I deduced my presence in the district has put his nose out of joint. He considered himself quite the ruler of Appleton and the countryside for ten miles in each direction."

"So Sir Henry finds himself outshone," Julius said.

When she would have pulled her hand away, he tightened his hold.

Ripley shrugged. "I don't intend to get in his way. What would be the point? It would gain me nothing but enmity. I brought Connie here for some peace and quiet, so I would hardly want to tussle with the local dignitaries."

Julius nodded. "I wish for a private word with my betrothed, if you please."

His lordship got to his feet. "I'll stand guard. You have ten minutes. No more, mind, Julius."

"Yes, sir."

Those words were the first respectful ones she'd heard from Julius, but he spoke them with such a sardonic air she did not think he meant them. Wondering at the relationship between the men, but putting her doubts aside for another time, she watched Lord Ripley leave the room.

Her tension rose once more when Julius took both her hands in his. Shocked at this display of freedom, her head still reeling from the rapid succession of events, Eve sat perfectly still, not responding to his clasp.

Julius bit his lip, gazing at her. "Eve, should you not wish this betrothal to go ahead, you may cry off at any time you wish, and nobody, least of all myself, will condemn you for it."

"Then why did you do it?" she blurted.

"Hush, sweetheart."

Heat rose to her face at the endearment. She liked it too much, and she had not deserved it. "I cannot be your sweetheart. We barely know each other."

Glancing to the side, he located her fan on the sofa when she'd dropped it after he had taken her into his arms. With a practiced gesture, he flicked it open and fanned her gently. The cooling breeze helped a little. "I will not be crying off," he said steadily. "I want this. The moment I saw you I wanted you. After ten minutes' conversation, I had made up my mind. But I do not come without encumbrances." He paused and watched her as if studying her. "You know my personal circumstances. I'm a widower, and so you would be taking on my daughter as well." He smiled wryly. "My mother considers her a little madam. I love her dearly. She's six years old, and while she's a handful, she is bright and beautiful. But you may not wish to mother her."

He paused, and a mask seemed to drop over his face, a realistic one with his features, but without meaning or expression. The change only lasted for a second, but the sight chilled her more effectively than her fan.

"I have a great deal to tell you, but we have no time now." He paused and animation returned, his eyes warming. "None of it matters beyond the fact I…desire you. I can take the best care of you, as you deserve. But you might not want me. I am, I believe, strong enough to bear your rejection. At the least, our betrothal will help you to escape an awkward situation."

"You will not rush into marriage, then?"

"There is nothing I would like more," he said, "But I will wait on your convenience. I want you to enter this union as sure as I am."

Eve exhaled, releasing some of the tension holding her rigid. He was right. This betrothal meant she would not have to talk to Sir Henry or refuse his offer. After all, she could not marry two men. If Julius didn't hold her to their agreement, she wouldn't have to marry anyone.

But she wanted to marry him. She had to admit, if only to herself, the thought of him holding her, making love to her, filled her with pleasurable anticipation.

Her only doubts were practicalities. Julius had flung himself into this situation, and she could not consider so short an acquaintance to be a sensible basis for a lifelong union. However much he appealed to her—and that was very much indeed—she had to consider the long term. She must assure herself he could truly care for her and give her the security she needed. "You know I have no portion to speak of." She had no other way of telling him. Better she said it bluntly, so he understood.

He smiled, showing no doubt in his face or position. "That's of no matter. I'll ensure you are well taken care of for the rest of your life."

"I have nothing, Julius. Only myself."

"That is more than enough." Leaning forward, he placed a careful kiss on her closed lips. "There. That is to seal the bargain. We will leave this room as a betrothed couple, but we will not have the banns called until we are ready. You could come to Derbyshire and stay with my parents while you accustom yourself to the idea. Should you like that?"

"Very much," she said without thinking. "You need time to inform them, do you not?"

He smiled. "Yes, I do, and I will. So you agree?"

She could do nothing but give in, particularly because she wanted to so dearly. "I agree. Thank you, Julius."

"No, thank you. You honor me, Eve."

Chapter 7

She was beautiful, his Eve. As Julius left the small room and led his bride-to-be back to the throng of well-wishers, pleasure gave his step an extra spring and lifted his mood. Alex swung into step behind them, as if he'd been with them all the time. His flat mouth and hard glare told Julius what he thought. He was not looking forward to the inevitable discussion that would take place once Alex had him in private. Considering how Julius had helped Alex with Connie, Alex owed him a favor or two.

As soon as he had delivered his proposal, a sense of rightness had settled on Julius's shoulders. He'd met a woman of grace and beauty, one with the kind of sensibilities that would make her an outstanding duchess in the fullness of time. He desired her desperately, but this development meant he was one step closer to confessing his love for her. The weeks he'd spent trying to calm himself were useless. He still felt exactly the same way about her.

Julius toasted his betrothed with the indifferent wine a stern-faced Sir Henry offered and wondered when they could take their leave. Mr. King had already departed. After several others also left, Julius asked Eve if she too was ready to go.

Alex offered to take them home. Consequently, his cousin handed an awestruck Mrs. Merton and then Eve herself into his carriage. Since they were wearing hooped skirts, they took some time to arrange themselves, even on the wide seats of the luxurious interior, but once they had overlapped their hoops to fit, and Eve had a lapful of Rosa's pink silk, Alex swung in and settled himself on the seat opposite. It was a small fold-down affair, obviously not meant for the owner, but they could do nothing but allow him. By then Julius had mounted his horse, which was stamping impatiently, waiting for his exercise. While Alex showed a smiling face to the ladies, his impatient movements revealed his true emotions to everyone who knew him, and most certainly included Julius.

The coachman whipped up the two matched greys and the vehicle jolted into action, rolling slowly down the drive of the hall towards the village and then to Alex's house. Julius was tempted to take Alex up on his offer and occupy a bedroom there. The service could hardly be worse than at the vile inn, which, after the initial novelty, he had come to dislike with an intensity the establishment hardly deserved. The situation must be as his mother had feared. He was atrociously spoiled. Although his parents had shown little interest in his childhood and upbringing, his nurse, and then his governess, and then his tutor most certainly had. Then society had treated him as a privileged member of its ranks. He grinned. It was a wonder he wasn't completely ruined. Perhaps his self-imposed task had prevented his complete destruction.

He urged his horse into a trot and clamped his hat more firmly on his head. This was not the first time he had ridden in evening dress, and while distinctly awkward, he could accomplish the feat. He'd brought his riding boots and had pulled them on before they set out, shoving his evening shoes in a saddlebag but ensuring the pistols he always carried with him at night was still readily to hand.

The ride would give him time to settle in his head what he had just done. Infuriating his mother, for one thing. It was almost worth going through with the marriage to ensure that. He could take Eve to the infernal house party his mother had arranged, although he would be sorry to disappoint some of the young ladies who would be present. They did not deserve such treatment. But then, neither did he.

His lips curved in a wicked smile. His brother Augustus was returning for one of his infrequent visits home. He could go to the damned house party.

He rode ahead of the carriage, enjoying the spring freshness of the breeze coasting past his ears. He was still smiling when he caught a slight movement in a small clump of trees to his left. When he paid it more attention, he could make out a figure. One, or more than one? Would he have the sense to let them pass by?

When the rider moved into the path of the carriage, Julius sighed. Apparently not. He slid his pistol from its housing, holding it under the skirts of his coat, pulling back the hammer to make it ready. The click as it settled into place sounded loud, despite the wheels of the carriage and the clop of the horses.

The highwayman rode out from the trees, a pistol in each hand, the reins held in his teeth. The carriage came to a halt, and Julius cursed. It should have continued on its way, but Alex would have ordered it to stop because Julius was there, and vulnerable. Baring his teeth in a vicious grin, Julius prepared for action. His spirit exalted. Now he could act.

Julius slowed his horse to a walk and faced the man. Predictably, their attacker aimed one of his weapons at him. He had others stuck in his belt. At one shot each, he needed them, but they would weigh him down.

Julius did not have to exchange words with Alex to know he would be aware of the attack. The coachman would have a series of knocks by which he could convey danger. If he had not done so, he would not remain in Alex's employ for much longer.

Keeping most of his attention fixed on the highwayman, Julius allowed himself a glance at the carriage. Darkness had fallen, but the lights that had glimmered inside the vehicle were extinguished. Julius could not see the shadowy heads of the female passengers any longer. They were probably lying on the floor.

Alex knew, all right.

Heartened by the knowledge, Julius narrowed his eyes and studied their attacker. He seemed *au fait* with his weapons, holding the pistols easily, his fingers barely touching the triggers. That in itself was a threat, since the weapons could go off by themselves if they were of the cheaper, more volatile variety. Julius's sword hung by his side, but he made no move to unsheathe it—yet. Without making his movement obvious, he pushed his heavy coat back with his elbow to expose the hilt. That action would make grasping his spare pistol easier, should he need it.

"Stand and deliver!" the man called. Well at least he had a sense of humor, coming out with that old saw. "Git down from the coach! You!" He waggled the weapon aimed at Julius. "Dismount. Don't let me see your 'and anywhere near that sword hilt!" Julius nudged the horse forward a few paces and made to dismount, shaking the stirrup free with one hand. At the same time, the door to the carriage opened, and Alex climbed down. Julius used the distraction to slip his pistol into his pocket.

"And the ladies," the man said. "I saw 'em."

He might be doing a good job mangling the English language, but he could at least be consistent. His accent was somewhat fugitive, as if he had to remember to use it, and it wasn't West Country. It had the nasal twang of the London ne'er do well rather than the burr of the West Country man. A foreigner, then, and not a man accustomed to using a heavy accent.

The answer came to Julius immediately. King, the mysterious neighbor who had made a play for Eve. He was the only Londoner Julius knew hereabouts, and the only man he had failed to discover much about. He had suspected the man of being an agent of either the Stuarts or the Dankworths, and now that suspicion firmed. The devil was, Julius didn't know which party. The Stuarts would kill her, the Dankworths would capture her.

A string of curses circled in his mind, but Julius clamped his lips together, refusing to give them voice. He did not want this man dead. He wanted him under his control.

Leaving his weapon in his pocket, Julius took his time dismounting. Before he released the reins, he glanced to Alex, who nodded. Julius's cousin's face was set, his attention fixed on their attacker. "The ladies are shaking with terror," he said. "Do you really need them to get down?"

"Yes," the robber said.

Alex lifted his shoulders in an exaggerated gesture of submission and fumbled with the door of the carriage.

A shot hammered out of the door, taking the man's horse. The animal screamed, reared, and then collapsed, as if a giant fist had felled it. Whoever had fired the shot had excellent aim. With the sound of the retort ringing in his ears, Julius released his horse and slapped its rump. It bolted forward, wild from the unexpected noise, its eyes gleaming in the light of the moon. It galloped away, sending up a shower of loose stones and dust from the road, threatening to charge straight across where King was sitting on his horse.

King had no choice but to drop one of his pistols and grasp the reins to move his mount aside.

Julius rushed him from one side, and Alex came up on the other. Used to working in tandem, Alex grabbed the rein farther down, jerking it from King's grip, and Julius went for the man. He leaped, grasped a handful of coarse fabric, and dragged the man off his horse.

Julius's own horse was half way to the village, the faint sound of his alarmed neighs filtering back to them. Alex had King's horse firmly in his grip, and Julius had King. The man struggled, but Julius overpowered him, twisting his arms behind his back, the sound of King's shouts of pain manna to his soul.

"I'll git yer," King mumbled. "See if I don't."

"For God's sake, man, enough of the false accent," Julius said calmly. His chest rose and fell as he sucked in deep breaths of the cool night air, but he forced his voice to remain steady.

King issued a string of foul curses, but at least he'd heeded Julius's admonition to drop the accent. "How did you know?" he said. "Were you lying in wait? And why didn't you get away while you could?"

"And leave my cousin to protect my betrothed?"

Julius's words had their effect. King went still.

"Your cousin?" King said.

"You know who I am. You recognized me almost as soon as you saw me, did you not?"

"As soon as I heard your name, I knew you were with them," King admitted. "But I didn't know for sure. I thought you were mocking me, trying to smoke me out by using his name. I don't know Winterton by sight, only from the caricatures and the engravings."

"Oh, I'm Winterton," Julius said. He glanced at Alex. "I think we should proceed to your house, rather than taking the ladies back to the village."

Barely out of breath, Alex jerked a nod. "Agreed. "I'll take charge of the ruffian inside the carriage, you get up with the driver. There might be more of them in wait."

Julius thought the eventuality unlikely. Surely King would not have attempted this alone if he had accomplices. He guessed that the man had been sent as an agent, to spy. Maybe the news of his betrothal had spurred him into action. "So who is your master?" He shook the man's bound arms, tempted to inflict a little pain, but thinking better of it. He would have plenty of time to do that later, if he needed to.

"Who wants to know?"

"Me. I'm guessing it's Dankworth rather than Stuart. Am I right?"

The man clamped his lips together.

Julius continued in a conversational tone. "You wanted to abduct one of the ladies and take them to your master. Or would you have killed her?"

He remained silent.

Julius sighed. "I so hate when I have to take the brunt of a conversation. Never mind. I'll discover which it is. Would your master tell the other party, I wonder?" Northwich and the Young Pretender were supposed to be allies, but Julius had seen how much that meant recently. They did not trust each other one bit. Moreover Northwich's oldest son, the Earl of Alconbury, was playing his own game. There were more sides in this fight than on a complex mathematical figure. "I may go to one and tell him and watch for his reaction. How about that?"

King sniggered.

Alex nudged the man in his back with the tip of a wicked-looking pistol. "Get in the carriage. If you utter one word, just one, I'll kill you. The ladies will avert their eyes while I do it, I'm sure."

He glanced at Julius, who nodded in agreement. "My poor horse should find its way back to the stables it came from. I am at your mercy, cousin." He met Alex's eyes and shook his head. He did not want Alex to talk to the women about him, not yet. He needed to tell Eve himself.

Alex grimaced, but nodded. Not only was Alex Ripley his cousin, he was Julius's best friend. Alex was one of the few people Julius let into his closely guarded private life, one that was opening to accept one more member.

Julius clamped the man's hands behind his back and hustled him none too gently to the carriage. Julius glanced at Alex, who nodded and mimed using one of the pistols they'd liberated to knock him on the head. That would keep him quiet until they reached the house.

But the ground was uneven, and Julius stumbled, losing his balance and tumbling forward. A flash of light attracted his attention, and he groaned. The bastard had a knife. Why hadn't they discovered it?

He tried to roll, found an obstacle at his back, and prepared to die as the knife descended toward his chest. Determination grooved lines deep into King's features, and Julius read death in his eyes.

A shot exploded. King's head followed suit, the top bursting open. A shower of warm liquid sprayed Julius.

* * * *

Eve's hand shook as Lord Ripley gently eased the smoking weapon from her grasp. Her mother had fired first, and she'd taken out the man's horse. But when the attacker swooped, his large knife promising instant death to Julius, she had not stopped to think. She took careful aim and fired.

When she saw the result, her head swam. So much blood! At first she thought she'd caught Julius, and her heart plummeted, but then he moved and scrambled to his feet. Lord Ripley jerked his head around, his eyes glittering in the moonlight, and then swung into action, moving to stand between the body on the ground and the carriage, blocking their vision of the gruesome sight. When the coachman threw a cloth down, Julius threw it over the body, taking little care over the task. A dark pool formed around the dead body. A highwayman. Out of the blue, death had arrived. It had happened that quickly.

His lordship shouted something to Julius, who nodded and headed for the coach. His stride was steady, but he didn't open the door and enter the vehicle. Instead, the carriage swayed as he swung himself up next to the driver.

Lord Ripley climbed inside the carriage and slammed the door closed. He laid the incriminating pistol gently next to him and gripped the leather strap when the carriage began to move. "He's fine," he said directly to her. "You saved his life. Julius is well capable of taking care of himself, but he was taken off guard. That man could have killed him."

"W-What happens now?"

Ripley frowned. "We will contact the magistrate and give him an account of what happened."

The implication of what she had done slammed into Eve. Tears of shock sprang to her eyes, and she pressed her hands to her stomach as nausea roiled in her belly.

His lordship touched her hand gently. "Your action was defensive, my dear. You have nothing to worry about. There will probably be an inquest, but I will do my best to hurry matters forward."

"Are you sure Julius is all right?" she faltered.

"Perfectly. But he did not want to disturb you with his appearance. He took the brunt of the…results." He gazed at her. "That was an excellent shot, ma'am. Have you been practicing?"

Her mother sat, stiff as a ramrod, next to her. Eve's mind refused to work properly except for that one imperative—to save Julius. Belatedly recalling Lord Ripley's question, she answered him. "I'm a country girl, sir. I know how to shoot."

Her mother joined in. "Her father accounted her a fine shot." She sounded steadier than Eve felt, even though it had been she who fired the first bullet into the horse. Lord Ripley had furnished the carriage with abundant weapons, so they had helped themselves, glad to discover the pistols were primed and ready.

"We will go straight to my house," he said. "You may stay there until we have sorted out this business."

Although Eve longed for the comfortable familiarity of her bedroom at home, she appreciated the hospitality offered by his lordship, and she had no mind to demur. Neither did her mother. When Eve leaned back and covered her mother's hand with her own, she discovered she was shivering.

Lord Ripley's residence was about as far from Sir Henry's house as the hall was from the village, so it took an hour by the large watch that hung in a holder. The roads varied enormously, from the wide, smooth road leading towards Bath, to the jolting, stony ones joining places of interest. This was barely a pathway, only just wide enough for the carriage. But the driver knew his business, and he steered the matched pair unerringly. The lights of the Manor glowed over the smoothly cropped lawns at the front of the house, the scene calm and serene.

On their arrival a footman threw the front door wide, casting a broad beam of light over the stone steps. Julius leaped from the carriage and ascended the stairs, speaking rapidly to the man. As a well-trained servant should, the man bowed but showed no agitation, merely called inside for another of his colleagues.

By the time Lord Ripley had handed the women down, Julius had disappeared inside the building. As they climbed the stairs, his lordship murmured to Eve, "He will clean himself and come to you, if you have no objection. Should you like your mother present?"

That was the last thing she wanted. Eve shook her head. She wanted him now, gore and all, wanted to touch him, assure herself he was unhurt.

The Manor was beautiful. Even in her agitated state, Eve recognized that as a maid led her with her mother to bedrooms on the second floor, either side of a wide corridor. From the scent of lavender polish to the watercolors and understated landscapes on the walls, this house exuded style.

The maid apologized for the small size of the bedroom she showed Eve to, but explained these chambers were aired and ready, and the master had wanted them settled quickly. The woman efficiently helped Eve undress, wash and dress in a night rail and silk dressing gown and then left to attend to the other two ladies.

This room was far more elegant than her own at home. It was at least three times the size, too. A large bed with pale blue drapes dominated the space, but the mahogany dressing table, side-table, and night stands gleamed with careful polishing.

After her first swift glance, Eve took no notice of her surroundings. She paced, wringing her hands. Julius could have been killed tonight. The ruffian would have destroyed them all, wrecked her life for a handful of gold and some jewelry. Something about him had seemed familiar, but she had not made out his face.

A sharp rap sounded on her door, and Julius strode in. He wore a long enveloping banyan, and for the first time since she'd met him, no wig. His fair hair clung damply to his well-shaped skull. He strode across the room and closed his arms around her. When she lifted her chin, he kissed her.

Relieved he was safe, she dissolved into tears. Julius led her to the bed and sat, still holding her. She perched on his lap, the closest she'd been to a man in her life, sobbing into his chest. At one point she managed to choke, "I hate criers. I'm sorry!" but Julius only thrust a handkerchief under her nose and bade her blow.

After, he mopped up her tears, dropping soft kisses on her cheeks and lips as he did so. His gentle treatment had its desired effect, and she stopped crying, although she didn't move. He felt too comforting.

Eve had rarely felt so protected, so safe. "I'm not usually a watering-pot," she confessed shakily.

"I'm not usually so indebted to a woman," he answered. "Between us, we'll muddle through this."

The shock of the evening, his proposal, the attack, swamped her with sensation. Her confused mind refused to accept any more or to complete her thoughts, but stray thoughts chased each other around her head. She snuggled closer, his heat enveloping her. "You're not hurt at all?"

"Only my pride."

"You can't be used to handling situations of that nature."

He laughed, the sound harsh. "I live in London. I should have been better prepared. But my heart was full, and I wasn't thinking properly."

Swallowing, she refused to look at him until he tucked his fingers under her chin and urged it up. This close, his eyes were even brighter than she recalled. They held an emotion she found hard to interpret, but he was smiling warmly. "Thank you," he said softly. "Alex told me you fired the shot that saved me." He paused, and his smile disappeared. "I have something else to tell you, sweetheart."

She didn't know how much more she could take tonight, but she remained silent.

"The highwayman was Mr. King."

Shock thudded dully in her heart. She lost her breath. "Why would he do such a thing?" And why was she not more surprised? "I only knew him for a few months. Not long, and sometimes he said things that didn't make sense. He said he was a gentleman from Newcastle, but then he didn't know about the smuggling rings there, when Sir Henry was discussing them. That kind of thing." She nibbled her bottom lip, but he deserved the truth. "Better him than you. I would have killed ten Kings for you." It was only the truth. He had threatened to kill Julius. Whoever he was, while she had a gun in her hand, she could not allow that.

He gazed at her without speaking, and then, with a groan, he kissed her.

This, at least, she knew. As he'd taught her, she opened her mouth to him. He touched his tongue to hers, taking her with a gentle insistence as seductive as any passionate encounter. In this kiss she could lose herself, forget the horrible events of this evening. He had her safe. She pressed her hand against his chest, and his heart thudded strongly under her palm.

Slowly he bore her back until she was lying on the bed, and he was next to her. He kissed her all the way there, only pausing when they were fully reclined. Then he lifted up on one elbow and gazed at her. "Thank you for saving my life."

"Will you thank me by answering my question?"

He sighed. "I wish you'd forget that for now, but you won't, will you?"

She shook her head.

His mouth flattened. "Very well. King was a representative of someone who wanted either to abduct you or wanted you dead."

When she nodded he raised a brow.

"You don't seem surprised at the news."

"I think I know why. My mother told me a long time ago."

"Then tell me," he said softly. "Let's see if our stories coincide."

Her parents had sworn her to secrecy, but if she couldn't trust this man, then she couldn't trust anyone. "I'm not the true daughter of my parents. They…acquired me in Rome. They were told I would be in danger if I remained there."

Julius stroked her hair and watched her, but said nothing.

"They took the baby, and when they got home, claimed me as theirs. My parents swore me to secrecy. The people in Rome gave my parents a sum of money, which they put into an annuity."

"Do you know the lady's name?"

"Maria Rubio. My father could never find any trace of her." She swallowed. "So I am the daughter of a lady called Maria Rubio and an unknown gentleman."

"Did the maid give your father any documents?"

"I've seen some, but they could easily be false, could they not?"

"They are not." He spoke quietly, but a hard edge appeared in his voice.

"How do you know?"

"My brother is a scholar in Rome, and he came across some copies of documents. One of them had the name of your parents on it." He paused. "I came here for you."

"To find me?" So he hadn't been attracted by her charm? Her mouth twisted. She was such a fool. And here he was, soothing her, holding her gently. All because of her parentage.

He bent his head and kissed her. She should push him away, she really should, but she could not. His kisses seduced her, made her weak. He lifted away, his eyes gentle. How many people had seen him like this? The openness of his expression made her feel privileged.

"Yes I did," he said.

She curved her hand around his neck. His hair was drying, and the curls tickled her fingers. He had curls? Opening her eyes, she saw them, a halo clustering around his head.

He drew away. "What made you smile?"

"Your hair."

"Ah." He grimaced. "My curse. However short my valet trims it, it still curls."

"I like it. It makes you look like a Roman emperor."

This time a grin flashed over his austere features and then was gone. "Better than a cherub, I suppose, which is what my relatives occasionally claimed. As long as you don't mean Claudius." His face stilled and he nodded. "Appropriate, in the circumstances." He leaned up enough to look into her face. "I am an Emperor, of a sort. Did you wonder about my relationship with Alex?"

Of course she had. Their familiar conversations were nothing like a man would have with his employee. "Yes. What man calls his superior by his first name?"

"A cousin." He watched her carefully, his face clear of expression now.

"You're related to Lord Ripley?"

He nodded. "I fear so."

She couldn't imagine being in bed with the grand Lord Ripley, a baron and heir to a great earldom. "Peers have relatives in all walks of life, do they not? They're not all peers of the realm, even if they are related to one. That's true, is it not?"

He did not answer her immediately, but studied her as if she had said something profound. "Yes it is. We're a large family." He licked his lips as if they were dry. "Does it make a difference?"

"To what?"

"To us."

Eve closed her eyes, forcing back her pain. "There is no us, is there?" He had proposed to her because someone else wanted her. He could keep her safe that way. He'd come to her tonight to explain. That was all.

"Even more so now."

When she would have moved away, he held her tightly, spread his arm around her waist and restrained her.

"Please don't go. Eve. If you'll have me, then my offer stands. If you discover you will not, I will let you go, but with the greatest reluctance.

I will ensure you are safe and that any knowledge of your mysterious origins is suppressed."

"Why would anyone want me? I have nothing to bring to a marriage." He laughed, far too carefree for her liking. "You have everything. Have you looked in the mirror lately? Listened to yourself? I came here to ensure that Maria Rubio's daughter was safe. You had remained hidden for all these years, so if you were still safe, I planned to leave you alone. But I became enchanted by your sweet self. Now I don't care who your parents are, only that you want me as much as I want you. When I proposed marriage, it was to you, not to some daughter of Rome."

She should not believe him. In her heart she did, but her mind said no. There was something about him, and there had been from the start, an air of command, of getting his own way. He could be using her for some end she wasn't sure of.

Every consideration paled into nothing when he kissed her and touched her. She craved more, and still more. "It's about my father, isn't it? Or is Maria Rubio an assumed name, and she was a great lady?"

"You are right. It's about your father." He watched her, his clever eyes observant, taking in all her moods. Julius missed nothing.

"Please, may we leave the matter there, at least for tonight?" This matter wouldn't die, she knew that, but she didn't think she could take any more tonight. "No more secrets, no more revelations."

He pushed back a strand of her hair and curled it around his finger as if reluctant to leave her. Gazing into her eyes, he said nothing for a minute. "We'll marry. Then I will keep you safe for the rest of my life."

Tension stirred in the pit of her stomach. She had to know the truth. "You said you wanted me, not what I represented. Julius, I need to know. Is that true?"

With any other man she would have accepted his offer and been glad of it, but with Julius that was not enough. She had once thought she wanted a husband who would be her partner, but with him, she wanted more. If his concern for her was lukewarm, she would not be able to bear it. She was afraid she was falling in love with him. She might even be there already.

"Yes, it's true, Eve. Now I've met you, I can't imagine having anyone else as my wife."

He hadn't said he loved her. Julius was a private person. She understood that already. He rarely showed others his feelings, but here, with her, he was being open and honest. He had not hidden from her, and he'd answered her honestly. Either that or he was the best liar in the world. This close she could see every fleeting emotion, or she thought she could.

Accepting his proposal would be the biggest decision of her life, changing it forever. Gazing at him, she weighed the other possibilities.

Could she let him go? Would she be happier without him?

He waited, perfectly still, watching her. Waiting for her answer. In a flash, she knew it.

"Yes," she said. "For the second time tonight. Yes, I'll marry you."

Warmth grew in his eyes and slowly, a smile curved his mouth. An unshadowed smile, one without the sardonic twist he used with most people. An intimate smile, as close and sweet as any embraces they had shared. "Thank you," he said simply, and he kissed her.

Eve gave herself up to him. Eve never did things by halves. When she made a decision she went into it wholeheartedly, and she did that now. She was his, whatever that meant. A burden eased from her shoulders as she did so, but another took its place. She would make him happy.

She would start now. Curving her hand around the back of his neck again, she sank into the kiss, let him take her where he would. He touched her, smoothed his hand up her barely-clad body, and exhaled, a deep breath heating her cheek and her left ear.

With his hand resting on her rib cage, under her breast, he finished the kiss. "Madam, I will ensure your contentment. I will do everything I can to make you happy."

"I'm happy now," she murmured softly.

"Could you be happier?"

"I don't know." She tilted her head to one side, as if thinking. "Could I? Is there a limit to happiness?"

"I've never tried the theory. Perhaps we should." He grazed her cheek with the tips of his fingers."

She enjoyed his flash of light-heartedness. It surged through her, raising her up. The other side of his sardonic cynicism, the wry sense he was observing—this engaged him completely.

She had learned another thing about her husband-to-be. When he gave himself, he did it without stint. That he had retained this quality spoke much about his character, his determination, his full engagement in whatever he undertook.

"I will leave you, sweetheart," he said, but he made no effort to move. He lay over her, his legs either side of hers, his body barely separated from her. That part of him that had made itself apparent before did so again, a rod of hardness and heat pressing against her belly.

"Do you have to go?" Thus, with a few words she committed herself. Her heart beat faster, but she was certain now. She wanted him.

He blinked, glanced at his body, and back up at her face. "That entirely depends on you."

"But what do you want?"

"Me? You matter most."

She caressed him, rejoicing in her freedom to do so. "But you are offering to share your life with me."

"I am. All of it." A shadow crossed his eyes and then was gone. "So, Eve, what is your will?"

She swallowed. A vivid recollection of her actions that night returned to her, as clear as if it was happening anew. "I don't want to be alone tonight."

"Then I will stay. Where will I stay?" He glanced over at the sofa set by the window.

"Do I have to say it all?"

"I fear you do. You must not provoke me if you do not wish for this. A man can only bear so much. Now is the time. Do I stop?"

With heat rising to her face, she shook her head. She trusted him, but more than that, she trusted herself. Whatever happened next, she wanted this. "I killed a man." A lump rose in her throat to choke her as for the first time she articulated what she'd done.

"You saved me," he said gently. "There was no other course you could take. If you had hesitated, you would have seen me dead. He had a knife."

"Yes. I saw it in the moonlight. It flashed, and I didn't stop to think." She gripped his arm. "Make me forget."

"I'll do more," he said, and he laid a kiss so soft she hardly felt it on her lips. It felt like a promise.

She returned the unspoken promise and let Mr. King slip from her mind. At least for tonight. This time was theirs, and nothing and nobody would break into it. She willed it so.

As he deepened the kiss, she curled into his warmth. He kissed her until she relaxed under him, opening herself to his caresses. He stroked her, gently at first, until she realized he had unfastened the sash of her robe. Shyly, with fumbling fingers, she performed the same office for him, unfastening the elaborate frogged toggles at the top of his banyan and then the buttons.

Underneath, he was naked. An aroma of soap washed over her senses, combined with a trace of the cologne he used, blending with the scent of his arousal, darker and muskier than she had expected. Excitement made her aware of every inch of his powerful body.

He lifted away from her, unabashedly displaying his firm, musculature, his arousal darker, hard and virile. When she looked back at his face, he was smiling.

"Your turn," he said.

Swallowing her nervousness, she sat up as he rose, leaning back on his heels as she dragged her arms from her robe and stretched to tug the fine lawn night rail up her legs. Only when she had bared herself to the tops of her thighs did he catch her wrist and turn it so he could unfasten the little pearl buttons at the cuffs.

"I could have got myself in an awful tangle," she said with a nervous laugh.

He only smiled. "I wouldn't have let you."

Before she could think herself out of it, Eve finished the job, pulling the fabric over her head and tossing it aside. Her hair fell forward, so she had to scoop it out of her face and push it back.

Their eyes met. His were smiling. "I chose well," he said softly. "You are so beautiful, Eve."

"So are you." She spoke the truth. Julius was perfectly formed, his proportions magnificent. Broad shoulders gave way to a powerful chest, the gleam of fine hair delineating the muscles. The hair on his head was fair, the color of sunshine, but his brows and his body hair were brown. The sight of him took her breath away.

When he moved, his muscles rippled with coordinated power, leashed for her. He leaned over her, and she obligingly went back against the pillows. His gaze fixed on her breasts. As if he commanded it, her nipples hardened. Sensation washed over them when he bent down and deliberately breathed over them, blowing streams of air on first one and then the other. She gasped, her body lifting involuntarily, begging him for more.

He gave it. He swooped lower to kiss her breasts, one after the other. He drew a nipple into the heat of his mouth and sucked.

"Oh, Julius!"

When he growled, the vibrations rumbled through her breast, to her chest and stomach, and lower. He touched her, smoothing his hands over her, cupping her breast and tweaking her nipple into startling awareness. He could mold her how he pleased, as long as he didn't stop.

When she flung a hand over her mouth, stifling her cries, he lifted his head. She looked down at him; he was propped on his elbows, gazing at her over the crest of her wet, tight nipple. Arousal rioted within her, thrilling her to the core.

"Take your hand away. I want to hear every sound, every murmur." He lowered his voice. "Every whisper." He spoke normally again. "Nobody will hear you. Nobody but me. Your mother has a room on the other side of the house, and so do Alex and Connie. Let this be free and honest. It excites me, to know what I'm doing to you, and how I make you feel."

Eve had never allowed herself to dwell on the intimacies between men and women, considering they were not for her. But now she could let herself go. She jerked her head in a nod, her eyes filling with tears and her heart with emotion. She reached for him. "Show me."

He stretched over her until his shaft grazed her stomach. The faint smile on his face slipped away when he kissed her. He touched his mouth to her lips, her cheeks, farther down to caress her throat. Every part of her begged for his touch, for him to relieve the unbearable tension holding her captive.

Then he slipped his hand between her thighs. Eve opened her legs for him, and for the first time in her life felt someone else's hands there other than her own. He stroked her, gently at first, caressing the sensitive skin at the top of her inner thighs, and then higher, until he nudged open the folds protecting her most delicate parts.

"You're hot and wet," he murmured against her breasts. "If I don't have you soon I'll burst with longing."

"Oh, don't do that. It could be exceedingly messy."

His laugh was soft and intimate. He worked her carefully, easing his fingers along her crease, stopping just short of her opening. At the front of her sex lay a tight knot of flesh. Eve was already aware how responsive it could get, but it had never felt so big, so central to her being before.

"You are so sweet," he murmured. "I knew your skin would be like this, better than the finest silk. You're gorgeous, my lovely one."

When he inched farther up the bed so his shaft pushed between her legs, she moved to accommodate him, raising her knees and bracing her feet on the mattress.

She had never felt so intimately linked with anyone before. Sometimes she'd imagined it, lying in her bed, fingering her sensitive flesh. But that act was more of relief, relaxing her rather than the febrile excitement coursing through her now.

"I may have to hurt you a little."

She knew that much. "If you stop now, I'll kill you."

He paused, stopped moving, and gazed at her. "I should not do this. We should wait."

She couldn't believe his doubts. "You are joking, aren't you?"

His laugh rang around the room, glorious in its uninhibited splendor. "I think I must be." When he laughed, his erection moved against her, nudging slightly inside.

Her breath caught in her throat. "What do you call it?"

"What do I call what, sweetheart?"

"Your…erection, your shaft, your member…"

"My cock."

The room rang with their laughter, and while they were still laughing, he thrust inside her.

A twinge of sharp pain shocked her into awareness and then it was gone. Julius took a deep breath and pushed farther in. Her body clung to his, the intimacy astounding.

"Hold on."

"I'm not going anywhere." But he did pull out, only to thrust back in. Propping himself up on his elbows, he gazed at her, his smile completely gone. The muscles in his arms bulged, and his features tightened. "You feel wonderful."

"So do you." The breathless quality of her voice surprised her, but she went with the flow.

"Now close your eyes. Let me love you."

She kept her eyes open, wanting to watch him, to see what this glorious experience did to him. "How many times have you done this?"

"Never," he said firmly. His strokes grew more powerful, hard and insistent, increasing in strength as her body opened to him, accepting his whole length.

"You have a child."

"Never with you. With you I'm starting anew."

Tears pricked her eyes, but she refused to let them fall. This experience was too wonderful to spoil with weeping. As he drove in, she pushed against him, arching her back to achieve a better angle, where she could accept every part of his shaft. Their rhythm grew closer, became one, accepting and giving in equal measure. Sweat gleamed on his body, sticking his hair to his chest. Their bodies slicked together, but neither gave up.

Every part of her responded to him. Heat built inside her, prickling up her spine, blossoming in her head and her breasts. When his chest abraded her bosom, her nipples sharpened, nudged against the power of his body, sending tongues of fire licking through her. "Julius, oh!"

"That's it, darling. Let it happen, feel it."

He sounded breathless. Never had blue eyes been hotter. Their bodies slapped together as the sensations inside her grew and swelled to an unstoppable peak. Where she would end she didn't know. She cried out, screamed his name, everything except what they were doing lost in a pale imitation of this cataclysmic act.

All her emotions joined in a swell, the biggest tidal wave in history, sweeping over her, taking her, drowning her. And she didn't care. Only he never stopped.

With a great cry, he dropped his head, his forehead pressing against the pillow beside her as he throbbed and finally let go. Heat and wetness seared her as he filled her with his essence.

He slumped over her. Exquisite manners and control were gone, forgotten, leaving only the vital, pure man who was Julius Vernon. Eve's lover.

After sucking in half a dozen deep breaths, Julius rolled to one side, taking her with him, his arm around her waist. They lay tangled up in each other, the sheets twisted around them. Eve let herself sink into the moment, trying to memorize this for all time.

Fear clutched her. With this act, she'd tumbled completely and utterly for the man who had led her into this new world. Vulnerability shivered over her for a scant moment before she closed her eyes and let oblivion take her.

Chapter 8

Julius awoke in his favorite way—with a warm female in his arms. Giving himself a moment of indulgence, he luxuriated in the sensation. Light arrowed in through a crack in the curtains, but it was early yet. What had woken him was the infernal racket of the dawn chorus. Birds tweeted outside the window at an astounding volume, at least it seemed that way.

Turning his head, he gazed at the woman sleeping peacefully. They were tangled up together, as they had been last night. Seeing her so vulnerable, her hair curling over her shoulders and his chest, touched him at a level he hadn't known existed before. Recalling her sweet surrender, Julius felt at peace with the world. Except for that part of his anatomy that had recalled only too well how she'd responded to his kisses and what she tasted like. His cock rose, ready for action again.

Only then did guilt strike him. He swallowed. He could not regret what they'd done, only when they'd done it. She deserved that she lost her virginity on her wedding night, not before. But last night had weakened his resolve so much he could not think of anything but losing himself in her body.

Loath though he was to admit it, King's death had shocked him to the core. He had coped, because he had to, but the full force of reaction had hit him when Lamaire was sluicing his back and they were on their third basin of hot water. His knees had buckled and he'd shaken, gripping the washstand to remain upright.

But he'd had to see Eve, and he had to remain strong for her. He might have spoken bravely, but inside he was a mess. Taking her had been his affirmation of life and his claiming of her. As far as he was concerned, they were now married. Only the formalities remained.

All he had to do was tell her who he was and what he could give her as Countess of Winterton. But should he deliver another shock so soon after this sequence of events? He could not lose her now. He refused to consider the possibility.

He balked at breaking the joy they had discovered together. As usual, he took his emotional response and examined it for rational truth. She'd had enough shocks already. He wanted her to process what had happened before he laid another set of circumstances on her. She had killed a man—for him. She already knew she was not the biological child of her parents, which was good. At least he did not have to catapult her into the madness. But she did not know who her father was, and she did not know who he, Julius, was.

Telling her might drive her away, and he would do anything to avoid that. Even the thought of it made him cast wildly around for a way to persuade her not to do it.

He took a few minutes to make his plans, test them, and make a decision. Having done so, he rolled over on his side, reluctantly easing his bed partner on to the sheets. He would not make love to her again until they were married. He would set that in train today, and he would ensure her safety with it. Marrying him would protect her, would bring her under the aegis of the Emperors.

He might not love her, but he liked her, desired her, and respected her. Love? Not as he understood it, and he was glad that particular madness had not affected him again.

She stirred, moaned, and opened her eyes. Before they were fully open, he kissed her, unable to resist her potent appeal.

Throwing an arm around his neck in a way Julius was coming to enjoy enormously, she kissed him back, her enthusiasm palpable. Forgetting all his good intentions, Julius swung over her, straddling her, reveling in her warm and welcoming body. And she was wet, he discovered when he slipped a hand into her heat.

She flinched. The small movement was barely apparent, but he felt it all the same. When he drew away, leaning over her to gaze into her face, she made a small sound of protest and tried to drag him back, but her reaction had succeeded in bringing him back to reality. He smiled. Even now, tousled from his loving and sleepy, Eve possessed the kind of rare beauty few people ever saw. Julius counted himself as fortunate. More so because of her personality. He'd found a peach, and he wasn't about to let any other man take a bite. Glancing at her breasts, full and ripe, he was tempted to do exactly that.

"Don't stop," she said softly. When she blushed, the delicate shade of rose travelled to her breasts…and beyond for all he knew.

He would discover that later, he vowed. "It was your first time last night. I want you to rest and recover."

She spluttered with laughter. "You make it sound like a penance. It was far from that. Julius, before you say anything else, don't forget there are two of us in this bed. I wanted it as much as you did."

The corner of his mouth kicked up. "I doubt it," he said. "I don't know if it's possible to want you more. But I intend to find out."

He saw the moment when recollections of the night before came to her—before they'd met in this room. A shadow entered her eyes, but she forced a smile.

He touched her lips. "Don't," he said. "What happened here was joyous. Nothing should spoil that. But what we did could have consequences."

She nodded.

He took another kiss before he spoke again, keeping the caress brief because he dared do nothing else. "Don't look so worried. What we have done has brought our plans forward, that is all. We will be married, and if I can arrange it, in less time than it takes to call the banns." July was well advanced. He had barely two weeks before he was due at his father's house. And if they had made a child last night, he wanted no shade cast on it.

"But what about him, the man I…?" She swallowed.

"King?" Julius wouldn't have that name lying between them. The man deserved what he received, and Julius refused to regret it. "What you did was in self-defense. We'll receive a visit from the local magistrate, I daresay. Alex will inform him, and then he may hear your story."

"Here?" Her eyes rounded.

"I want you safe. You're too vulnerable in that little house. You must stay here."

She smiled wryly and stroked the back of his neck in a way he was beginning to enjoy hugely. "You're very free with Lord Ripley's hospitality."

"He will not object. I promise you." *Quid pro quo.* Julius had sheltered Connie when Alex had needed him to. Now it was Alex's turn to return the favor.

She bit her lip. He kissed it better, so they lost a few more minutes. He loved the way she moaned into his mouth. If he was fortunate, she would agree to share his bed every night once they were married.

One thing at a time.

He drew away slowly, watching her as he did so. "Your mother should have called you Adora."

She shrugged, a pretty movement of her pearly shoulders against the sheets. "Maybe she did."

He would burn every one of her night rails, so he could see her rosy and naked every morning. "Sweetheart, you are adorable." Still careful to keep a little distance between them, he swung out of bed. "I will leave for London today."

Her shocked gasp echoed around the room. "Why?"

Cupping her cheek, he caressed it in a gesture more reminiscent of soothing than arousal, although it threatened to turn that way if he did not take care. "To get us a special license. Unfortunately at least one of us has to apply for the license in person, otherwise I would stay here with you." And he could take care of one or two other matters while he was in town. "I will be there and back in a week."

"Julius we are in Somerset. The journey to London is a full four days."

If I travel fast and light I can cut that to three." Maybe two if he travelled through the night, or used some of the fine horseflesh he'd seen in Alex's stables. "It takes but a day to get a license." About twenty minutes in Doctors' Commons filling out forms and making declarations, and a day to wait for them to complete the paperwork. Less if he found an official who was open to a little golden persuasion. Julius was impatient to complete the matter and to have her in his bed again. "While I'm away, you must take heed of what Alex says."

Swallowing, she nodded. "I lived for years in comfortable obscurity. Now everything is changing, like sand shifting under my feet."

He understood that feeling. At some points in his life, like when he'd left the schoolroom to become the center of public attention, just because of who he was, he'd felt that way. Or when he discovered the sordid truth behind the story of the children of Maria Rubio and vowed to make it his particular business. The knowledge had made him look on the world in a very different way, turned his comfortable, secure existence on its head.

"Don't let it shift. You have friends who will help you. You will never be alone, least of all here."

He could tell her one thing. If he told her all his secrets at once, he would overwhelm her. "Darling, I have to confess something to you."

Her hold on him stilled, and her smile was forced, a mere expression rather than a reflection of her soul. "Go on."

"I came here with a purpose, more than my visit to Lord Ripley." Watching her carefully, he selected his words. "I have been engaged in a matter of extreme delicacy. You know that his lordship is one of the family known as the Emperors of London?"

"I'm not that ignorant. The neighborhood was agog when he first arrived. They said that."

Alarm spiked through him. "Did you do much reading on the subject?" Had she recognized his name?

She grimaced. "No. My mother did, though. She read all about them in every publication she could get her hands on. My mother is a dreamer. I took little notice."

Then why had her mother not made the connection between the Emperors and the Vernons? The answer came swift on the heels of his question. He was known everywhere by his title, not his surname. Besides, the gossip sheets often referred coyly to "Lord W—" instead of a full name, either in a feeble attempt to avoid prosecution or more likely to encourage speculation. And there were more Vernons than titles.

In any case, if he told her, she would tell her mother, and she would tell everyone. Relief surged through him when he hit upon a plausible excuse. Eve would be far safer if nobody knew she was affianced to Lord Winterton, at least until he returned. Then he would tell her.

Doggedly, he continued with his story. "The Emperors have undertaken a special mission." He dropped a kiss on her lips. "You know that the Stuarts were exiled?"

Her eyes dilated and she went still in his arms. "Of course."

"What you may not know is that the son of James II, the man commonly known as the Old Pretender, married twice. He had a clandestine marriage that resulted in a number of children their mother was careful to hide. My research indicates that you are one of those children."

She blinked, then shook her head. "Then why have people not come for me? Why am I not living in a palace?" It was clear she did not believe him. Her derisory smile said as much. She was humoring him.

He smoothed the hair off her forehead, holding still, watching her. Better that she had not believed, but now it was time for her to believe. "People did come for you. Mr. King, to be precise."

"What?" She gripped his arms hard enough to bruise. Not that Julius cared.

"I believe he was an agent of one of the parties searching for the children. You are a legitimate child of the Old Pretender."

When she tried to move away, he held her steady. Distress filled her eyes, and she frowned. "Then this is just to protect me?"

"No!" How could she think such a thing? "My mission was to discover you and protect you. Not this! This is us, Eve, nothing else."

He held her still when she struggled. "Please believe me. There is no advantage in my marrying you. I could ensure your safety without that, but I want you very much."

She stopped fighting. "Are you sure?"

He held her and soothed her, murmuring words into her ear, touching gentle kisses to her skin. His body demonstrated the truth of what he was saying, but the task took some time. "I can't pretend this passion. Eve, the moment I saw you, my good intentions flew out of the window. I wanted you so badly I stayed to court you."

Eventually she paused and bit her lip. At least she had not wept. That she knew meant he would bring one less shock to her.

"I need to talk to my mother."

"Yes, you do. And I need to set out for town."

But he lost his good intentions when he kissed her.

He needed her. Desperation flooded him. Would she allow him back? He had to convince her that he meant everything he said when he told her how much he cared for her.

When he probed between her legs, his cock hard and ready, she opened them, and he slid within.

He did not stop, but thrust inside her. She was wet enough to take him, or he would have stopped, far gone though he was.

Embedded deeply within her, he paused and gazed down into her eyes, open and wide. "Does this feel as if I'm here from duty? Eve, I have given up caring who you are. I just want you. I will keep you as safe as I can, but that's not my concern now. I want to make a life with you."

With a groan she curled her legs around his thighs, pulling him into her.

He set up a regular rhythm and watched her all the while, even when she closed her eyes. Her mouth opened on a gasp, and triumph seared him when he recognized her arousal. She could not resist him any more than he could her. "This is what matters," he said, his back arching as he probed her body. "No other consideration. I want you, Eve Merton."

"Julius," she moaned, reaching for him. "Julius."

Holding his own peak within him he brought her to a shattering orgasm, working her carefully, her surrender roaring through him and driving him to his own culmination.

He lay over her, shuddering. She turned him to malleable putty. He would do anything for her. Except let her go.

He raised his head. She was staring at him, wonder in her eyes.

"Do you doubt me now?"

She shook her head, swallowing. "No."

"I must go." He snatched a kiss and then another before he gently withdrew from her seductive heat. "I want to start the next part of our lives as soon as possible. Sweetheart, soon it won't matter what name you call yourself, because you will be Eve Vernon."

With determination born of his need to care for her, he swung off her and out of the bed. If he paused for much longer he would make love to her, despite his decision to let her rest.

Telling her the rest of his secrets was out of the question now. He ignored the relief he felt when he realized that. Next to what he'd just told her, his status was trivial, something he would help to become accustomed to.

After gathering up his clothes, he began to dress, grimacing at their crumpled state.

When she laughed, he turned to raise a brow in query.

Eve was leaning on one elbow, the sheets barely covering her unclothed form. Her dark hair tumbled over her shoulder and arm, and her bared skin made his mouth water. For two pins he would go back to her and damn the plans. But that would also be to ruin her reputation and he didn't want to do that. Already he heard the faint shuffling from downstairs, audible evidence of the household stirring.

He only went back to her when he was respectably clad. Cupping her chin, he leaned over and kissed her, making it luscious. She returned it in full measure, as always. His Eve never did anything by halves.

"Take the greatest care of yourself, my sweet," he said. "I would have my bride in one piece and as beautiful as ever when I meet her at the altar."

Which would probably not be an altar at all. He would marry her in the village church if she insisted, but Julius had a deep reluctance of making his private life public spectacle. He preferred to take charge of his appearances and his reputation.

Hooking her arm around his neck, she made the most of his kiss, almost drawing him back into bed. Only a stern mental reminder persuaded him away.

At least she knew one of his secrets. The other would not be too difficult.

He stopped at his own room, where an impatient Lamaire waited. Discouraging superfluous conversation, Julius let the man shave him and then changed into something more suitable. Still plain, but at least uncrumpled. His man eased a pair of perfectly polished riding boots reverently on to Julius's feet. Clearly the valet had had too much time on his hands recently, as every garment in Julius's possession was primped to the edge of perfection.

"Do not discuss me with anyone," he told the man, reverting to French. "Pack me a small bag. I'm going to London. I only need enough for the journey." Ignoring the valet's small moan, he continued, "I'll be back in a week, maybe less. I'll use the clothes I have in London while I'm there."

He smiled wickedly when his valet paled, but the man knew better than to say anything. "Don't worry, I won't be wearing anything too fine."

"That, *monseigneur*, is what worries me," said Lamaire as he got to his feet, having adjusted the boots on Julius's feet to his satisfaction. "You have a reputation we should try to keep up."

Julius switched to English, knowing he had the man at a considerable disadvantage in doing so. "I am my own person. If I choose to wear sackcloth and ashes, I will make a fashion of it. Don't pack anything I will regret leaving behind in London."

He left the room and went downstairs for breakfast.

In London, most of the fashionable world breakfasted at noon, or even later. Here in the country, where everything started and finished earlier, he would find something in the breakfast parlor, even if the full buffet had not been set yet. On his way downstairs, he encountered a footman and gave him a message to send to the stables. He would use a travelling chaise and four horses, which would make his journey much faster. Time was racing past, and he wanted to be away before half past seven.

Visions of spending night after night in the arms of the delectable Eve drove him to make haste. But when he entered the breakfast parlor, as well as a promising selection of food, cold and hot, he found Alex. Trying to appear cool and collected, he filled a plate and accepted Alex's offer of tea. He sat at the table. "It's early for you, isn't it?"

Alex shrugged and finished the mouthful he was consuming. "The baby wakes early. Although we have a wet nurse to help with the feeding, Connie grows restless near the time he will wake."

"I never noticed any such propensity from my mother," Julius remarked.

Alex grinned. Julius's mother was not known for her maternal feelings. "I suspect she had the nursery set up at the opposite side of the house to her bedroom."

"I daresay she did," Julius said blandly. A miniscule prick of hurt needled him but these days the emotion was so insignificant he could ignore it easily. Matters had not always lain that way. He sipped his tea. "I have a favor to ask of you."

"Ask away. I'll see what I can do."

Julius grinned. At one time Alex would have joined him in any kind of folly, but a wife and child had settled him into domestic complacency. "Take care of Eve for me while I'm gone."

"Where are you going?"

"London."

"What for?"

Julius attacked the pork chop on his plate, cutting off a piece before spearing it with his fork. "A special license." He chewed his savory mouthful and watched.

Alex put down his own cutlery and gave his cousin his full attention. "I'm not entirely surprised," he said.

"Because of my action at the ball?"

"Because of your action after you returned here. I walked over to your room last night for a quiet chat, but what I heard sent me back to my side of the house. Really, Julius, you should know better than to take up with a screamer. You will have no peace, and the caricaturists will have a field day."

He had not exactly kept quiet, either, and he'd enjoyed every thrilling moment. Rather than subdue Eve, he'd put up with anything the cartoonists threw at him, if their engravings did not embarrass her. He would have to rearrange the placement of their bedchamber in the houses he owned. "I see." He cut another piece of the succulent meat and ate it before he spoke again. "I want my betrothed to be properly cared for. See nobody disturbs her, and monitor her visitors, if you please. Connie is hardly in a position to supervise, so I fear that task must fall to you."

"I expect you want me to give her mother house room too?" Alex said blandly.

"Most assuredly I do. She could be in danger too." Julius took a bracing sip of coffee. "I told her about her birthright. It appears she already knew some of it. Her mother told her. But she hadn't known the identity of her father."

Alex grunted. "At this rate, all my relatives will be members of a royal house." Several of their cousins had already married into royalty, so Alex's comment was only a slight exaggeration. "The Emperors seem to be morbidly fascinated with the Stuarts."

"Perhaps the Stuarts are trying to move up a rung," Julius commented.

"Did you tell her who you are?" Alex leaned back with a broad smile on his face. He was enjoying Julius's dilemma, damn him.

"No," he said shortly.

"Oh, and maybe you want me to tell her?"

That would ruin everything. He would give her time to absorb the first piece of news first. "By no means, and warn the servants I will not tolerate any tattling. Nobody else in these parts knows. King realized last night, or perhaps he knew before, but nobody else is aware that I'm one of *those* Vernons. I will tell Eve both salient facts when I return, license in hand."

"You do realize you are doing it again, Julius."

Julius frowned. "Doing what again?"

"Marrying in haste. Are you sure you will not repent at leisure?"

Julius was surprised to discover he would not. So certain was he that he would rush his union with Eve rather than lose her. Yes, he had done it before, but there were differences.

"The events of last night and the news about her father have shocked Eve deeply. I would stay to care for her if I didn't trust you with my life. With my future wife. That is why I chose not to tell her I am Winterton. She cannot take so many shocks at the same time. I will tell her, but not yet. Let her get over her father's identity first and the death of King."

A jug of cool beer stood on the table, condensation running down the engraved glass on the outside. Alex hefted it and poured some for himself. Julius refused the offer with a shake of his head. One drop fell on the linen tablecloth as Alex returned the jug to its tray. Julius stared at it.

Eve was entirely different to Caroline. He was doing the right thing this time. He was older and so was she, old enough to know their own minds. His parents would not be pleased, but he was indifferent to the way they felt about this matter. He wanted Eve, and he would have her. Nobody would gainsay him. But she still did not know she was marrying Lord Winterton.

Alex was one of the few people he would trust to care for her, but short of rushing her to town, that was all he could do. The magistrate might take it amiss if he spirited her away, even if he returned to the village, and Julius had no mind for his wedding to have more guests than he had invited. He would arrange matters to his liking first, as he always did.

Hence the journey to London.

"Tell the magistrate I have been called away on urgent business but I'll return within the week. I am merely another witness, however, and a necessarily biased one, so I would not be a good person to call in the eyes of the court."

Alex gave a long whistle. "You won't get to London and back in a week."

"I will if I use your livestock."

"What?" Alex sat bolt upright, gripping the arms of his chair. You're serious, aren't you?" Sighing, he released his death grip on the wooden arm rests. "I suppose you want the travelling chariot, too."

"I've already ordered the horses put to it."

"Feel free to order my horseflesh as you please, my lord," Alex said with a wry twist to his mouth.

"You won't need it," Julius said briskly. "And you know I will take good care of it. I'll have one of my own vehicles brought back with me, so I have a conveyance suitable for my bride."

"And how will you explain the crest on the door?"

"I will have told her by then. I should tell her before we are married, should I not?" Taking care, as he always did when something touched him dangerously closely, Julius showed every indication of control, as if he had planned everything. He finished the chop he no longer wanted and drank his tea before he spoke again. "I'm sure Eve will be delighted to discover her new circumstances."

In fact he was far from sure Eve wanted to be a countess. Left to herself, she would probably prefer to become the wife of a gentleman, even the Cit Julius had led her to believe he was. When he considered losing her, a premonition crawled up his spine. The marriage service itself made no mention of titles. She did not have to know until the deed was done. Then he would have her, and he would make good and show her what she could be.

In the fullness of time she would make a magnificent duchess.

He pushed back his chair, gave Alex a civil farewell, and made to leave the room. Just before he did, Alex said, "Do you know who the magistrate is?"

He turned, keeping his features carefully schooled into mild interest. "I feel sure you are about to tell me."

"Sir Henry Fulworth."

"Ah. He will not create problems."

"He might, if he knows who you are and why you came here."

Julius shrugged. "Then don't tell him."

* * * *

Eve slept far later than she was used to, but then, she'd had a tiring day. A tiring night too, come to that. She had slept much better than her wont, held closely by the man she was to marry. Rolling on to her back, she tucked her hands behind her head and stared up. In the modern style, the bed had a canopy suspended from the ceiling and no posts at the end, only at the head.

The details of the lovely room imprinted themselves on her while she lay and thought and tried to make sense of what had happened. Last night she had killed a man, someone she knew. Had thought she had known, she should say. But when she tried to recall the scene in detail, other images intervened. The sight of a naked Julius prime amongst them. The image swam before her eyes, much more vivid than anything else. She would never forget the moment he had come inside her for the first time, watching her all the while, that tiny crease between his brows.

She had to admit, even if it was only to herself, that she would have invited him into her bed whatever his intentions.

One day she would bear his children. He had a daughter already, one she had not met, but Eve would have few problems with a six-year-old. She had planned a governess career. Now she would be a wife.

Her children would be related to royalty. She turned the idea over, examined it. Found she cared little. She would never acknowledge the connection. What good would it do? It would only plunge her and her children into turmoil, and that was best forgotten. One thing he said had resonated with her. When she married, she would be Eve Vernon. She could leave the rest behind. If anyone caught up with her, she would laugh them to scorn.

Someone scratched at the door. Startled, she said, "Come!" and a maid entered, the same one as the night before. She bore a tray with a pot of tea and a plate of toast.

"Good morning, madam. If you wish to dress, breakfast is being served below."

Staying in this lovely house certainly had its advantages. At home, she would have got her own food, or at least helped the maid set it out. The maid who also cooked. They employed all of two maids and one footman. They sent out the laundry, and Eve and her mother helped when they could.

In a week, her life would change. In a week, she'd be married. She shook her head. No, it still made no sense. She couldn't believe it. Not until it happened, if it ever did.

The maid brought in an armful of silk and draped it carefully over a chair. Eve gazed at it in wonder. The fine green fabric was probably fashioned in Spitalfields and rippled over the chair in a rarefied way that breathed "costly."

"Her ladyship sent the gown for you and hopes it will serve," said the maid.

"Could someone go to my home and collect my belongings?" she asked.

"I believe his lordship has already given the order, after talking to your lady mother," the woman said.

Goodness, what time was it? Her attention flew to the delicate clock on the mantel. Nine o'clock! She'd never slept so late before.

She had better accept the use of the gown or she might offend her ladyship. That would never do. That was why she allowed the maid to array her in the gorgeous gown. It fell over a quilted petticoat, in lieu of a hooped skirt, and so would be deemed undress, but when she examined her appearance in the mirror over the frankly indulgent dressing table, she looked more imposing than she could ever remember being in her life. There was even a little lace apron to go over the top, as unlike any apron Eve had ever owned before as a tent was to a palace.

Instead of Eve's customary linen cap, which kept her hair tidy for the day, the maid pinned a little lace piece of nothing that only gave everyday caps a slight nod of acquaintance. She had coiled Eve's hair into a shining knot at the back of her head, leaving a lock at the back to curl flirtatiously over one shoulder.

Only one thing marred Eve's delight in her appearance. Julius was not here to see it. She'd stayed awake until the wheels of a coach rumbling down the drive indicated his departure. Eve had gritted her teeth against the urge to rush to the window and watch the vehicle depart, as if she were some kind of lovesick female.

Which in a way, she was. The wonder of the night before remained with her. Even the knowledge the maid who changed the sheets would see the evidence of her downfall and no doubt transmit it to the rest of the staff did not cloud her sunny mood as she followed the maid to the breakfast-parlor.

Sun streamed in through the windows, illuminating the golden hair of a woman sitting at the table. As Eve entered, her ladyship looked up with a smile as bright as the day. "Good morning."

Eve dropped a curtsey. "Good morning, your ladyship."

Lady Ripley grimaced. "Connie, if you please."

Her mother sat primly on the other side of the table, so when Connie indicated the chair next to her, Eve had to take it.

Lady Ripley—Connie—was breathtakingly beautiful. A clean linen fichu was pinned around her neck, tucked into the neckline and fastened the front of her gown in lieu of a stomacher, but her cap was as frivolous as the one Eve wore, only bearing long lappets teasing her shoulders. Her pearly skin gleamed in the light, and when Eve took her seat with the help of the footman standing silently by, she could smell Connie's gently perfumed presence. Like another being had descended from Olympus and settled in this pretty room.

Connie surprised Eve by offering her hand. "I believe we are to be related in a short amount of time."

Eve cleared her throat. "Yes." She took Connie's hand. "Mr. Vernon didn't tell me he was related to the Emperors of London until last night. I thought he was a businessman."

"Well, he is. We all are," Connie replied affably, but her eyes narrowed and she shot Eve a glance that spoke of curiosity, or speculation. "Before my marriage I was a country widow, living quietly in Cumbria."

That came as a surprise to Eve. "So you met Lord Ripley by chance?"

Connie laughed, a merry ripple of sound. "You could say that. We met at my godfather's house, and Alex wouldn't leave me alone. Not that I wanted him to." She paused and glanced away. "A few weeks later we met again in London, and the die was cast. Would you like some tea, coffee, or chocolate?"

The aromas of the beverages mingled with the mouthwatering scents of freshly prepared bacon, eggs, and kidneys. "I would love some tea." Eve smoothed her hand over the front of her gown. "I understand this comes from you. I am deeply grateful. I only had my evening gown." Which, after she had rolled it in the dirt last night, was probably ruined. "I will return it when my own clothes arrive."

"Pray do not bother," her ladyship said. "It looks much better on you than it does on me. Besides, I shall prevail on Alex to buy me a new one. At the moment he can deny me nothing, so I might as well take advantage of it."

The son, of course. "Congratulations on the birth."

"Thank you. It was a little fraught at the time, mostly because Alex was so worried and wouldn't leave off pacing in the room below, but the midwife assured me it was a good birthing. We came here because it is not too far from Bath, and he could send for medical help if I needed it, but of course he did not tell me until I had recovered." She laughed. "Not that I had not worked it out for myself."

A love match indeed. Like her own, except Julius had not told her he loved her. A niggle of doubt remained at the back of her mind.

"I shall not inflict my child on you unless you should wish it," Connie said. "Nursing other people's children is of all things tedious. He is a healthy boy with a lusty set of lungs that he uses to great effect several times a day. I expect he will be as robust as his father. And as difficult to handle."

Lord Ripley was tall, dark, and built like a bull. Handling was not on Eve's mind when she looked at him. But Julius, despite his fair coloring, could stand next to him and appear to advantage. They did not look in the least like relatives. Eve tried to recall what she'd read about the Emperors of London. A family of one son and five—or was it six?—daughters, they had vowed to name their children after great emperors of the past. The head of the family was a duke. At the back of her mind Eve recalled one, after marrying a peer, for her second marriage chose a Cit, a businessman from the City of London. Perhaps that was where Julius fit in. She had never paid much attention to the gossip, not taking an interest in such matters, but one could hardly pick up a newspaper without one or other of them popping up.

If Julius was a child of the marriage to the Cit, that meant he was cousin to earls, viscounts, and marquesses. Eve could never hold her head up in such company. What did she know of such matters?

A footman entered the room and glided over to his mistress, offering her a note on a salver. It was not sealed, merely folded over. Eve applied herself to her breakfast while Connie read the note.

"Bother."

"My lady?" Eve's mother enquired. "I hope it is not bad news?"

"In a way." Connie put down the note, giving Eve a glimpse of handwriting she knew. "It says the magistrate is outside with the constable." She addressed the footman. "Pray take this to his lordship."

Eve laid her knife and fork neatly side by side on the plate, her appetite entirely gone. Slowly, she got to her feet, trying to remember to be poised and graceful. She wouldn't get through the ordeal any other way.

"You could let my husband handle all this."

Eve shook her head. "They will want to interview me. I did the deed, after all. But I will not see them on my own."

Connie nodded. "Very wise."

Eve sat still until the message summoning her to the study appeared, borne by the same footman who had brought the original note.

Recalling all her deportment lessons, keeping her hands folded before her, Eve followed the footman, feeling like a condemned woman. Although everyone had insisted she would not face prosecution, Eve wasn't so sure. If Julius had made an enemy of Sir Henry, this meeting would spell out her fate.

The study was a cheerful room, with books in glass-fronted cases and a sturdy yet fashionable desk gracing the space. Alex had taken his station behind it, and before the desk sat Sir Henry. Behind his chair the local constable stood.

The men got to their feet when she entered the room, and Alex walked around the solid walnut desk to greet her. He smiled briefly. "Do let me show you to a seat."

Eve took her time spreading her skirts and then presented Sir Henry with a nod of greeting.

Sir Henry harrumphed and sat once more, making a fuss of pushing his coat skirts out of the way. A glass of sherry stood on the table, and the squire took a sip before breaking the silence nobody seemed too eager to spoil. "Miss Merton, in my capacity as magistrate, I must ask you some questions pertaining to the events of last night. Lord Ripley has already informed us you were the instigator of the incident."

"No I did not," Alex said softly, yet commanding the attention of everyone present. "The man we thought was a highwayman started it."

Another heavy throat-clearing followed. "Miss Merton, would you tell us what happened, in your own words?"

What other words would she use but her own? Eve obligingly did so, from the time they left the ball to the time they arrived at this house. From time to time she had to stop, but the men waited until she was ready to speak again. "We had no idea the robber was Mr. King until Mr. Vernon stripped the mask from his face." A small distortion of the truth.

Sir Henry was on his second glass of sherry by the time he was ready to announce his verdict. "There will have to be an inquest, of course, but I see no reason to detain you. If Mr. King had thought to play a jape, it was in exceedingly bad taste, and he deserved what he got. If he truly intended to rob you, that is doubly true." He totally ignored the poor constable, who had remained standing, but at least the man would serve as witness. "I will outline the matter and inform the court of my decision. As far as I can see, you acted with commendable promptness."

Relief swept through Eve, easing her tension and bringing her frozen mind back into play.

Sir Henry put his empty glass back on the table, but shook his head when Alex proffered the decanter. "Now we have dealt with the main business, I would like a few words with Miss Merton in private on a different matter."

Here it came. She nodded her permission to Alex, and he took the constable out of the room. "No more than ten minutes," he said, as if he were a practiced chaperone.

His edict relieved Eve. She did not want to have the conversation she guessed was coming, but she must. Sir Henry had considered her as good as won, but in a dizzying short passage of time, everything had changed.

Sir Henry got straight to the point as soon as the others had left. "Lord Ripley told me you are firm in your decision to marry Mr. Vernon."

Eve schooled her features into impassivity. "I am, sir."

"May I ask you why?"

She frowned. "No, you may not."

His face reddened at her small defiance. He should have spoken to her first privately and then proceeded with the business of Mr. King. That was a tactical mistake, because he could not go back on his word now. He could have threatened her with a court appearance.

"Really, madam! You are not unaware of my intentions towards you, I am sure. I had intended to use the ball last night to announce our betrothal. Mr. Vernon was both importunate and inappropriate. He mauled you. We could overlook that small transgression. I am sure I can persuade people they saw nothing, or I rescued you from a marauder."

"You did not, sir, and I will not say that." She folded her hands neatly in her lap, her signal to herself she should remain on her best behavior.

"Why not? We have had an understanding for some time, Eve. I allowed you your little jaunt to Bath, but you must have realized you could not sustain the position of governess."

She tilted her head to one side. He *allowed* it? "I appreciate your kindness." Or his avariciousness.

In a flash of intuition, she saw what he had done. Nothing. If he was telling the truth, he had set his sights on her some time ago, but waited for her to catch up with him. He had done nothing to prevent her making an idiot of herself in Bath, trying to fit into a profession she thought was her only option, and then watched her live in that little house, once her father's transgressions became known. "Sir, are you saying your regard for me was of long standing?"

He flashed a look of dislike at her, his mouth straight, the lines either side deeply grooved. "Naturally, but I considered you needed a little time to learn what the alternatives to our union would be."

She wouldn't marry him now for all the tea in China. Even if Julius proved false, she wouldn't do it. How could he watch her struggle all this time and do nothing to help? "Sir Henry, I fear you were outdone by a more decisive candidate. I accepted Mr. Vernon's offer because I wanted to. No other reason. He has gone to organize the event. I remain determined to continue my course." Remaining in the same room as this man sickened her. If he had proposed after her father's death, even before that, she would almost certainly have accepted him and been spared the ordeal in between. "Why did you not ask me before?"

"You needed to be brought to your senses, Eve."

Brought to her knees, more like.

"That way you would settle to the life I can offer you. I could never be sure you wouldn't take some notion into your head to behave otherwise than you should. Your foolish efforts at independence were always doomed to failure, but you needed to learn it."

Eve got to her feet. She did not try to control the tremble in her voice. Sir Henry should see something of her rage. "I have learned, Sir Henry, a person who cares for another would not allow her to go through the agony that has been my lot in the past few years. I did not relish the only career open to me, and it hurt me to see my mother immured in that cottage with the mice and the spiders. You should have tried to save me from that. You have better houses in your gift you could have offered us." Recalling Sir Henry's position as magistrate, she held her tongue except for a stiff, "Good day, sir," before she swept out of the room in what she hoped was a dignified manner.

The man was a dolt.

Chapter 9

Back in London, after a journey when two of the hired horses dropped shoes and one was a complete slug, Julius found some consolation in coming home. He'd left the house open and fully staffed to receive his brother Augustus, but unfortunately Augustus had not yet arrived from Rome. That came as a blow, because Julius had wanted to speak with him. He might have to delay his journey, because Augustus had information Julius was eager to obtain.

In the end he had relented and taken Lamaire with him. The valet gave a cry of delight when he walked into the bedroom and immediately chivvied the maids to launder the clothes Julius had used in the country. Julius suspected that, if he were left to himself, Lamaire would have dropped the offending articles in the nearest waste-heap, but he instructed the man to prepare them for his return.

"But surely that is of no consequence now, my lord!"

"I am returning within the week with the clothes I brought with me. You may, however, pack some of my usual garments and have others shipped to my parents' house. I will be taking my bride there after the ceremony. You are to speak to no one about that part, you understand? The penalty is instant dismissal. I will not have town gossip about me or the woman I have chosen to marry."

If his parents heard of Julius's plans before he'd accomplished them, they would do everything in their power to prevent them, especially his mother. If that happened, Lamaire would take the blame unless he heard otherwise. That should keep his valet in train.

The dapper man moved about Julius's room while he sat at his dressing table idly polishing his nails. A couple had broken recently, and his hands were certainly not as soft and white as fashion dictated.

He did not give one jot.

He could get his business in town over within a day or two and head back to the country. Accordingly, he gave his valet conniptions by snapping out orders. "I'm going to Doctors' Commons and then the club. Clothes, please. The hyacinth-blue ribbed silk and the white waistcoat with roses."

A long wail came from the dressing room, but Julius ignored it. "The green will do," he called through and waited for the inevitable result. A long moan. Lamaire was definitely the most amusing valet he had ever had.

Lamaire chuntered his way through dressing his master, but at the end of the process, Julius felt like himself again. The snowy wig, carefully curled and set, not a hair out of place, the gold-braided cocked hat, the coat—the blue, as Julius had known it would be—and the waistcoat, together with a pristine carefully tied neckcloth made for the perfect image of the man about town. Sliding the long sapphire pin into the folds of his neckcloth and a carved emerald signet ring gave him a sense of rightness, that he had replaced something missing.

Julius settled his small sword about his waist, glanced in the mirror, and took his handkerchief, quizzing-glass, and snuffbox. Lastly, he tilted his chin in the arrogant pose most recognized in him. He was back to himself again, and he felt much better for it. Simple garb was interesting, but he had missed Lamaire. He must be sadly spoiled, but he had done his best to atone for that by taking an interest in current affairs, particularly the affair of the Jacobites. A shame that did not make him feel any better, but there it was. That was not why he did it.

With a word of thanks to his man, Julius left and prepared to face the world.

Here, in fashionable London, he was a leader. Here was the place he belonged. How would Eve feel about it? He remained uncertain as he strode through the streets towards Doctors' Commons in Lincoln's Inn Fields. The walk was a fair one, but he'd become accustomed to walking recently, and the distance was no trouble to him. He had time to think.

Thinking was highly overrated, he surmised, after he had turned a few corners, greeted a few acquaintances, and continued on his way. He could reach no conclusions, and nothing about his situation told him he could expect to reach any soon. Used to making plans and then ruthlessly carrying them out, he was still no closer to his objective of smoking out whoever had dared to send King to attack or abduct Eve.

He trusted Alex to keep her safe until his return. King was probably not the man's name, but either party, the Young Pretender or the Duke of Northwich might have found amusement in using it. King had settled in Appleton for a few months, so why had he not made his move before?

Because Eve was not pursued by anyone until Julius arrived. Perhaps the man only meant to keep an eye on her until his master had spared enough time to decide her fate.

Julius halted, causing the man walking behind him to curse and dodge around his now static form. He stared at the sky, the fluffy white clouds making shapes seemed sinister to him all of a sudden.

That would mean a letter. He was in the wrong place. He should be gaining ingress to King's house, not wasting time finding out what he could here. Except he had to apply for the special license. For only that reason would he have left Eve. Would Alex have the sense to search King's house? Probably not, since he had a new heir and the two guests to take care of. And Connie to cherish, something Alex did ruthlessly, to the exclusion of everything else.

Julius continued his journey.

An hour later he had filled out the requisite forms, paid the fee, and was on his way to White's. Ladies had their drawing rooms for gossip, men had the clubs and coffee houses. If women had their own coffee houses, they would be unstoppable in their power. Julius only hoped they never realized that salient fact.

He rounded the corner by the Park and strolled down the street towards the club, pausing to glance at the red brick façade of St. James's Palace. The royal family rarely stayed there these days, using it as a formal meeting-place, but one of the princesses was fond of it. God knew why. In Julius's not so humble opinion, the place was hideous inside and out, the rooms invariably overheated and stuffy, and the decoration dull or outdated or both.

The palace seemed quiet, so presumably the King was at Kensington, a smaller palace he vastly preferred to any other. Julius didn't blame him. Kensington was away from the soot and bustle of London and a more modern, neater building.

Across the road stood White's Club. A substantial establishment, compared to the previous one and the coffee house before, it dominated that part of the street, presented a dignified, imposing presence in that part of the area. Totally unlike the activities that went on inside.

Julius pulled out his watch. Two of the afternoon, a time when the club would be humming, except this was July, and London was, although the most populous city in the world, described by the great and the good as "thin of company."

Passing through the entrance, he nodded to the porter. He handed his hat, gloves, and sword to the footman, half wishing he could leave his coat, too. The comfort of the place enveloped him as he strolled through the main rooms. This place was a far cry from the rough-and-ready coffee houses of the City, furnished with upholstered chairs and sofas, the tables polished mahogany rather than the three-legged ones or the trestles used in other establishments.

Comfort beckoned along with the cloying scents of brewing chocolate and pipe tobacco. Without obviously scanning the main rooms, Julius found many of his acquaintances there. Shouts of "Winterton!" came to him, but he headed for the man seated by the side of the empty fireplace, one elbow propped on the small table beside him, reading the newspaper.

His cousin Valerian Shaw glanced up as Julius approached and then got to his feet, grinning. "I thought you'd left town, Julius," he commented, motioning to the empty chair at the other side of his table.

"I'm back on an errand." Julius shook his hand briefly and dropped into the chair, motioning to the waiter, who obligingly brought an extra cup and a fresh pot of coffee. Val was a member of a sprawling and noisy family, a son of the Marquess of Stretton, and twin to Darius. "I had thought you obeyed my mother's summons and you'd already be at the Abbey."

Val grimaced. "I'm heading there later this week. I've been avoiding it, to be honest. Then it's to my father's house for the shooting season."

"Then you may attend the celebrations of my nuptials," Julius said. He took care to keep his voice low.

Val's startlingly green eyes opened wider. "You're giving in to your mother's persuasions?"

Julius shook his head. "Entirely the opposite. I plan to arrive at my family home already wed."

Val broke into a gale of shocked laughter. He ignored the heads turning in their direction, pulling out his handkerchief and mopping his eyes. "Then I'll leave for the Abbey earlier than I planned. This I have to see!"

"I doubt it will be pleasant." Julius leaned back in his chair and observed the gleaming silver buckles on his shoes with a thoughtful air they did not deserve.

"When the displeasure is not turned on to me, I daresay it will make for a wonderful spectator sport. You will oblige me, Julius, by not announcing your intentions for a few hours. I will get excellent odds on the prospect of your marrying in the next four weeks."

"The minute the entry appears in the betting-book with your name on it, the gossip will start," Julius said, resigned to his fate. After all, he'd visited Doctors' Commons that morning, and if anyone had seen him there, the gossip would already be spreading.

"Your mother has invited so many eligible young females to her house party that mine will not be the first bet." Val picked up the plain white pot, a remnant of White's coffee house days, and poured a cup for them both.

"I suppose that's the truth." Julius did not generally concern himself with gossip, unless he could use it to gain his own ends, but he would rather avoid it this time, for Eve's sake.

"So who is the fortunate candidate?" Val asked, seemingly idly, but his gaze was sharp. Val missed nothing. Most considered him lost in dissipation and idleness, but not Julius.

"Nobody you know, but she is related to people we have been pursuing." Val had been of significant help with tracking down the errant Stuarts.

One finely arched eyebrow went up. "You don't say! Trapped, Julius?"

"Snared, more like." Julius sipped his coffee.

Val nodded. "The difference is subtle, but it's there. I understand your meaning. Sometimes a man may choose his snare."

Julius grinned. "Precisely."

"Why?"

From almost anyone else, Julius would have refused to answer, but he made an exception in his cousin's case. "She needs me." Keeping his voice low, he outlined as much of his predicament as he thought wise for his cousin to know.

"Julius to the rescue." Val toasted him with his cup, his expression gleeful. "The biter bit."

"And how is the beauteous Charlotte?" Julius enquired innocently.

Val had been betrothed to the solemn Charlotte for nearly a year now, and he'd been dodging the nuptials valiantly. The match was supposed to settle him down, cure him of his gambling, drinking, and womanizing. "She's fine, as far as I know."

Not the words of a passionate lover, but Val avoided his gaze, so maybe Julius was wrong. Maybe Val did have feelings for Charlotte, enough to spare her from a match that did not augur well.

Julius shrugged. "It's time, Val. I didn't need my mother to tell me that. While I object strongly to her cold matchmaking, I am not averse to remarriage."

"Especially to a governess."

"As you say." Julius replaced his cup in its saucer with a hard clink.

"You did not come here today merely to kill time until your license was ready, did you?"

"I came for the gossip." No point beating about the bush with Val. He tended to see through any subterfuge. "I told you what happened and why the matter is now urgent. Who was King working for?"

Val saw his point at once. "You mean did King plan death or abduction for her?"

"And possible rape. Do you think Northwich's sons would balk at that when the prize is so great? If seduction does not work, I doubt they would hesitate." Hatred filled him with caustic poison. When he thought of the Northwich family it was always that way, but due to the nature of his self-imposed mission, Julius often found himself in their company.

Julius had not realized he was holding the newspaper until the sound of a rip came to his ears. He dumped the crumpled mess on the table. Fortunately, the paper had been ironed, so his fingers had not turned black with unset ink. "They cannot be allowed to tear society apart. They will do anything for their own ends, anything at all." He remained certain of that fact. If he had one constant in his life, it was that. The Dankworth family and their machinations. His determination to defeat them, to make them pay—no, not that. Julius regarded himself a sensible man, never led by his emotions. That would remain the case, whatever it cost him.

He would never lose his temper again, ever.

Forcing a pleasant expression to his face, an exercise he had become adept in over the years, he tried to alleviate the damage. Val would not have missed his violent reaction, whatever he said and whatever excuse he offered. So he gave none, only changing the subject. "If you hear anything, please contact me."

"This affair holds more than your usual interest, and that is saying something." Val reached out but then pulled his hand back. Men did not hold hands or pat. Not in public, at any rate.

Julius nodded. "Since you are here, collecting gossip, I believe I must move elsewhere and see what I can gather. I plan to return to the country in a day or two." He frowned. "It's a pity Augustus is still at sea."

"Augustus is coming home?"

"Not for long. He enjoys his life in Rome. He's paying a visit only, mostly to appease our parents, although I will be glad to see him." Julius got to his feet. "I fear I have much to do, so I must leave you, but I greatly appreciate your help. It eases my mind to know you're here and helping."

Val laughed, but his mirth turned to a groan. Turning to see what had caused his dismay, Julius found a man standing at his shoulder, and not one he would have chosen to meet. The son and heir of the Duke of Northwich, his long face stern, nodded to him.

"Winterton."

"Alconbury."

While Julius would have welcomed meeting him somewhere less public, here was not the place to do or say all the things currently crowding into his brain. Their cordiality was for the benefit of the people sitting avidly around them, their ears flapping.

Alconbury stepped back, seemingly no more enthusiastic to see Julius than Julius was to see him. A nod sufficed for greeting, but the men did not take their eyes off each other, like prize-fighters waiting for an opening.

Alconbury was clever, quick, and dangerous. That much Julius knew, but there was much more about this man that puzzled him. Although ostensibly devoted to the Jacobite cause, as was his father, Alconbury was playing a different game, one Julius had not yet uncovered.

Alconbury's dark eyes flashed. "The matter concerning your coming to town was not of our doing," he said. "The lady is safe from us."

Julius caught on at once. First, Alconbury knew why Julius was in town. Or he thought he did. Either way, Julius would give all the guineas in his pocket to find out who had told him. "I'm in town to arrange a few personal matters."

Alconbury nodded. "Just so."

Recently the man had rendered Julius and his cousins services that told Julius all was not perfect in the Northwich household. The old man had begun to rely on his second son, William, rather than on his heir, embroiling William in plots that were either too much for Alconbury or Alconbury refused to consider.

That was a very dangerous game. Northwich had more than one son, and his heir could only be deposed by death. Northwich was so single-minded, so fixed on his purpose, that Julius had no doubt he would dispose of an inconvenient child if he had to. Julius had no idea what Alconbury was up to or why he would consider such action, but what Alconbury did was none of his business. Unless his actions affected what Julius wanted to achieve.

He trusted nobody with the surname of Dankworth. This might be a two-pronged attack, one man lulling him into trusting him. Hell would freeze over before Julius would do that.

Alconbury's jaw was set and his eyes held the dark gleam of menace. He was no more pleased to see Julius than Julius was to see him. That expression was no way to befriend someone. "Tell the lady I mean her no harm. Neither, as far as I can tell, does my father."

If he had mentioned Eve's name, Julius would have knocked him through the wall. He clenched his fists, his nails biting into his palms. "The lady is not your concern."

Alconbury bowed. "I agree." He closed his mouth with a snap, as if he planned to say something else, but had thought better of voicing it.

So they knew about Eve, or at any rate, Alconbury did. Did his father? Were they acting independently?

"I wish you good day, sir." With a swish of the full skirts of his coat, Julius turned away and left. Once he'd reclaimed his things, he wasted no time, heading at a spanking pace in the direction of his house. He would dine quietly, collect the license in the morning, and return to Appleton.

"Sir."

Fury spearing through him, Julius spun around to confront his adversary. "You followed me? Do you really want to provide a spectacle for the great unwashed?" Flipping back his coat, he let the jeweled hilt of his sword catch the light. "This time I have the means to stop you."

Alconbury bared his teeth. "You can try." He lifted the edge of his own dark green coat, revealing the cream lining and his own weapon. "I will meet you any time you choose, but you will have to be the aggressor, because I have no such intention."

Damn the man to hell and back. Julius would have enjoyed releasing his temper in a flurry of slashes and thrusts. He'd been irritable ever since his coach had lost a wheel, forcing him to miss a day's travel. "Then why pursue me?"

"To speak more plainly." Alconbury lifted his head and flexed his shoulders, in the manner of a man spoiling for a fight. "With all those ears flapping in the club, whatever we said would have been all around London by nightfall."

"Sooner," Julius said dryly. At least they could agree on something. "So what did you want to say to me…plainly?"

Alconbury took the stance of a fighting man, legs apart, coat thrust back to expose the hilt of his sword. If he drew it, Julius would meet him, but until Alconbury did, Julius would not make the first move.

He glanced toward the club, since he was the one facing it. A few men had wandered out in Alconbury's wake, seemingly casually, but Julius knew better. They would love to have some amusement to enliven their day and give them something more substantial to bet on than the progression of flies on a wall. Many of them had longed to see a fight between two men who were reckoned equally matched. Julius did not particularly want to oblige them today.

"Say what you need to." He retained his stance, but took a deliberately relaxed pose. He would still be ready to strike, if necessary, but he would not do it unless provoked.

"Very well." Alconbury gazed at him, his brown eyes dark in the bright sunshine. "I know of your lady, and do not waste air telling me she is not your lady. I received word there was an incident with someone."

"How would you have heard that?" That was what came of losing a wheel on the road. It gave others a chance to overtake him, and the news had reached London before he had.

"How do you think? I had a man in place. I knew that area held something of interest."

"Does your father?"

"Not as far as I know."

Alconbury kept his gaze on Julius, as if the minute he looked away, Julius would strike. Julius knew exactly how he felt. Tension thrummed between them, as tight as a drum. "Let that stand. I know what happened, and somebody died. That person was nothing to do with either my father or myself. Is that clear enough for you?"

"So you know for sure your father wasn't involved in it?"

Alconbury raised his eyes to heaven, as if to find answers there. "Exactly. Someone like that would need substantial investment. We have no house in that area, and no funds went out of the family. I cannot put the matter any clearer. If you wish to protect this lady, do not waste your time looking in our direction."

Julius's blood ran cold. If this was true, Eve was in worse danger than he feared. The Dankworths would want to capture her, to force her into an unwanted marriage. The Young Pretender would merely wish to take her out of the problem completely.

If he could trust this man. Alconbury was the son of his family's worst enemy, the man who wanted to destroy them. Something lay in their past that had started the feud, but the current generation, Julius and his contemporaries, had no idea what it was. Did Alconbury?

They were done. Julius jerked a nod to Alconbury, choked out, "Obliged, sir," and went on his way, ignoring the groans of the men waiting to watch a fight.

Alconbury's chuckle came to his ears before he strode out of earshot. The man was altogether too self-confident for his own good.

Chapter 10

"I cannot imagine your so-called betrothed is coming back," Sir Henry said after church. Two Sundays after Julius left, Eve was in private and quiet despair, desperate to hear from him. But very little had reached her.

The past week had driven her nearly demented. Julius had written to her, but only a short note to inform her he was delayed, and it was included in a much longer one to Alex, the contents of which he did not share with her. However after the arrival of the letter, by messenger and not carriage, no less, Eve was rarely alone. Even in the house a burly footman trailed after her, looking uncomfortable as he did so, but doggedly protecting her.

The footman was standing not six paces from her now, while she spoke with Sir Henry after Sunday service. Exasperation filled her. This was too much, having her watched as if he were afraid someone would leap out of the nearest bush.

"My dear, I am concerned for you." Sir Henry touched her arm below the single ruffle of lace she wore.

She refused to take more from Connie, despite her new friend's insistence. She would hardly have time for finery if she found herself back where she started—living in a small house on the village green, looking for work as a governess. While she had taxed her mother with the knowledge of her parentage, and her mother had confirmed it, Eve did not see what difference that would make to her life. It had not so far, so why should it do so now?

"You should not be concerned, sir," she said. "You know who Lord Ripley is, and his credentials could hardly be better."

"That family is somewhat irregular." Sir Henry leaned so close, the sweetness of his breath wafted over Eve's senses, mingled with the sickly scent of rotting teeth. If he did not suck pastilles all the time, he might not have such bad teeth.

Sir Henry had not repeated his proposal, but he had continued to visit, insisting on ensuring Eve's safety and that of her mother. While Eve appreciated his care, she could have done much better without it. He appeared at the Ripley's house with alarming regularity—like a vulture, Connie had said in one of her more unguarded moments. A well fed, smug vulture, waiting for Julius to let Eve down and abandon her.

His plumage today was his favorite russet, the color of the country, he had often said, with a green waistcoat that bore definite traces of breakfast.

Eve gritted her teeth, smiled, and nodded. "Lord and Lady Ripley have been very kind. They wish me to remain with them until the wedding."

"Ah, but will there be a wedding?" Sir Henry smiled as if he were teasing her. "He promised to return within the week, and more than two have passed. How many more before you give up?" He lifted her hand to his lips, brushing the back.

Recalling the way Julius's lips felt on her skin, Eve shivered, delicately but without the possibility of preventing her instinctive reaction. Sir Henry felt nothing like her betrothed. His breath was too hot, his lips too hard.

"I will be waiting," he promised. "What happened was an aberration. A practiced seducer visited us and was then gone, all in an instant. Like a folk tale. You were always meant for me. You must know that now. I will wait, but not too much longer. There are more young ladies than you waiting for me to say something to them." He followed the last remark with a grisly version of a teasing smile.

Did he truly believe the young women of Appleton wanted nothing more than to be mauled by him? True, he was in possession of a comfortable fortune, and he was not known for profligacy in any form, but was that enough? His increasing girth promised only to flourish in the coming years, and his sense of self-importance stifled Eve. He could not conceive of anyone more important than he was. He was monarch of the district and had been so for some time, regarding Appleton as his own private fiefdom.

Lord Ripley might have bought a house, but he was of no consequence, holding no local offices and wielding no influence. At least, in Sir Henry's rigidly restricted view of the world, one where, like the old map in Hereford Cathedral, he was the center of the universe instead of Jerusalem. In a few years he'd be bellowing across the hunting field, demanding his rights as Master of the Hunt, and inviting his cronies to the hall to drink the night away. What was she thinking? He did that now.

He would merely continue, as he always had, and when he died he would leave a son to carry on the family tradition. For if he did not marry Eve, he would find someone to warm his bed and take care of his house. That was all a wife would ever mean to him.

"Unhand my bride, if you would, sir," came in the soft, refined tones of a man of fashion, a man confident of himself and his place in the world. The voice she had longed to hear ever since he had left.

"Julius!" At once she condemned the eager girlish way she cried his name, but she could not take it back now.

Sir Henry blinked at her once, but his hold on her hand slackened. Eve took advantage of his inattention and moved away to the man she had ached to see most in the world.

Heedless of the congregation who had lingered to gossip after the service, he took both her hands in his and raised first one, then the other to his lips, removing the taint Sir Henry had placed there. "And how is my lady?" he asked.

Eve swallowed. She should scold him for his tardy appearance, or at least behave with propriety. After all, they were standing outside a place of worship. "I'm perfectly fine," she said, her voice girlishly breathless. She needed to learn to be more circumspect, but she could not prevent the sheer joy coursing through her when she saw him and felt his touch. His fingers warmed her through. She should have put her gloves on directly after the service, but faced with a glorious day, she had refrained from doing so. Now she was glad she was still bare-handed, as was he.

"I am so sorry I couldn't come to you earlier," he said, "But I hurried here as soon as I was able."

"He did," a deep voice chimed in with feeling.

Eve tore her attention from Julius to the man standing by his side. He wore a similar fashionable outfit, but the effect was very different. His brutish strength showed through the coat of mid-green dull satin, and—were there cherubs embroidered on his waistcoat? His eyes, though, they were the same as Julius's, the dazzling blue of forget-me-nots.

In other respects, though, this man was…more. An inch taller than Julius, maybe two, where Julius was all athletic grace with powerful, sleek shape of a greyhound, his companion was packed with muscle. Not in a clumsy way, but with the same assurance.

She hazarded a guess. "Your brother?"

The corner of Julius's mouth quirked in a smile. "Indeed. May I present my brother, Augustus Vernon? It was partly his fault I am tardy with my return. That, and a few necessary duties I had to accomplish."

He released her hands long enough for her to make an acceptable curtsey. Mr. Augustus Vernon returned the salute, his bow perfunctory but good, his eyes filled with a kind of sardonic glee. "So you are the lady who has snared my brother? About time, I say. Our mother will be delighted."

Eve doubted that. She was not looking forward to meeting the lady and confessing she had married her son out of hand, and she had no fortune at all. What Julius was willing to overlook, his mother would probably not. What mother would?

She wouldn't say anything, though, in case she put her foot in her mouth. "Thank you, sir," she said demurely.

"It is partly because of this marriage I have come, but I intend to accompany my brother to our parents' house after the wedding." Augustus spoke English almost too perfectly, as if he were out of the habit of using the language.

She turned to Julius, her brows lifted in query.

His mouth tightened. "I fear we should make our way there after the ceremony. Our mother expects us. Expects me." His smile brightened. "But from tomorrow onwards, we will be as one."

What would he do if she refused him now? They had spent a night together, it was true, but there would be no immediate outcome. Her courses had arrived right on time. This union was by no means certain.

The avid attention of the bystanders burned into Eve. She hated when people stared at her, but if she was to spend the rest of her life with Julius at her side, she had probably better get used to it. With a smile, she took his arm. "Would you care to walk to the carriage with me?"

That in itself would draw opprobrium. The villagers preferred the Sunday tradition of walking to church, but Woolton Manor was too far away for them to walk, Alex had declared, and sent a carriage.

Eve's gaze clashed with Julius's. He was watching her, his eyes blue flames. He could not have made his desire for her more obvious.

He led her to the carriage and handed her inside with delicate ceremony. The action sent a wave of shyness through her. No longer on solid ground in more ways than one, she smoothed her skirts automatically as her betrothed sat beside her. Sir Henry was standing by the church railings, staring at her, his gaze fulminating.

These interlopers had ruined his plans for the village he had always considered his, invaded his little kingdom without compunction.

Julius and his brother appeared not to notice until the carriage had jolted off. With Eve's mother also aboard, the equipage was now quite full, and Julius had Eve's skirts over his lap, to make room for his brother who was seated next to him. Indeed, Augustus Vernon could take up a whole seat on his own. As it was, he was sitting almost sideways.

As the carriage went on his way, Augustus observed in a dry tone, "I see your presence has not gone unnoticed, Julius."

"I'm sure it will settle down once we are gone," he said.

"And the congratulatory visits?" Augustus twitched the cuff of his coat into place.

"They can cope with the interruptions. But we will not be here to see it."

Eve cleared her throat but could think of nothing useful to say. The sound was enough to bring Julius's attention back to her. His face remained almost devoid of expression, but his eyes glowed. Were her eyes revealing as much to him, or was her quickened breathing giving him the clue? She fought to control her breathing. "Tomorrow?"

He nodded. "I obtained permission from the vicar to visit him later today. We marry tomorrow."

Augustus shifted. The carriage rocked, though whether the road was the culprit or this big man, was unclear. "Our mother will be delighted. At least I will not be the center of her displeasure. I had feared all her recriminations would fall on me." When Eve shot him a startled glance, he gave an unrepentant grin. "I only speak the truth, dear lady. Our mother is rarely content with anything, so believe me, you will not be unusual in that respect. Who knows, she might welcome you, and then where would we be?"

"It is of little matter." Julius did not take his attention from her while he answered his brother. "She will have to remain content. If she distresses Eve, I will take my wife away."

The word shuddered through her, but if Julius noted it, she showed no sign, instead addressing her mother. "Would you care to accompany us? I understand you are welcome to stay with Alex as long as you please. Perhaps you would prefer the storm clouds to abate before you join us."

Mrs. Merton granted Julius a cold stare, one he accepted with a polite smile. "I will go wherever my daughter needs me. I can think of no reason why I should cower from anyone. But perhaps your mother would prefer not to have extra guests foisted upon her?"

Augustus spoke, his deep voice rumbling through the small space. "Our mother is a lady of uncertain temper. I have an errand in Oxford first, but I am at Mrs. Merton's disposal after that. I would be honored to escort you to our family home."

Eve's mother gave Augustus a considered nod. "Thank you, sir. The respite will give me time to arrange our affairs here." Such as closing up the house.

The coach jolted over a hole in the road, forcing Eve off-balance. Julius steadied her by grasping her shoulders, as if he already had the right to touch her so intimately. In front of her mother, too. Heat rose to her cheeks, but she merely thanked him and leaned back. He did not linger, but nodded and turned back to her mother. "I would not stay above another two nights at the Manor, since we are expected elsewhere. My brother's tardy arrival delayed us." He turned his head and snared Eve's helpless gaze. "Unless you wish to do otherwise?"

Mutely, she shook her head.

His warm smile rewarded her. "Then it is agreed."

He was taking their lives out of their hands, arranging them to suit himself. Or his mother. He had spoken as if his female parent was a despot to be appeased. What about his father? All Eve knew was he was alive. Was he henpecked? From what Julius said, she certainly suspected as much.

Under cover of her voluminous skirts, Julius found her hand and grasped. That small gesture did as much as anything to reassure her. He had come back.

On arriving at the Manor, Augustus stepped down first, helped Mrs. Merton to alight, and then headed for the house. That left Julius to help Eve, which he did with great care. He raised her hand to his lips before he placed it on his arm. Once inside the house, he led her into a parlor at the back of the hall, the room bright with morning sunshine.

He closed the door quietly, leaving them together in a place far too small to accommodate his presence. Lifting her left hand, he concentrated on removing her glove and then placed it gently aside on a table. Then he shocked her by going on one knee. Before Eve could beg him to stand, he lifted her hand to brush it against his forehead. His skin was smooth, seductively warm. "Miss Merton, I never formally requested your hand in marriage. I do it now, and I promise to abide by your decision." He glanced up at her and their eyes clashed. "I will, however, reserve the right to pursue you. I can't help it, Eve. You draw me in. I truly wish to marry you. Will you take me?"

"I'm not pregnant," she blurted out.

A shadow passed over his eyes. Was he disappointed, or relieved? She could not say. She hardly knew this man, except he had wooed her with determination and a seductive intensity she had not been able to resist.

"That is immaterial. One day, God willing, you will bear my children. I missed you while I was away. Answer me, sweetheart."

There came that word again, the one he had used in bed. Oh, Lord, why had she thought of that now? But looking at him, she could hardly think of anything else. "Yes," she said.

He rose to his feet. When he smiled into her eyes, she was lost, lifting her head to receive his kiss. Why did she even try to resist him?

They kissed, sweet and engrossing. Her body heated and dampened, as if he had taught it to prepare for him. Eve could not have prevented her reaction. She didn't even try. Her hand slid around his neck and she spread her fingers, his heat and strength more reassuring than his words.

He lifted his head and gazed into her face. "I swear I will do everything in my power to make you the happiest woman on earth."

Here, now, held securely next to him, Eve believed every word. "And I will do my best to be a good wife." Her voice surprised her with its huskiness. "You won't regret this."

"I know that already." He moved away, releasing all but her right hand. "Shall we join the others for breakfast?"

She tugged him back. "We leave tomorrow?"

"On Tuesday. Once we've paid our respects to my parents, we may leave for my house, should you wish it."

His reassurance calmed her, but he still reminded her of the horrible events after the ball. "They still don't know why Mr. King attacked us in that way. Sir Henry suggested he might have planned an elaborate jest."

He shook his head and gently folded her into his arms. "No jest, my sweet. I have much to tell you." He bit his lip, gazing down into her face. "I will do it in the coach on the way to my parent's house. It shouldn't take us too long to get there, long enough for me to introduce you to your new life. We have to travel to Derbyshire, so it should not take more than three days. I've taken the liberty of engaging a maid for you, but if you don't like her, we can change her easily enough."

She bit back her immediate response. Was a maid really necessary? Although he was related to some very grand people, he was still a Cit, and Cits' wives did not always need a maid solely to attend to their needs.

"We are in a strange stage of flux. My mother cannot continue to live in the village, can she?"

He shook his head. "I'm sure I can find something that will suit her better." He kissed her palm. "For you, my lady, I have plans, and they do not include your mother."

That hot flame returned, and she could not resist him when he kissed her once more. "Never doubt I want this with all my heart," he said when they finally separated.

She was glad, because she did.

*   *   *   *

As they swung down from their horses the next day, Alex stopped Julius going into the church. "We have a few minutes. Julius, are you sure about this?"

"Positive." The more he thought about the issue, the better it sounded.

"You have told her who you are?"

Julius paused. Trust Alex to hit on his vulnerability. Many people considered Alex bluff and without guile. Julius would say his cousin incised to the heart of the matter and did not concern himself with subtleties or prevarications. He shook his head. "She knows I'm an Emperor. I will tell her the rest after the ceremony."

Alex frowned. "That's unlike you, Julius. You prefer to face the truth and to be fair in your dealings. Do you not wish her to enter this marriage knowing everything?"

"How could she possibly know?" he snapped, without considering what he was giving away. "How can anyone, until they are in that situation? It would make no difference, and it will only confuse and upset her. She has the character to cope. I know that for sure."

Alex tilted his head to one side slightly. Julius knew that gesture. Alex was thinking of something new, something that had not occurred to him before. "You're afraid if you tell her, you'll lose her."

Julius's heart sank. Yes, he was, but fear was not an emotion he met often, and he did not know how to cope with it. The tension that invaded his body every time he considered telling her he was the heir to a duke paralyzed him.

"Are you in love with her?"

He took one more step to confessing his secret aloud. "In love? That is a madness I will never tumble into again. I know you will understand this, and my determination never to lose myself in anyone ever again."

Alex knew more about Julius's previous marriage than anyone did. He regarded Julius now with a grave air. "Do not judge one person on another's behavior. Do not make Eve suffer for your late wife's mistakes."

Julius's mouth tightened. He wished Alex had not mentioned her on this day above all. "I won't, I promise you."

He turned to enter the church, but he heard Alex's next comment, although he feigned deafness. "You already have," he said.

On entering the church, Julius was startled to discover half the village had attended.

Everyone turned around and stared at him as he made his way to the front pew. This place of worship was a small one, holding barely a hundred people, if they chose to cram into the pews and stand at the back. Sir Henry sat in his customary place on the opposite side of the aisle, his family by his side. He glared at Julius. Julius offered a nod and a smile, taking his usual aristocratic position, now he was out of view of the others in the church. He crossed his legs, leaned back, and tilted his head to one side, gazing at Sir Henry without meeting his eyes, as if the baronet would be presumptuous to do so. Sir Henry looked away sharply.

A stir at the back of the church told him his future wife had come in. He stood and waited for Eve, nerves unexpectedly churning in his stomach.

* * * *

Eve felt steadier than she'd imagined she would when she took her first steps into the church. The throng surprised her, but warmed her with their kind regard. They had come to see her hurriedly arranged marriage. Whatever they thought of the hugger-mugger way the marriage had been arranged, they had come to witness her joy.

And she did feel joyful. Happiness suffused her, and she almost danced up the aisle. No doubts remained. She loved him. She had risen that morning with pleasurable anticipation of the day to come, not with any misgivings, and while she dressed in the new gown Connie had given her, her spirit only became lighter.

Alex remained at the back of the church, waiting to hand her over to his cousin and friend. Julius stood next to his brother, waiting for her to join him. The smile Alex gave her warmed her, but she sensed a wariness about him. She dismissed the shadow it cast on her day. Her mother sat just behind the front pew, sending Eve a small, reassuring smile. Eve took her place by Julius's side.

Connie was here, too, having been churched the day before. She was now officially back in society, her respite over, although Alex would not allow her to tire herself out by receiving visitors and going about the district. Not that she wanted to. She had only reluctantly left her son in the care of his efficient nurse, but she had declared she would not miss the marriage for anything. She was, of course, the finest dressed in the church, although she had made an effort not to appear so.

When Eve laid her hand on Julius's arm, it was completely steady.

She made her responses in a clear voice, not faltering once. Julius followed suit, although his tones sounded colder as they rang around the old stones of this building, which had been here longer than any other in Appleton. The place had witnessed many weddings with varied results throughout the centuries. Eve vowed this would be one of the happiest.

As the vicar pronounced Eve and Julius man and wife, a shaft of sunlight poured through the only stained glass window, the one behind the altar, made of the fragments of glass recovered after Cromwell's men had paid a visit a hundred years ago. Dappled shades of blue and red dazzled them and sent Julius's face into a riot of cool blue, intensifying the shade of his eyes when he turned and gazed down at her. A faint smile curved his lips when he slid the ring on her finger.

The sermon and blessing done, they stood to go into the vestry and sign the parish register. Julius murmured, in a murmur meant for her ears alone, "You are mine now. Nobody can take you away from me."

Why would anyone want to? His fierce tones, so possessive, thrilled her to the core. The sheer passion in his words filled her with excitement. Her pulse throbbed, her heart beating so hard it shortened her breath. "You want me so much?"

"Never doubt it." He sounded calm, but she knew better. He was better at controlling his outward appearance than she was.

They still had to endure the wedding breakfast and consequent celebrations. Eve didn't know if she could bear waiting much longer. Every time he touched her, her body went seeking, as if of its own accord, for that magical night that at one time she had thought would never happen again.

But it would. This time they need not worry about pregnancy. If it happened, that was all to the good.

Julius helped her into the carriage and sat next to her as rigid as a statue. They drove up the main street in silence. The gardens and the sides of the road appeared more populated than usual, and people stopped what they were doing to watch the carriage pass by. Eve smiled and waved when it seemed appropriate. These people, her neighbors, would probably never see her again.

A new life lay ahead of her, one she had no experience managing. However, she would do it, if only for her husband's sake. She savored the word. Husband sounded too domestic for Julius, with his wild streak and his passion, but that was what he was. Would he stay faithful to her?

The thought of him in bed with someone else made Eve's stomach tighten and nausea roil inside.

Immediately, he was there, leaning over her. "Is everything all right, sweetheart? Are you well?"

She managed a shaky smile. "I'm fine. I let my mind wander, that was all."
He turned his attention away from the people on the street and fixed it on her. His total and complete attention. "Tell me." The words were more of a command than a request.

She couldn't look at him. "It only crossed my mind. I'm sorry. I don't know what I was thinking."

"What?" His grip on her hand tightened. "Tell me."

She swallowed, but she would have to tell him. She could not devise a convincing lie. He compelled the answer from her. "How long will you remain faithful?"

His grip slackened and his breath gusted out in one long sigh. "Is that all? Sweetheart, look at me."

Lifting her chin, he met her gaze. He touched her brow—she must be frowning.

"Forever. I admit, I have had mistresses in my time. But when I was married, I never strayed." He paused. "Much though I had provocation. And I am doubly sure I will not with you. Our one night together convinced me you are everything I will ever need."

"How can you know?"

The corners of his mouth flattened. "This is the second time this topic has arisen. I did not want the subject of my first wife to mar the day, but I fear if I do not tell you, it will damage more than the day."

Their carriage had cleared the village, and they were rocking along the road leading to the Manor.

Julius drew her into his arms and leaned back against the squabs, so she was resting against his shoulder. She was not wearing powder on her hair, something she had done rarely in her life, so she would not mark the cloth of his fine green coat. He gazed at her as if he would kiss her, but then he started talking.

"I will tell you the brutal truth about my first marriage. It might help you understand me better. And maybe, my mother's reaction when I introduce you to her. I fear she may not at first welcome you, but my father will do so. I promise."

Eve listened, concentrating on every word so as to forget nothing. The sound of the wheels on the road and the horses' hooves melted into the background as he spoke, until all she could hear was his voice.

"My first marriage was arranged. Caroline was of good family, a good match on paper. They would probably not have chosen her for me, but the bland miss they at first selected would not have suited me at all, and

I fear I would not have done for her." He smiled wryly, but that soon disappeared, and a bleak expression shadowed his eyes.

Eve wanted nothing more than to kiss it away, but she had to let him speak. He was letting her deeper into his life, revealing another of his secrets.

"Caroline was beautiful and spirited. She had starts when she would race into a frenzy of activity. She shopped, danced, engaged in every entertainment London could offer, but I was a doting husband and I indulged her, assuring myself she would settle down. We soon conceived our first child. My wife wanted the child named for her, and I had no objection. Charles for a boy, and Caroline for a girl. We had a girl, or rather, she did, after a day and a night of labor. The birth went hard with her, and she was not a natural mother. I adored Caro from the moment I saw her. I still do." He paused, studying her face. "I love my little girl. She is six now. I hope you can prove a good mother to her, Lord knows she needs one."

She gave him what she hoped was a reassuring smile. "I was planning to become a governess, remember?"

He shook his head. "You would never have succeeded. You're too beautiful."

She blinked. "Do you mean governesses can't be beautiful?"

He kissed her, a swift touch of his lips. "Yes. The governess is a powerful temptation. She is educated and closer to the family than the domestics. Mothers tend to shy away from employing a lovely, graceful woman to take care of their children, for fear she would corrupt the men of the house. It has been known to happen, you know. Either that, or the man will seduce her."

"So I should employ a plain woman as governess to our children?"

His smile warmed her heart. "For my part, I care not. I will not be looking at her. Employ whom you wish, as long as she is good at what she does." The smile faded, and a frown replaced it. "That is something I would wish you to do, as a matter of fact. I have never yet persuaded a governess to stay. My daughter is lively, an intelligent child, and she pushes too many of the women too far."

"I could do it."

"No you cannot. You, my sweet, will not have time. I intend to keep you very busy."

He leaned toward her, and slid his arm around her waist, drawing her inexorably close for a kiss that lasted considerably longer than the last one. She made a small sound into his mouth and opened for him, touching her tongue to his, arching up to him as he groaned.

Julius made quick work of her filmy lawn fichu, pulling it out of her bodice so he could touch the upper slopes of her breasts. He covered them with his hands, stroking lower, until he dipped beneath in search of her nipple.

His touch made her twitch and gasp, shocking but in a good way, awakening her senses, bringing her body to life. She curled her hand around his neck, stroked the bare skin, before pushing up, under his wig. Impatiently, she shoved it out of the way to feel his heat, cupping the back of his head and holding him in place, demanding more.

Their response to each other drove them hard. How could anyone make her so aroused so quickly?

He pulled away with a gasp. At first she barely noticed, following him, pleading with him without words, moaning her need for more.

He laughed, a carefree sound she had rarely heard from him. "We'll be arriving at Alex's house soon. Do you really want us to fall out of the coach like a couple of savages?"

Brought to a belated sense of propriety, Eve shoved her fichu back into her bodice. With a reproachful click of his tongue, Julius helped her, making a much neater job of the task than Eve would ever have done, even without her agitation. "How could I have forgotten all sense of decency to almost make love in a carriage?"

Before he arranged the folds of the fabric over her breast, Julius dipped his head and dropped a kiss there. "Exactly as I did. We may try that particular exercise before the week is out." He chuckled when she squeaked in shock. "We will be travelling for two or three days, my sweet. We have to find something to do on the journey."

"I could not—I would never—"

"A carriage with glass windows and blinds can afford much privacy." He leaned back and examined his handiwork, twitching one fold into place before he was satisfied with the effect. "The activity is recommended by many. A sense of danger adds spice to an encounter, do you not agree?" He glanced at her. "Perhaps another time. I'll enjoy teasing you with the possibility."

He adjusted his neckcloth with no help from Eve, placing the folds precisely in place by touch alone. For the first time she noticed the pearl pin he used to hold the fabric in place. The gem was as large as a pea. "Is that real?"

"Naturally." His answer came automatically, as if he did not have to think about it. Sweeping his wig from the seat behind him, he settled it back into place, grimacing, although she had no idea why he would do that. The wig was not an extravagant one, such as men of fashion customarily wore, but a modest, tie-back one in a soft shade of white.

"Do you not like wearing a wig?"

He stared at her, arrested. "I have always worn one. Yes, I believe I do. The custom leaves me free to crop my hair beneath it, and as you've noticed, my locks have an alarming tendency to curl. Some of my cousins wear their own hair, but theirs is straighter, or the curl drops out when the hair is grown. My brother is considering following suit, since he has, as he says, little time for fripperies."

"I thought he was particularly well turned-out today."

He regarded her curiously. "Do you? I was hard put to it to persuade him not to outshine me, I confess. He spends his time abroad for the most part, but our mother demanded his presence."

The more she heard about Julius's formidable mother, the less Eve looked forward to meeting her. Mrs. Vernon sounded like a woman who disliked being crossed, to say the least. Autocratic might have described her better. Eve preferred to reserve judgment, but Julius's mother's character was becoming more settled in her mind.

By the end of the week, she would know the worst.

But today, Monday, she was newly married, a fate she had considered she would never experience, with a wedding night to look forward to. Would she have anticipated sunset with such eagerness had Julius not shared a night with her before? Eve did not know, but she presumed she would feel nervous at the very least. In fact, her anticipation did have a touch of nervousness, but that only added excitement to her mood.

The carriage swung into the drive leading up to Woolton Manor, and with a final glance at her, Julius picked up his hat from the seat opposite whence he had tossed it after they'd got into the coach, and sat bolt upright, as if he had done so from the church right up to the door of the house.

He helped her from the carriage himself. As she placed her hand in his, he winked at her, out of sight of anyone else. Eve tried not to giggle. That would not be at all proper in a woman of her status.

As she entered the portals of the now familiar house, she wondered at how easily she had grown used to the grandeur of Woolton Manor. She assumed Julius's house in London would be more modest, as town houses tended to be, and was secretly glad of the fact. But not as small as the house by the village green.

Chapter 11

"Not too much of an ordeal?" Julius entered Eve's bedroom by the private door joining her room with his, startling her into dropping her hairbrush.

She had dreamily been stroking her hair for ten minutes, ever since she had dismissed her new maid. The maid, a sweet girl of probably eighteen or so who went by the name of Taylor, had proved efficient at her task. The only time she had paused was when she had mistakenly addressed Eve as "my lady." That sounded passing strange, and Eve had quickly told her "madam" would be sufficient.

Taylor had nodded, bobbed a curtsey, and continued to fold the gown Eve had removed, using exquisite care, but also an efficiency of movement that showed her experience and expertise. Once Eve had addressed the subject of her wardrobe, she would find other tasks for Taylor, for she would not let such a good maid go.

Her hairbrush fell with a clatter on to the silver tray holding some of the magnificent items that had appeared on her dressing table. As far as she could, tell a whole set was displayed there, with powder boxes, hair boxes, mirrors, brushes, and even a haresfoot for the application of rouge.

Eve had never used rouge, but perhaps she would experiment. A little face paint could not be considered over-vain, surely.

Laughing, Julius crossed the room and stood behind her, resting his hands lightly on her shoulders. "I trust you won't try to deny me when I tell you how beautiful you are."

"No," she said. "But it is a gift—or curse—I was born with. I did not have to strive for it, and therefore I have never valued it. Until now," she was compelled to add, in response to his expression. "I have tried to learn what I can and to keep my temper. I value those things because I worked for them."

"A worthy answer." He pressed his fingers into her shoulders in a caressing movement that eased the muscles that had tensed at his entrance. "But you will not mind me taking pleasure from your beauty. I trust the day didn't tire you out?"

She laughed. "I would be a poor creature if that were the truth!"

"Before you tell me about the women toiling in the fields or in their attics spinning wool for a little extra money, get to your feet and kiss me. Tonight is ours, my lovely one, and I intend to make the most of it."

She rose and turned, enjoying the swish of her new dressing gown. She had found it together with a night rail of fine lawn on her bed when she had come up here after bidding farewell to the last guest.

To her relief, Sir Henry had not availed himself of the invitation to the wedding breakfast. He had watched her marry and then taken his leave, so she could answer truthfully, "The feast and the dancing were no ordeal at all. I enjoyed seeing my neighbors so happy. Why did you not invite any of your family apart from your brother?"

"They know of our wedding, but since we are to see them soon enough, I did not expect them," he said, but darted his gaze away briefly before returning to hers, his eyes bearing no sign of the flint she had imagined she had seen in them. "They will love you."

Before she could respond, he kissed her. His first kiss was sweet and persuasive, taking over where they had left off in the carriage. But this time they would not stop. The bed beckoned, already turned down and ready to receive them. He changed his position slightly, and still in the kiss, lifted her and carried her to the bed, laying her down almost reverently. Some wag had put flower petals on the sheets, roses and scented violets.

He broke the kiss, and still standing by the bed, gazed at her.

He unfastened the tie of her robe and gently spread the sides apart, sucking in a breath when he saw her. Her fine linen night rail was indecently transparent, but Eve found no shame in it, only pleasure that she should affect him so much.

"I—I sometimes find I cannot express my feelings too easily. I will try, Eve."

Those cerulean eyes blazed the truth. He had not hidden from her. Happiness suffused her.

Eve had no doubts about reciprocating his sentiment. "I love you."

He bestowed a warm, unshadowed smile on her. "I'm glad," he said simply.

They undressed each other. When he had drawn the night rail over her head, once she had shaken her hair out of her eyes, Eve found him gazing at her with untrammeled delight. "You're so lovely," he murmured, as if to himself and then met her eyes. "We have some way to go, sweetheart, but we will get there."

"Not too soon, I hope." She had a little difficulty unfastening the elaborate frogged toggles at the top of his robe, but the task did not take too long. "I want to have plenty of delightful diversions on the way."

"I am sure we will." Julius smoothed his hands over her body, pausing only to shake the robe from his arms. The magnificent garment fell, disregarded, to the floor. "We will make love, and laugh, and make children together." He gave a mock sigh, but his eyes danced with merriment. "That is a skill we should try to perfect, I think. Starting tonight."

At last he climbed into bed to join her. She rolled on to her back, letting him come over her, his powerful thighs either side of her more slender ones. The heat of his body surrounded her, overwhelming in its potency. His shaft rose, long and thick, the head already glistening. A few drops of clear liquid emerged from the tip. Unashamed, he scooped them on to one finger and held them to her. "For you," he said. "My body worships you."

Leaning up, she claimed the bounty with a swipe of her tongue. The flavor was unexpectedly delicious, sweet and spicy at the same time.

Julius groaned. "However did I live without you?" He kissed her.

He thrust his tongue into her mouth, claiming her with unmistakable imitation of what was to come, in and out. She sucked and tried to retain his tongue, but he finished the kiss after one deep plunge and continued to her throat. "This is mine," he said as he kissed her neck and the pulse throbbing at its base. "And this, and this."

Kisses as light as caresses joined deeper, claiming ones as he moved farther down her body. When he sucked a nipple hard, biting her softly, she moaned aloud, the threat of a sting of pain adding to the tingles rioting through her.

Wrapping her arms around his broad shoulders, she stroked him, claiming him in her turn. She pushed her fingers through his close-cropped fair hair and to his neck, where his tendons flexed easily as he tugged on her sensitive flesh with his mouth.

She wanted to belong to him, for him to claim her in every way possible, but she needed something else in return. "Are you mine?"

"Every part of me." He muttered her name between kisses.

She slid her feet against the sheets, lifting her knees, unashamed of the display. The aroma of arousal filled her nostrils, intimate and mildly embarrassing, enough to add spice to the emotions rioting within her.

Eve no longer doubted they belonged to each other. They had tonight and as many nights as they wanted in their future. Questions rioted through her head, only for his caress to take them away. Eve stared at him as he kissed and explored her body. She sensed a desperation, or maybe that came from her. When he dipped his tongue into her navel, she flinched and cried his name, immediately clapping her hand over her mouth to stifle the sound.

Reaching up, he pulled her hand away. "I told you before. I want to hear every whisper and every scream. I want you to let me know what I'm doing to you pleases you. If there is a need for quiet, I will deal with it. Trust me."

The last two words were barely above a whisper, but they seared their way through her. She would trust him. He would take care of her. Then she could do the same to him.

"Yes."

Their gazes met in a look as intimate as any of his caresses.

Julius kissed her, working his way inexorably to the heart of her, where he paused. "So lovely." His breath swept over her thighs and the part between, and finally, he bent his head and kissed the knot of flesh at the front of her cleft. It throbbed for him.

Shock leaped through her. He would do such a thing, but then, as his tongue worked its magic, thrills chased each other, starting where he was concentrating and encompassing her body. With each deep suck he drew her farther into his orbit. She clamped her thighs either side of his head, pressing against his mouth. Even the sounds he made did not force modesty on her. Modesty had no place in this room.

The thrills fused together to become one huge surge of sensation. Eve lost her mind, screaming his name, when he thrust two fingers inside her and did something that forced her up higher.

He did not relent until he had drained her of all feeling. Then she could only lie back and gaze at him as he lifted his head and prowled up the bed to her. Glancing down gave her the image of a predator, powerfully male, his hard throbbing member red and engorged, once more wet with his arousal. His mouth hung slightly open, revealing sharp white teeth, his lips still wet from the intimate kiss he'd given her. Kiss? He had torn out her heart with his teeth.

He kissed each of her breasts, drawing her nipples deep, licking the sensitized tips, before he resumed his predatory prowling.

Opening her arms, she let him in. "Everything I am is yours. Everything."

"This is our time," he said as he brought their bodies together and filled her with hard masculine need.

His cock forged its way into her. Following instinct, Eve wrapped her legs around him, lifting them so her heels rested on his buttocks. When he powered deep, his muscles clenched and then released when he had found his home.

"I am so glad you're not a virgin," he murmured and then he kissed her.

She sucked on his tongue. Vestiges of her intimate flavor remained with him and she took that too, the taste lifting her arousal. A moment ago she had thought she was done, that he had only to take his pleasure now, but she was wrong.

Her eyes shot open as she recognized the signs of arousal deep within her.

At first he took his time, thrusting deep and then sliding out in a sure, steady rhythm, accustoming her body to his loving invasion. Then she understood his words. If she was still an innocent, he'd have had to take more care with her, would not have been able to drive inside her without pain. She felt no pain tonight, only unutterable joy.

Pleasure rippled through her as her body prepared itself for another peak of sensation.

He lifted away from the kiss, gazed at her as he worked his erection in and out of her, studying her. A faint smile curved his lips, warmly encouraging, and he murmured her name. "Eve," had never sounded so seductive, so perfect as it did in his distinctive tones. Even in bed he had the edge of refinement, as if innate, born with him instead of bred into him. "Is this good?"

"So good!" she rasped, her throat slightly sore. Only then did Eve realize how loud her screams must have been. But she had no time to speculate on who had heard her, if she had embarrassed anyone, before Julius took her on another journey.

She went with him. She always would.

He built her arousal, driving hard into her, until he had quickened his thrusts to hammer-blows of sensation. Every part of his shaft connected with her inner walls, sending fresh thrills rippling through her. She kept her gaze on his as he worked her. His pupils expanded so the brilliant blue became a rim around the fathomless depths within.

Caught in the whirlwind, she gasped, "I can't bear it!" as the sensations built to a peak. She could sense the place where they merged, but as wildly as she grasped for it, she could not get there.

"Then don't bear it." His voice had a rough edge, one she only heard in this circumstance. "Let go, darling. Don't fight it. Don't work for it. Just let it happen." He spoke in staccato pants. A sheen of sweat covered his body. Even his hair had darkened.

Gazing at him, paying attention only to Julius, she did as he demanded. She let go.

And tipped over the edge.

Sensation engulfed her, swallowed her whole. His mouth landed on hers, and he took another kiss, one she gave gladly but could do nothing to reciprocate.

Then he broke away and gave one harsh, sharp cry, like a wild bird descending on its prey. His shaft throbbed, and wetness anointed her cleft, her thighs, and the sheet beneath them.

Julius slumped, but as he did so he twisted, so they were lying on their sides and she was not bearing his full weight. He eased her leg down, so it curled around his calf, and then turned them so he could perform the office on her other side.

He was still embedded deep within her. His eyes alight with passion and unholy amusement, he thrust again. He was still hard.

"How is that possible?" she demanded, brought back to where they were and what they were doing.

"I have no idea, but I intend to make the most of it. You're a fever in me. I knew it would be like this between us. That loving would encompass us completely. I have missed you over the last days. I never want that to happen again."

"Neither do I."

"Then let us pledge now. Every night and every moment of the day we can spend together, we will. We will never let the sun fall on a quarrel, never let anything outside our bed destroy what we have here." He punctuated his words with a series of shallow thrusts that felt different than before because they were lying in a different position.

She gave her pledge gladly. How could matters lie any different between them? "I promise."

"So do I." The kiss he gave her then was more than carnal. It drew her spirit from her into him, but he gave it back, intact, when he opened his eyes and gazed at her with the look of love.

* * * *

Julius held his wife close as she slept. Her soft, pliant body delighted him, and his love of all things beautiful rejoiced at the sight of her naked. Much though he enjoyed seeing a beautiful woman well dressed, he preferred Eve naked. If society allowed it, he'd keep her exactly like this.

Devil take it, he had fallen for her hook, line, and sinker. That had not been his intention when he embarked on this course. He needed a wife, someone who could provide him with heirs and help him care for little Caro. To that end, he had been prepared to take one of the women his mother had lined up for his perusal, much though the process had gone against the grain to fall in with her plans. After his first bout of fury, he had thought about it. Then he had come across Eve, and manna had fallen into his lap. He had wanted her from the first, but physical attraction was not the same as this encompassing need to make her happy.

She had told him she loved him, but he had balked at saying the words back to her. He was deathly afraid of that happening because of the consequences of the first attempt, but he was willing to let her in so far. After, no. He would retain a part of himself, keep it apart so he never, ever went through the experience again. He had tried so hard with Caroline, but nothing he did made any difference. She'd still died.

He tightened his arm around Eve, so much she moaned. Perhaps he should have told her his identity before the wedding, but he had longed for this night, untrammeled by anything. If he had told her, she might have balked or treated him differently, and he could not have borne that. The frustrating weeks apart had done nothing to ameliorate the desire he felt for her. If anything, as the days passed his desire had increased. He missed her, to hold, to love, to talk to. And to look at, of course.

Surely his identity would not make that much difference to the way they felt about each other. If anything, she would be glad that he had ample means to provide for her and her mother and to protect her from the forces ranked against her.

He would not allow himself to put off the unpleasant task any longer. Today, when the vicar had announced his full name, Julius Caesar Vernon, he had held his breath, but she had not noticed. He had squeezed her hand at that point and smiled into her eyes. Perhaps that had distracted her enough. If she heard his full name she might realize who he was. He was damned fortunate she had not noticed this far. He'd picked a wife who did not spend her life with her nose stuck into gossip sheets. If she had demanded it of him, he would have told her.

Tomorrow he'd tell her for sure.

* * * *

They had no time the next day to make love before they had to get up and leave. Eve regretted that she'd slept so late. Julius was already up before she had awoken. When she glanced at her father's old pocket watch, which she had commandeered after his death for her own use, the faded dial told her eight o' clock was nearly upon them. Curled in his arms, she had felt safe and wanted and lulled into sleep.

Grimacing, Eve climbed out of bed as the door to the powder room opened and her husband came in. He was in his shirtsleeves, and his waistcoat still hung open. Eve was naked.

His eyes darkened, and he stepped towards her. In instinctive reaction, Eve reddened and cast wildly about for her robe, but he got there first. Gently, he wrapped it around her and helped her thrust her arms through the sleeves. He kissed her neck, and slid his arms around her waist from behind.

"Never hide yourself from me. I love to look at you. Don't you want to give your husband pleasure?"

Eve hung her head, letting her tangled hair cover her face. "I will try."

"No trying. I would have kept you in bed all day, but we need to get on the road. If you are able, I would like to travel until nightfall." He urged her to turn around to face him, and he kissed her. "I'll send your maid to you. Would you like me to order some food sent up?"

Nobody had ever done that for her before. At home, food was for the parlor, dining room, and kitchen only, for fear vermin would invade the house if it were spread around. But there were servants here aplenty to ensure the mouse population was kept down.

"No," she said softly. "I'll be down directly. I won't take long, especially with my new maid."

"If you wish it, just tell me." He touched her chin. "I will make it happen for you."

An hour later they were ready. After blowing her mother a farewell kiss, Eve accepted her husband's hand and climbed into the carriage Alex was lending them for the journey.

Once in the coach and bowling along the road, Julius drew Eve into his arms, so she rested her head on his shoulder. "Rest, sweetheart. At the first staging post, we'll change to my carriage and send this one back to Alex."

"You had your own carriage brought to Somerset?"

He smiled at her, brows lifted as if he were surprised she asked. "Yes, of course. We have to travel in comfort. I cannot arrive at…the house in a borrowed carriage. Besides, Alex may need it."

Forestalling any further questions, he kissed her. He was doing a lot of that. Eve wanted him to carry on doing it.

Did lovemaking usually make a person so soporific?

Now she could relax. Now only the two of them existed. Once she woke from her nap, he kissed her and helped her tidy herself up as they approached the first stage on the road. They stopped in the early afternoon, drew up in the yard of a large coaching-inn, but she did not catch the name of the town. They would pass through many on their way to his parents' house. Meeting them was something Eve preferred not to think about. She would worry about that confrontation nearer the time. Tomorrow she would ask Julius about his parents and how she could help ease the meeting. Eve did not shy from confrontation, but she preferred to make such matters as easy as possible. She felt a new air about Julius this morning. He seemed more self-assured, less concerned with others around him, except for her. The attitude put them in a bubble of their own, made her feel she was sharing a place with him he normally inhabited alone.

Today was the day after her wedding, and she determined to enjoy it.

Julius had ordered a couple of rooms for them to use in the hour it would take to switch between Alex's coach and his. For the first time, Eve wondered why he had not had his coach sent to Alex's house.

Her maid was not travelling with them. She had gone ahead and would meet them when they stopped for the night, so Eve had little to do.

When she decided to leave her room, a footman escorted her to the coach. He took her to a shiny black vehicle with glass windows that looked new. The door was already open, and the man helped her into it without comment. On the seat opposite sat a wicker basket. Four matched greys stood ready in the traces, stamping and huffing, obviously eager to be away, and a coachman sat up on the driver's seat. He tipped his hat to her, but said nothing, eyeing her with a speculative air.

Eve sat back, feeling somewhat of a fraud. She did not belong in this magnificent vehicle. She had thought Alex's carriage grand, but with its burgundy leather upholstery and shining accoutrements, this vehicle easily outshone it. She could not deny the seat she had taken was the most comfortable coach seat she had ever used. Surely the upholsterer had not used feathers in the construction?

While she was arranging her skirts, a stir on the other side of the yard caught her attention. She settled to watch. A man in a snowy white wig and cerulean blue coat laced with gold, the skirts stiff with buckram, had his back to her. He was waving and chattering to another man, whose mouth did not stop moving. The second man remained in her vision, as the first went out of sight, but she could still hear them.

They were speaking in French. She recognized that much, even though the rapidity of the exchange defeated her knowledge. She had thought herself conversant in the language. She had even taught it to uninterested schoolgirls, but perhaps she should rethink her ability to speak the language, as she could barely understand one word in three.

As far as she could gather, they were talking about clothes. The man facing her was volubly complaining about something, until the man she could no longer see ordered, "*Taisez-vous!*"

The rapped out command proved who was in charge of the order. The smaller man closed his mouth with a snap and finally the first man came into view.

Eve's jaw dropped. Under that curled and pure white wig, wearing the magnificent gold-braided coat was her husband. He was also wearing an easy smile.

"Eve, may I introduce my valet? Lamaire speaks little English, although he has promised to learn."

Eve blinked, closed her jaw, and tried for a smile. "Pleased to meet you." The words sounded inane even to her own ears.

The valet swept her a bow. "*Enchanté,* my lady." The last two words were so heavily accented, they were nearly incomprehensible.

Julius swung up and into the carriage. "Give the order to depart, Lamaire."

The footman folded the stairs, closed the door, and with the trumpeting of the yard of tin, they were off. The vehicle barely jolted, but when they tilted to one side to sweep around the sharp corner out of the inn yard, Eve toppled over.

Right into the arms of the scented, powdered, beringed man she had seemingly married.

She stiffened as he carefully restored her to an upright position. He released her, and, with raised brows, sat back, crossing one long leg over the other. "You have questions." He did not ask, he told her.

Of course she did. "Who are you?"

His blue eyes appeared even more brilliant than before. "Your husband, Julius Caesar Vernon."

Julius Caesar?

He sighed. "The Earl of Winterton. Which makes you my countess."

Shock speared her to her seat. "How can that be? Aren't you a Cit?"

His mouth flattened, deepening the creases either side of it. "No, although I do have investments in the City."

Rage simmered through her. It overflowed until she couldn't think properly any more. She took a deep breath, and another. They didn't help much, although she could finally speak. "Did you not think to tell me before we married?"

He reached for her hand. She forced herself to remain still, although she wanted to pull away. She let her hand remain in his. After all, he was her husband. He had the right to take her hand or anything else that took his fancy. She was his wife. She belonged to him.

Fool that she was, she'd given herself freely and without stint.

"I'm the same person, Eve," he said softly.

What was she, a pet for him to tame? "You are, at least to yourself. But to me, you're different. You're an earl, someone so far away from my world I can't even begin to reconcile myself to it." Images flooded her mind, of a way of life she had never coveted. From now on she would become a public figure, fodder for the caricaturists and the writers of scurrilous newsletters. She would have to behave perfectly at all times, dress beautifully, be gracious.

She did not doubt him for a minute, because this vision of him suited him. He was comfortable in his fine clothes in his gracious carriage, at home as she would never be.

As her temper receded, appalled realization returned, and her mind started working again. "You will have to instruct me on everything. Everything."

He squeezed her hand. "Not quite. In one sphere of life you are making more than satisfactory progress."

Heat swamped her. "Intimate relations are completely out of the picture now." How could she even consider sharing a bed with him ever again? "I don't know you." She contemplated the figure of the man she had married. He was exquisite, perfectly and expensively attired. "Why did you want to marry me?" Slowly a suspicion formed in her mind. Did he want someone he could control?

"Do you need to ask?" From the expression in his eyes, he meant the intimate part of their relationship.

He'd seduced her, then wed her under false pretenses. "Am I even your wife? I didn't marry the Earl of Winterton. I married Julius Vernon."

"Julius Caesar Vernon." He gazed at her, sincerity in his eyes. "That is my name, the essence of who I am."

But how could she trust him? The information he had given her was so earth-shaking she was having difficulty processing it.

She withdrew her hand. He let it go without resistance. Eve tried not to shrink back into the corner. With a desperation that tightened her throat, she longed to leave the coach at the next stop and not return. To go back to the miserable little house on the village green and molder in obscurity. Obscurity sounded really appealing right now. "You are a member of the aristocracy. You were brought up to fill a high station in life." Her voice quavered, and she took a moment to control herself. "That is part of you. You cannot distance the man from the earl. You are both." She closed her eyes and drew a deep breath. "I am neither. I can't do this, Julius."

Silence reigned. Eve kept her eyes closed, concentrating on regaining control over her senses. As always, his proximity affected her profoundly, calling to her in a way she would have found foreign to her nature until recently. Julius had done a good job of introducing her to the world of carnal passion, perhaps too good. She wanted to spend the rest of the day in his arms, to return to the way she felt about her marriage this morning.

But she could not. She would have to work hard to become what her new position required of her. She had no choice. Julius was right. She had married him and everything he was, which included the title he had not seen fit to disclose to her before now.

She made up her mind, opened her eyes, and met his. Anxiety rimmed them, the double crease between his brows deepening.

"I will be your countess."

He nodded, but the worry did not dissipate. "And?"

"And I will bear your heirs. But I cannot do both right now. Give me time, Julius. I need to accustom myself to all this. I want to know so many things. I never do anything half-heartedly, and I will make you as good a countess as I can." Anger still simmered deep inside her.

"In the fullness of time, you will be a duchess."

She shook her head, resisting the temptation to bury her head in her hands. The enormity of the step appalled her. How could she cope with this?

Another suspicion crossed her mind. "Did my parentage have any bearing on your decision to persuade me to marry you?" Even now she ached. She loved him so much and hated herself for doing so. He had used her weakness to persuade her.

The carriage jolted over a rut in the road, and Eve lost her balance. Tipping forward, she landed in his arms. His hold tightened about her, cinched her tight, as if he could not bear to release her, but in the next moment, he righted her and restored her to her seat. She took her time arranging her skirts and regaining her self-control. That telling moment had ripped through her, removed everything except what they had meant to each other last night, before he had dropped the devastating news on her head.

Knowing the value of silence, she met his gaze and kept it, although it cost her a great deal to do so. She ached for him still, but she knew better than to reach for the moon. His lovemaking overwhelmed her, and she could not afford that distraction. Not until she was more sure of herself.

Silence fell, a taut, straining tension snapping between them. Eve waited.

Julius sighed and shrugged, the fine fabric of his coat moving with the powerful muscles she had felt under her hands last night. "I would not have come to Appleton if I did not receive word of your existence. After that, fate took a hand."

"I don't know if I believe in fate."

"I did not until recently." He made his meaning clear, hiding nothing.

How did he manage in the world, if he exposed his feelings in that way? Perhaps he did not have to consider it, being an earl, with all that entailed. The warmth in his eyes threatened to overwhelm her. But if she allowed him to do so, she would never find herself in this new, confusing life that had been thrust upon her.

"You have changed me, Eve. I want to be as good a husband as I can possibly be. I love you, Eve."

Tearing her gaze away, she stared blindly out of the window, unable to look at him. "If you loved me, you would have told me." How could she believe that now?

"I have every faith in you, madam." His voice came coldly.

She ventured to turn her attention back to him.

The contrast between his openness a moment ago and his appearance now startled her. This man was an aristocrat, born to the purple, brought up to expect obedience from all his minions. And she was one.

He had enslaved her, and she could do nothing but go on with what would become of her life.

* * * *

Julius ached to reach for Eve, to hold her safe and reassure her. He would care for her and guide her in everything, should she wish it. He would move the world for her.

But he could do nothing, because he recognized the justice in what she was telling him. Eve would make a magnificent countess, but she needed to discover that for herself. He could not afford another wife who could not cope with the station in life he'd dragged her into.

Alex was right, although Julius hated to admit it. He should have told her before they married.

So why hadn't he?

A chill came over him as the implications of his actions solidified. As the scenery passed the window, he forced his mind back to its customary iciness. Apart from his daughter and his sister and possibly Augustus, he kept himself separate from the world. He felt safer that way. Since Caroline had ripped his life apart, he had kept his existence in neatly defined compartments, not allowing his different worlds to interact.

Eve had charged into his life, ripping his preconceptions wide open. In truth, he barely gave her origins a thought once he'd lifted her on to the saddle of the nag he'd hired and mounted behind her. His concerns should have been to secure the daughter of the Old Pretender, who had the potential to seriously unbalance the stability of the country, not to make her his own. All other considerations had flown out of the window from the moment he had talked to her and she'd enchanted him.

They were passing through a village, the pretty exteriors of the cottages no indication of the squalor within, if the ones he had seen were any judge. The comparison with his life hit him hard. Now he had a wife he did not want to love, but his wayward emotions had dictated otherwise. He had a wife who resented him for the life he was dragging her into. He only had himself to blame.

Would he never learn? He had made mistakes before and determined never to repeat them. He had fulfilled that part, but he was still making mistakes. As a callow youth he had fallen for a woman who had "disaster" written all over her. He had indulged her, refused to take advice to treat her more firmly, to guide her more securely. Caroline's volatility and their increasing separation had led directly to her death.

When he thought of the same fate falling on Eve, his blood ran cold in his veins. Despite the brightness of the day, he shivered. That, at least, would not happen again. He would do everything in his power to prevent it.

Even if it meant drawing away from her until she found her own way, he would do it.

Chapter 12

Tension racked Eve as they approached the house she would have to learn to call home. At the two inns they had stayed at on their way here, they had slept in separate bedrooms. Fully cognizant of the identity of their distinguished guests, the innkeepers and servants had bowed obsequiously and eased the hardships of the journey.

Eve felt cocooned from the real world. So this was how the upper echelons of society could remain ignorant of the suffering of the poor and disadvantaged. Separated from real life, they would have to make an effort to keep in touch with affairs. Where she lived—or had lived—reality was forced down her throat most days, whether she wanted it or not.

Already she had gained a polish she was not comfortable with, but paradoxically found an easy shell to hide behind. She could sit in the carriage in close proximity to her husband, pretend to read or sleep and withdraw.

The ease appalled her.

She could continue along the same lines and never discover the joy they had shared on the two nights they had spent together. She and Julius could live separately.

For his part, Julius did not attempt to break the new fences she was busy erecting, but coolly helped her out of the carriage, ensured her comfort and left her alone.

Why had he given up so easily? She had asked for the space and he had given it to her, but he had made no attempt to draw her closer, to seduce her, or talk to her. He'd answered her questions coolly and without emotion. She should appreciate that, but she did not. She only felt completely alone.

When she saw the house, all thoughts left her, swept away by the sheer magnificence of Edensor Abbey. The frontage took her breath away. The Palladian mansion dominated the landscape in a majestic sweep of pure grace.

Julius broke the uneasy silence. "My grandfather had the front constructed. The back of the house has an entirely different appearance. The house itself is much older. Once it was a Benedictine abbey, and then Henry VIII gave it to one of his courtiers, my ancestor. I can best describe my ancestors as opportunists. They waited until they were sure which way the wind was blowing before taking sides. That was with a few aberrations that halted the relentless progress of the family. Because, of course, family was all." He spoke dryly, as though he were a guide to the house, not a member of the family owning it.

The grey stone blended in with the greenery, bright dots of color indicating where flowers broke the lush landscape. As if reading her thoughts, Julius said, "My grandfather also had the grounds remodeled. My father is considering employing Capability Brown to change a few things. Your thoughts will be welcome, of course. You may choose to make the grounds your particular concern. It's up to you."

The notion swamped her. She had duties beyond imagining. How would she cope with this new grandeur? She set her mouth to a firm line. She would have to. That was all.

She dared not meet Julius's gaze. Not because she was afraid of him, but she was afraid the tenderness she had been accustomed to seeing in him would be entirely gone. She wanted to remember it, longed to see it, even though he had betrayed her so badly.

The question revolved in her mind. Why had he not told her? Why had he kept his true identity a secret from her, even when he'd asked her to marry him? Did he not trust her?

A notion occurred to her, shocking her back to reality. "Why did you not ask me to sign an agreement? A marriage settlement?"

He grimaced, a mere twitch of his lips, but enough to show his dislike of her question. "And reveal the extent of my wealth? I would have had to get lawyers involved, and the consequent delay would have been enough for you—" He broke off and recommenced in a cooler tone. "I considered it would be sufficient to deal with the formalities when we reached here. Over the next week, I daresay we will come to an agreement. Since you have no portion, we will provide one for you."

"No!" she said, repulsed at the idea of taking money or property from him.

"Yes," he said. "It will provide dowries for our daughters and settlements for our sons, as well as provision for your widowhood."

The carriage came to a halt outside the imposing double sweep of steps before the house. The doors swung open, as if someone inside were watching for their coming.

Of course they were. An important person had come home. Julius probably took this kind of treatment for granted.

When she moved, he glanced at her, long enough to keep her in her seat. She would have pushed the door wide and kicked the steps down, but in the last few days a servant had performed that office for them. This was no different, except the servant wore the livery that must belong to the family. His snow-white wig was almost as perfect as Julius's.

Once the footman had the steps down, he looked up. His eyes widened, but he said nothing. Instead, he held out his arm to assist her to alight, which she did without ceremony. Julius followed. Once his feet were on the ground, he shook out the full stiffened skirts of his ultramarine coat, laced with black braid today, and graciously offered his arm to Eve.

She looked into the face of a stranger.

Cold, his eyes icy, his mouth set in a determined line, Julius nodded once and led her up the set of shallow stairs leading to the front door, via a half landing. He held his arm out, so she had to lay her hand on it in a ceremonial way, rather than snuggling her arm up against his body, as he had done before his confession of his true status.

The man she had married had turned into an earl. She had lost the warm, loving man of her wedding night. He might have gone forever, since he never truly existed in the first place.

And what of Alex? He must have known who Julius was. They had deceived her together. But the real blame lay with Julius who should have told her. It was his responsibility, and he had failed to do so. Eve detested dishonesty.

They stepped over the threshold at the same moment to discover a man bowing low. His glance at Eve revealed nothing but disdain. Inside, she bridled. They should not look at her as if she were something scraped off their shoes.

A small woman not in the first blush of youth, dressed in a breathtaking gown of pale-pink embroidered with spring flowers approached them, her wide hoops barely swaying with her movements. She glared at Julius. "Winterton, what is this? You arrive late, and bring a…guest with you?"

At last, Julius responded in a way Eve recognized. His glance at her conveyed reassurance, warmth returning temporarily to his eyes. Then he turned his attention to the woman.

"You did not get my letter? That is, to say the least, unfortunate. Mother, I have the honor of introducing to you…my wife."

Eve swept into a low curtsey as Julius continued.

"Her mother will be arriving shortly. I sent word ahead of our imminent arrival."

"I heard nothing." The woman's curt tones rang around the huge space. An imposing marble staircase led up one side of the hall and stretched across to meet its counterpart running up the other side. White marble columns supported the stretch of hallway, and another space opened up beyond. The walls were polished panels, and above hung gleaming paintings, portraits of people in antiquated dress interspersed with landscapes. Two massive chandeliers were suspended above them. They looked as if they held a hundred candles each. The penetrating tones sounded as if they bounced off every surface before returning in accusatory echoes. "Is this your idea of humor, Winterton?"

Light streamed in through the windows at the front. Eve stared at a beam of bright sunlight on the floor as she straightened, and once she had regained control, lifted her head to confront the angry features of her mother-in-law.

Eve refused to look away. The stormy eyes, so like her son's, except the color veered toward grey rather than blue, gleamed in the sunlight.

Julius continued to speak. "While I regret you did not receive my message in good time, I can assure you this is my wife. We have been married for four days, but I have been courting her for some weeks. The moment I saw Eve, I wanted her, and I was fortunate enough to win her."

The Duchess of Kirkburton, her complexion smooth from the skillful use of cosmetics, her hair drawn back into a fashionable style and powdered lightly, was everything Eve was not—fashionable, poised, and confident. Watching her, Eve detected hesitation, and for the fraction of a second, a moment of doubt.

The duchess turned her head abruptly, one of her ringlets brushing the frill of lace fastened around her neck and leaving a trace of hair powder behind. "I consider your behavior reprehensible, Winterton. I have gathered the perfect candidates for your hand, so you go off and marry the first woman you find?"

"No, mother." Anger trembled behind his taut words. "I married the woman I wish to have by my side."

"And so you repeat your mistake when you married Caroline?"

"You helped to arrange my marriage to Caroline."

Although the mother and son appeared entirely unaware of the two footmen nearby and doubtless the ears pressed to the other sides of the doors leading off the hall, Eve was not. "Should we not discuss this matter in private?" she suggested as mildly as she could.

The duchess swung her gaze back to Eve, as if surprised she was still there. "If you wish. Perhaps it would be a courtesy to our guests." She spun around in a swirl of silk and addressed the footman goggling behind her. "Request the presence of the duke in my breakfast parlor, if you please."

The man bowed and glided away, his steps barely creating a sound on the chequered black-and-white floor.

"Come."

The duchess led them up the stairs and turned left, taking them along the spacious hallway and into a suite of rooms at the end. They were furnished in perfect taste and at great expense. Not a china shepherdess was out of place, and dust would not dare to show its face here. She stopped and waved impatiently to a seat.

Eve took another, a chair with broad arms upholstered in delicate yellow and white stripes. She no longer cared if she marked the seat with her travel-stained garments. The duchess had not even considered offering refreshment, and Eve wanted tea. She would have happily gone to the kitchens and made it herself, had it not been totally reprehensible to do so. For the rest of her married life, she would be castigated as the countess who did not know how to go on in society, who stopped to prepare her own food and drink. If only they knew! The knowledge would not be difficult for anyone to discover, but this family would probably try to hush it up. Good luck to them. Eve refused to hide her origins. Liars were always found out.

Goodness, she was making decisions about what kind of wife she would be to Julius without even realizing it!

She need not have worried, at least about the tea, because a maid appeared almost immediately after them, bearing a substantial silver tray containing all necessary items. She'd even brought bread and butter. If Eve hadn't been so afraid of her manners letting her down, she would have been overjoyed by the food.

She should learn how to start behaving like a countess, whatever that meant.

She disposed her skirts as gracefully as she could before she sat. It occurred to her that whoever she was, the duchess should perhaps have offered her a room to get rid of the dust of the road and refresh herself, but perhaps the trial should come first. They would not give a condemned prisoner a chance to refresh himself.

Eve sat up straighter and lifted her chin, refusing to allow anyone to intimidate her, even this formidable lady. If she thought of the woman as the Duchess of Kirkburton, she would quail before her greatness, but if she addressed the person she could see and hear, she had a chance at coherent speech and thought.

"Who are you, young woman?" the duchess demanded in stentorian tones that filled the large room effortlessly.

"She is—" Julius began, but Eve cut him off.

"I am the daughter of a country vicar and his wife. Until recently, I lived in a village called Appleton. I have a reputation that will not disgrace the position your son has elevated me to, but I have no personal fortune."

She felt rather than saw Julius relax.

The duchess poured the tea. Eve remained perfectly still until the maid brought her a dish, and then she took it with a smile and a nod, as she recognized the tactic. The duchess had needed to think. She turned to Eve with a polite smile, better than the frozen features she had offered before.

"Then my son fell madly in love with you?"

Eve raised a brow. "That would not be to the point, ma'am, would it?"

Another interruption occurred when a man entered. His face had the ascetic quality Eve had come to recognize in his son, and he bore the air of someone accustomed to power. Three other men followed him, younger, closer to Julius's age, but nonetheless still intimidating with their fashionable clothing and their quiet arrogance.

Julius got to his feet and bowed, and Eve stood and curtseyed, keeping her head bowed while Julius made the introductions. She met Lords Darius and Valerian Shaw, twins and the sons of the Marquess of Strenshall, and Lord Nicephorus Westwood. All cousins of Julius. Darius and Valerian had a dark beauty Eve would normally have admired, were she not still obsessed by her fair-haired, treacherous husband. Lord Westwood had an air of distance that made his unsmiling austerity attractive in a different way. The Emperors of London must be devastating to society. They all bowed over Eve's had, seemingly unsurprised by Julius's choice of wife.

Her grace spoke first. "I consider you deeply foolish, Winterton, to have taken this step without our approval."

Just as if Eve were not there. Obviously the duchess was not yet willing to let Eve join the family. The presence of the others increased her anxiety, but she hated the uncertainty plaguing her. She would not allow it to defeat her.

From his inside pocket, Julius produced some papers.

Silence reigned while his grace took out a pair of gold-framed spectacles, perched them on his nose, and perused the documents. He took his time, but eventually put the glasses back in his pocket and lifted his head. "The papers are in order. Winterton obtained a special license from Doctors' Commons and married in the parish church at Appleton. Miss Merton has lived there for years and so she fulfils the residency requirements." He addressed his wife. "Madam, we have a new daughter-in-law."

Eve lifted her head and stared at the duke incredulously. He was smiling, the first sign of a welcome she had received since entering through the doors of this great house. She ventured to smile back.

"You understand, my dear, we need time to get to know you," the duke said gently.

"Of course, your grace." Heat rose to mantle her cheeks when Eve realized she should probably not call him by his title. Then what should she call him? "Sir," probably. Her gaucherie knew no bounds.

"There is no room for her. Winterton does not have another bedroom close to his. We will have to move his rooms," the duchess snapped. "We have a house full of guests at the moment. How can we undertake such a major alteration?"

"We will share a room," Julius said smoothly. "I do not wish to inhabit my old rooms. I want a suite close to the nursery. To my daughter."

The duchess shot her a vicious glare. "You indulge that child too much."

"That, madam, is our concern."

Could Julius sound any icier? Eve could barely remember the warm, loving man he had been, the persona he had jettisoned along with his name. Why had she not read any more gossip sheets? Why had she closed her ears when her mother had read the salacious articles aloud? Serve her right for pretending superiority to such matters. If she'd listened, she'd have known who Julius Vernon was.

"You are not a private person, Winterton." The duchess took a delicate sip of tea before going on, replacing the dish in the saucer with barely a clink. "I take it you will be leaving Helena in our care now? You will hardly have time to care for her if you are concentrating on your family."

"Then you assume wrongly, mother. I will of course be taking Helena back into my house." A trace of anger quivered in his voice.

"How happy she is does not concern me. Helena will do her duty."

"That she will," Julius said. "However I believe we vary in our ideas of duty regarding my sister, madam."

The duke added his voice, his tones calm and reasoned, his features impassive. "Helena will do as she wishes. She is old enough to choose for herself."

This was turning into a family argument. Lifting her head, Eve met the sympathetic eyes of Lord Valerian.

His mouth tilted in a smile. "Welcome to the family," he murmured.

Eve smiled back.

"Eve is one of the daughters of the Old Pretender," Julius said abruptly. "Someone has already tried to kill her. Unfortunately he died before I could question him. When I went to London to obtain the marriage license, I tried to establish which of the two camps he belonged to." He paused and glanced at her. "I believe it is the more dangerous of the two."

"Which is?" Lord Darius prompted.

"The Young Pretender. Every child is a threat to him. He is hunting them down. Including my wife."

Eve took a deep breath and tried to calm her racing pulse. He was telling people the deep, dark secret her parents had warned her not to divulge to anyone.

"So you married her to protect her?" Lord Valerian raised a brow, his mouth curved in a sardonic smile.

"Partly." Julius reached out his hand and took hers. His warmth enclosed her, radiated through her. However hard she tried to put him at a distance, he found his way back into her life. "But I could have protected Eve without marrying her."

He glanced at her, and for an instant, the old Julius found his way through. Eve smiled back.

He said nothing further, but turned his attention back to the room. "Augustus is looking through the records held at Oxford on his way here. There is some confusion about Eve's birth certificate."

That was the first she had heard. She frowned. "Problems?"

"No doubt because you were born abroad." Julius waved his hand in a vague but elegant gesture. "A small detail, but my brother likes to be precise. It does not matter in the larger scheme of things. Charles Stuart believes you are his half-sister, born legitimately, and that is enough for him. The man is half-mad."

"Only half mad?" Lord Valerian put in, humor in his voice.

Julius shrugged. "Maybe all the way." He shot a glance at her again, and whatever he saw made him get to his feet and draw her up with him.

"Eve is tired. I wanted everyone to know the situation because I want her to receive the strongest protection until we hear. My hope is the Young Pretender will hear of our marriage and will cease his suit. He must know I have no pretensions to royalty."

Eve found her voice. "Neither do I."

After bowing to the company, Julius took her from the room. A hubbub broke out behind them, but he took no notice and led her on inexorably.

Once out of the room, he drew her closer, but that might have been because the corridor, spacious though it was, only allowed them to walk together in that way. But he kept her that way when he took her up the broad staircase. In silence, he led her along another corridor to a set of double doors at the end and into a bedroom that made her gasp.

Only then did he turn and face her, his grasp on her arms gentle, his eyes sincere, his face stark. "I would have done anything to spare you that ordeal."

She could not doubt the sincerity in his eyes. More fool her, but he had revealed himself too late for her to change the way she felt about him. She would have to learn to deal with this new person, this great lord. Either that or trail behind him as the wife from the lower orders, and that she absolutely refused to do.

"I'll answer every question you ask me as truthfully as I can." Regret traced the blue of his eyes. "I'm sorry, so sorry, Eve. In my arrogance, I assumed my position and consequence would come as a pleasant surprise to you."

Indignation swamped her shock, replaced her horror. "Why would you think that? I married a man who I could be comfortable with, who I could love, and what do I get? A public figure. Did you think me so downtrodden and poor that I would welcome that status?" A vision swam before her, of her mother laughing and sometimes deriding the behavior of the upper echelons of society. The brief indulgence gave them pleasure but meant nothing to them. However, these people were real, not figures enacting a play for their benefit. Now she was one of them. How could she live with that? How could she not? She had jumped into this situation, and now she had to deal with it.

She wasn't ready for the pressure, but she had to be, had to make herself ready fast.

"Promise me you will never lie to me again."

"I didn't lie—"

She wouldn't let him get away with that. "You lied. You knew what I expected." A lie by omission was still a lie.

He sighed, the breath heavy enough to lift his chest and momentarily press it against her breasts. Even that made them tingle. She should not allow it, but her reaction to his nearness seemed to be something she couldn't prevent. "Am I allowed small lies?"

"No." He was too tricky for her to allow him any concessions.

The trace of a grin flicked his mouth up at the corners before he turned serious again. "I promise. Eve, I cannot express how sorry I am all this is now forced on you. Otherwise, how could I protect you?"

She was very much afraid that she did. "I'm royal. Did you want a princess for a wife?"

He snorted. "Hardly. In any case, the Vernons have traces of royal blood from various sources. But you and your siblings give the Stuarts new hope. King George is ailing, his heir a boy and under the influence of unsavory individuals." He squeezed her hands. "A claimant free of the taint of treachery could force questions, could even affect the balance of power in Europe. Even if the Stuarts give up all pretensions to the throne, they can still affect decisions."

"It's nonsense. The law decides who is king. The Divine Right of Kings died a long time ago." A mirror was set on the wall, within her eyesight, she discovered, when she glanced around. This sunny, beautifully appointed room held treasures aplenty, and the elaborately gilded mirror was one. Eve saw herself anew. "Do I look like a Stuart?"

"You look like Eve."

She turned back to him. None of this seemed real, any more than discovering the man she had married was heir to a dukedom. It was all a fairy tale, and she would wake in her old room with the ill-fitting windows that she had to stuff with rags in the winter to stop the draughts. That was reality, not this.

"You said I was the third child of the Pretender that you have discovered. Did you want to marry them?" And she had siblings. She would ensure she met them. Perhaps together they could work something out.

"One is male."

She ignored the amusement that lit his eyes that she had found so irresistible such a short time ago. "The other. Would you have married her?"

He closed his eyes. "No. I would not."

Restlessly she got to her feet, took a few paces, and turned, her skirts swirling about her.

"Do you take part in politics? Is that it?" With the pretense of opening her modest dressing case, she went to the chest where it had been carefully laid. She had but a brush, a comb, and a small mirror inside, but she had inherited the set from her grandmother, and she cherished them. Now she stroked a finger over the tortoiseshell back of the mirror, comforting herself with the smooth texture, as she had so many times before. "You wanted a stake of your own?"

"I would not have the stability of this country disrupted by a worthless power seeker," he said softly. "James Stuart has no idea how to rule, only to scheme, and his son is worse."

"So you would claim the throne through marriage rather than see them in power?" Julius Vernon would not have done such a thing. He had a practical turn of mind that would have laughed at the very idea of becoming King. This person, the Earl of Winterton? Eve was not so sure. She didn't know him. Julius had only shown her part of himself when he had courted her and asked her to marry him. This man could have hidden so much more. A vaunting ambition to rule, for instance.

That would not be so far-fetched, not from the Earl of Winterton.

She had supposed her mother's stories to be fanciful at the least, but it appeared her parents had told her the cold, hard truth. The tortoiseshell had warmed under her fingers. She picked up the mirror, but kept its back toward her. "What prevents me from being a monarch?"

"Your brother, the one you have not yet met. Your grandfather, James Stuart, would want you to strengthen his claim. Your half-brother would want to destroy you."

The Stuarts really thought they still had a chance at the monarchy? "They're mad."

"They are indeed, but madmen often succeed where the sane fail."

She turned the mirror. Did she see the trace of the Stuarts in her dark hair and her long nose? Would others see it?

She had no answers, only more questions.

Chapter 13

Spurning Julius's offer of having a meal served to them privately, Eve went down to dinner later that afternoon. At her request, he left her to get ready on her own. Taylor attended her in silence. Better to face everything now than leave it festering. She had always been that way, preferring to confront obstacles and overcome them, rather than try to go around.

Eve had done her best, but even her burgundy silk could not compare to the gowns the women she met in the drawing room were sporting. Fine silks and brocades met her gaze, adorned with the best and most elaborate lace from Brussels and Vincennes, the threads so fine they could barely be seen by the naked eye. Filmy lawn gauze adorned the bosoms of the ladies, and cosmetics tinted every face.

Except hers. With little experience with face paint, Eve had decided against it, even turning down the offer of a patch for the corner of her eye. Her maid had retreated, disappointed, but Eve wanted the gossips to see her as she really was, not the person she might wish to become. Or not. She had yet to decide what kind of countess she would be.

The heads swiveling to shoot her hard and curious glances meant they had been talking about her. Eyes glinted, fans flicked out and wafted the air like a flock of fluttering birds. The colors of myriad silks swirled as they turned and reformed like dancers in an elaborate measure she did not understand.

One woman broke away from the group gathered in the center of the large room and came towards her, a welcoming smile wreathing her features. She wore her fair hair unpowdered and gathered in a gleaming mass on top of her head, a couple of curls allowed to escape and tease the bare skin of her shoulders. "Since no one thought to introduce us, I will do it myself, if you have no objection."

How could Eve object to this exquisite creature?

"You are my brother's wife." The lady bestowed a gentle smile on her, but it disappeared as fast as it came.

Eve found herself unable to speak. The news had travelled. At least she would not have to face the embarrassment of introducing herself. She had thought to find Julius here, but only women inhabited this room, and now she came to distinguish between them, only half a dozen.

Of course, society dined later than she was used to. Her mother would have told her, but her mother was not here yet.

Eve curtseyed. "I'm Eve." Should she call herself something else? Lady Eve? No, that was wrong. She was Eve, Lady Winterton. Surely too formal for before-dinner conversation?

"Helena." The lady smiled. "His sister. Tricky devil, isn't he?"

Exactly what Eve had been thinking. Her grin broke through her reserve and she nodded. "Yes he is. I fear I'm only just beginning to understand him."

"Oh, nobody understands him." Helena turned, so they were facing in the same direction. "Allow me to introduce you to the others."

In short order Eve met Lady McComyn and her lovely daughters Mary and Elizabeth, Lady Murtagh and her lovely daughter Charlotte, and Miss Sophia Kershaw. They were uniformly beautiful and coolly welcoming. The younger ladies were obviously here so Julius could select his bride from them, like chickens waiting to be plucked, or more likely hounds chasing a hare.

Except Julius was no hare. He would not want to be anyone's quarry. Whether he wanted it or not, he was being pursued. That would be enough to drive him into the arms of someone else. Her, to be precise.

The women eyed her with suspicion, but all bore smiles, none as welcoming as the one Helena had offered.

"Would we know your family?" Lady Murtagh said.

Eve took instant dislike to the fashionable drawl. "I doubt it," she said. "Until recently we lived in Appleton, a village near Bath. My father was connected to some notable people, but they never concerned themselves with us, and we were only too happy to reciprocate. Our lives did not intersect."

"I see." Her ladyship looked Eve up and down as if she were a prize horse up for sale. "I merely wondered what dear Julius was up to now. You are married, I take it?"

"Knotted tightly," Eve replied, working hard to prevent her teeth clenching. If only she could deny that small fact. She might have had a chance to befriend one of the ladies, to learn what she was to become, had Julius not taken the notion into his head to marry her quickly. Was he afraid she would get away or he would lose his nerve?

No. The answer came to her in a flash. He was afraid his family would not allow it. He married her because he wanted to defy his mother. Although Eve had barely met the woman, she had an inkling of how controlling the duchess was.

The village pond was no more. Now she had to remain afloat on a larger sea. Had to. Not for his sake, but for hers.

Thank heaven for Helena, who drew her to sit on a large sofa set by the fireplace, which was filled with fresh flowers, the weather being too warm to set the fire. The scent wafted over her, as did the perfumes of the ladies. When they moved, fresh aromas assaulted her nostrils. The gowns must be scented. Not the camphor or lavender, which would betray a gown that would be stored carefully and kept for Sunday wear, but flower scents mingled with muskier, headier aromas.

The soft upholstery gave under Eve's weight, its fabric far finer and newer than her gown. It had served her well, but its usefulness had come to an abrupt end today. No longer would it work as her dinner gown. Even less as a ball gown. What would she do now? She would have to suffer while she watched the other ladies parade their finery before her until she found the opportunity to order gowns of her own. Parade they would. Eve had no illusions about that. They resented her.

"Have you even been to London?" a girl asked, her plump lips forming a pout as she spoke. She must have practiced the gesture for hours, all to no avail.

The "even" added a sneering quality to her words. Eve turned a bright smile on to her. "No, although I will be rectifying that in the future."

"Oh!" Lady Mary widened her fine blue eyes. She possessed an air of fragility, enhanced by her ivory-colored gown and fine blond hair, which gleamed through its light coating of powder. "I have never met anyone who has never visited London before!"

As if Eve were some exotic creature. Eve gazed back at them, letting her eyes half close. "Really? What a sheltered life you must have led!"

Helena gave a crack of laughter. "Well said. London is not the center of the world, despite the way the fashionable talk about it."

"Don't you need to dress for dinner?" Lady Mary's younger sister, Lady Elizabeth, said. She was as fair as her sister, but with a more pointed chin.

Her features were more animated. She would probably take in society better than Lady Mary, which must be a sad trial to her older sister.

"This is it," Eve said, ruefully indicating her gown.

"I have ordered fabrics and gowns from London for my wife," said Julius.

Eve had not even been aware he had come in. She swiveled around to see him standing in the doorway, glorious in his favorite blue, but a different outfit to the one he had travelled in. Fortunate man. "If they do not arrive by tomorrow, that particular modiste will be in trouble."

"Goodness, Julius, you startled the life out of me!" Eve said without thinking. Despite his finery, for a moment the amused gleam in his eyes brought her right back to the man he had been before yesterday, the one she could share her thoughts with.

"I beg your pardon, my sweet."

While she was struck dumb by the public endearment, he glided forward, the heavy skirts of his coat swaying gently, the magnificent jeweled Order decorating the left side of his coat twinkling in the light pouring in through the windows.

"I should have hobnails put in my evening shoes, so you could hear my approach." He came to stand before her and bowed over her hand. "The last thing I want to do is startle you." He brushed her knuckles with his lips, his touch indicating to everyone present this woman—she—meant more to him. Usually gentlemen would bow over a lady's hand but end an inch or two above it. Not in this case.

"You have chosen clothes for me?"

"A selection. Take them all or choose the ones you want and send the others back." Retaining his hold on her hand, he sat next to her.

If they were anything like the clothes he owned, they would probably intimidate her on their own.

They sat twenty to dinner. That took three removes with at least a dozen dishes in each remove, the crockery, silverware, and crystal perfect examples of the tradesman's art. The china was porcelain, the silverware real silver, and the glasses were finely cut and engraved crystal. Eve handled them with care and ate sparingly. Her behavior probably castigated her as a provincial, but by this point she was past caring. Let them think what they wanted to. They would anyway. Anything she did would not alter that.

* * * *

Finally Julius saw the benefits of sackcloth, ashes, and self-flagellation. It had taken him over thirty years to discover the advantages, but finally he was there. He cared for Eve, hated to see her in such discomfort. He should have ignored his mother's house party and found somewhere else to take her, but here he could ensure her protection.

After an agonizing dinner, and when his mother had led the ladies away, finally his father asked him the question he was asking himself. "What were you thinking?"

Val leaned back and propped his feet on the table, crossing his ankles. "He's violently in love," he said.

"Or *she* is," Darius added. "Maybe he couldn't bear to disappoint the lady."

Val shot his brother a darkling look. "How would you know?"

Darius preferred men, a family secret most of society decided to ignore, but it wasn't like Val to mention his brother's proclivities in such disparaging tones.

Darius grinned. "Some of my best friends are female."

Val snorted and found a silver toothpick in his pocket, which he plied with enthusiasm.

"Carry on like that and you'll make your mouth bleed," Julius remarked. At last he could remove the heavy coat that hung on him like a woolen blanket. This day was far too hot for formal wear. "Or maybe I will." He tossed the coat over the back of his chair.

Val scoffed at him. Not that Julius could not take care of himself, but he and Val had taken each other's measure many a time in the fencing salon and found themselves evenly matched. "You have your hands full, cousin. You're far too engaged to waste time on me."

"I like her," Nick put in. "She has courage."

"She'll need it." Val glanced at the duke.

Julius's father ignored his nephews' comments but glanced at the gentlemen who were not members of the family, either to remind the others or to give a hint for them to leave.

Although Lord McComyn moved his chair, he did not leave. Likely his wife would make his life hell if he left now. He cleared his throat with a loud harrumph and reached for the brandy decanter. "New blood. Every family needs it now and again. Hybrid vigor!" Lord McComyn rode to hounds whenever he had the opportunity, rather more than was wise, if his wife spoke the truth about his activities. She usually finished with a sigh. "Oh well, it keeps him out of the boudoirs." That explained why his nickname was "Boudoir" McComyn. Few people called him that to his face, though.

Julius would rather have his wife discussed to his face than behind his back, although he planned to join her in the drawing room soon. With his sisters there, he could leave Eve for a short while. Helena would take care of his interests. Lucinda had a good heart, and would help if she could. "I saw Eve, and I wanted her. Consider it perspicacity and acquired wisdom I left it this long before marrying her."

"She's perfect." Darius accepted the decanter and poured himself a liberal measure. "She's old enough to shoulder responsibility, young enough to become a mother."

"And beautiful," Val added.

"Almost too much," Nick said. "It's exactly like Julius to find a ravishing beauty in the middle of nowhere." He glowered and downed his wine in one gulp.

"You have to know where to look." Julius could not help feeling smug. Once Eve had found her feet, she would be an asset to him and his family. That notion occurred to him for the first time, but he dismissed it with a careless shrug. He enjoyed looking at his wife, conversing with her and holding her close. The rest was not as important, certainly barely worth his consideration.

Why not?

He had long told himself the next woman he married, as he knew he must, would be elegant, young enough to bear heirs, and no trouble. Eve had been nothing but trouble from the start. True, some of the problems were not of her making, but the spirited woman tramping down the country lane had been a handful in more than one way. He would not have her any different.

He could barely wait to get her upstairs at the end of the evening. He could not expect any favor, but her tiredness bore him down, all through the interminable harpsichord playing and singing the women insisted on doing. He did not linger over wine and gossip.

Once he joined her in the drawing room, Julius sat determinedly by her side, giving every impression of the devoted husband. He ignored the daggers shot them by some of the younger women and remained with her, bestowing on her all the attention a wife should expect and then some for good measure.

He waited until six songs had passed and the youngest McComyn girl had played an interminable nocturne, no doubt because the piece was fiendishly difficult, although tedious in the extreme. After all, although Julius was out of the marriage mart, several other gentlemen remained. He did not envy his cousins their fortunes. While most would abscond to Stretton's house for the large hunting party that opened the season, some might choose to remain here and shoot his father's game birds instead.

He trusted every guest invited to the opening day of the season. However he remained aware of the potential danger to Eve. Any stray shot or one fired by an interloper could be fatal. His blood ran cold. Maybe he should take her away before the Glorious Twelfth. Anything less glorious was difficult to imagine.

Whatever Eve thought of him, however she despised him, and God knew she had reason to, he would protect her—with his life if necessary.

When her jaw tightened in an effort to stifle a yawn—he recognized the movement, having done it so often himself—Julius got to his feet. "My dear, we have had a long day. Allow me to escort you."

Blinking, she took his hand. No pretense at formality now. Before she could change her mind, he closed his fingers, trapping her hand as securely as he might a chick in need of care. He drew her to her feet. She stood silently, with no rustle of skirts. That would change in the next few days. Her loveliness already outshone all the other women in the room. He would ensure she became a woman society would never overlook.

She made her curtsey to the ladies, and, head bowed, accompanied him upstairs, her hand lax in his. She did not try to pull away, but she didn't respond to him, either. Julius despaired. He would not use her, refused to take a wife bent on obedience. Had he destroyed her spirit?

She said nothing until their bedroom door closed behind them. Julius removed his coat and tossed it over a nearby chair. When Lamaire entered through the door between the powder room and this one, he said one, curt word. "Out."

The valet did not stay to argue. Just as well because Julius was spoiling for a fight right now. How could he get through to her? "Eve, what does it matter what I am? I'm still the person you married."

She turned away, lifting her hands to remove her hairpins. The first clattered into the glass dish on the dressing table. "You are. That is true. But you are more than that. So much more I cannot imagine why you did this. You're a great lord. Everything you did tonight tells me of that. You are at home here as I never will be."

"Yes you will." Heedless of her frostiness, Julius crossed the room in two long strides and put his hands on her shoulders. She wore no fichu, only a frill of lace, so his fingers touched bare skin. As always, the thrill of touching her rendered him momentarily speechless. He could not afford that. He forced his mind back into action, as if all his blood had not flowed south. "You have it in you, Eve. You will become everything you need to be. Everything you want to be. I will allow nothing less."

"You will not allow it?" Her bitter tones echoed around the room as she turned to face him.

He dropped his hands to her waist, afraid if he let her go she would make her escape. "You deserve it. Eve, I will give you all I have and all you need. Doubt all I say if you wish, but not that part. I have faith in you."

"Then you are the only person in this house to show me such favor." Her eyes glistened with unshed tears.

She would not cry for people as worthless as the ones downstairs, and he included his reprobate cousins. Even worse that she should think of crying over him.

Julius had never made a more serious mistake in his life as when he had decided not to tell her his true name and status. He began to speak, trusting his instincts. His reason had failed him spectacularly, so why not? What more did he have to lose? "Eve, I would have done anything rather than hurt you. I should have thought more, should have considered your position. But this is the safest place I know. I have servants loyal to me and my family. I can care for you here, until I contact the man responsible for this and make him stop. More than anything else I want to ensure your safety. I need it. Eve, do you understand that at least?" Desperate tones edged his voice, but he didn't care. Since Caroline died, control had become vital for his existence.

He should respect Eve more. He should show her how much she meant to him, abandon any thought of hiding from her. He'd promised not to keep anything from her. "Ask me any question you wish. I will answer, I swear it."

"But what should I ask? How do I know what you know, how many secrets you hold about me?"

"You have them all, my love."

"Don't call me that!"

Her vehemence took him by surprise, and he blinked, but held on to her. "Why not? It's what you are to me."

"Am I? Would you treat the woman you love in that way?"

He swallowed. What had he done? Had he wrecked everything by his wretched secretive behavior? "I wanted to protect you."

"Then inform me, Julius."

At least she'd used his name. All night she'd referred to him as "my husband" or, copying his mother's example, "Winterton." He hated it, curls of acid roiling in his stomach when he heard it on her lips. "Everything. I swear. We may go into the country and live quietly, if that is what you wish. I have some business to conclude, but if that is what you want, that is what we will do. Apart from the title, we may behave as any other country gentleman and his wife."

"Would you let me go alone?"

Would he? If he was sure she was safe, he might have to. That would prove the bitterest pill of all to swallow, to know he could have had her but he'd thrown it away. "Have I lost you, then? Can you no longer trust me or even spend time in the same house as me?"

She bit her lip. One large tear tumbled from the corner of her left eye and trailed down the side of her face, creating a glistening path for others to follow. Desperate to prevent them from falling, he tried again.

"If you wish it, I will do even that. Nobody will trouble you. You may live with your mother as if I had never come into your life. Except I will make you financially stable. I will never abandon you, Eve."

She closed her eyes and took a steadying breath. When she opened them again, the depths were darker, the pupils wider. "No, I do not want that. I wanted to know how you would answer me. God help me, Julius, but I love you."

She spoke as if the words were torn out of her.

Relief powered through him, lightened his heart while he stared at her. He did not deserve this. Still sore from recognizing his mistake, he would do anything for her, to make this right. Desperation chased the relief. "Then we will make this marriage a strong one. We have everything we need. I'll make arrangements for us to leave as soon as possible."

"What about your parents?"

"They will not have a say in our lives. We do not have to see them or this house ever again, should that be your desire." He dared to move his hands, slide them farther about her waist. She pressed her breasts against his chest, the movement making them swell above her low-cut neckline.

Julius tried to keep his attention away from the luscious bounty spread before him. She did not move away or make any protest. A little more relief slid through him.

Eve lifted her hands from where they had hung limply from her side and curved them around his upper arms. She kept her attention on his face, watching him closely. "No, we cannot do that. Even tonight I saw what you were, what you could become. What you *should* become. How can I deprive people of that? You cannot waste your talents."

"For intrigue and scheming, you mean?"

"No!" Her denial was vehement. She shook her head, and more curls came loose, the hairpins falling out from the relaxed style. She did not appear to notice, but Julius did. "You are a great man. You have power and influence and the ability to make people listen to you. Not once tonight did you raise your voice, but everyone paid attention when you spoke. Your ideas were taken into consideration, although you said nothing of me. By the end of the evening you almost had them reconciled to me." She glanced down, as if fascinated by the buttons on his waistcoat. "Those women—your mother intended one for you, did she not?"

He smiled ruefully. "Yes, she did. When I met you, I was running away from this house party. I knew I would have to marry again, to make an heir or at least try to, but I did not wish to do so. The idea of marrying a woman of her choosing terrified me."

Her attention returned to his face. "You, terrified?"

"Very much. She had backed me into a corner. I had no redress. Then I met you, and I knew in short order I wanted to be married more than anything else in the world. But only to you."

Unable to prevent himself any longer, Julius lowered his head and kissed her. His lips touched hers and pressed until she opened her mouth under his, and he could give her his tongue. Not in passion, not yet, but in pure, heartfelt love. Eve responded eagerly, sucking his tongue and stroking her own against it. She lifted up on tiptoe and he slid one hand to her backside, bringing the other up to support her upper back, holding her securely while they exchanged caresses.

With that kiss he made her a silent promise. This woman was too precious to be a possession, whatever the law said. She was his equal, his partner, his wife. She would be a part of his life—the center of his life. He would never keep anything from her again.

Slowly the kiss grew in intensity, as their mouths opened wider, the better to explore and possess. The world tightened, shortened, and folded in around them, until nothing mattered but the woman in his arms. Julius would have kissed her forever, but other parts of his body were making themselves known. His erection rose, hardened, and trapped a fold of his underwear, so it rubbed uncomfortably, but anything against that organ would have irritated him, except the hot, wet heat of his wife's body. Nothing else would do.

Julius would not call himself a roué, but he was certainly experienced. Eve made him feel like a lovesick schoolboy, clumsy, far too anxious to get her naked to concern himself with finesse and ensuring her comfort.

But she behaved the same way. She pulled at his shirt, even before he had his waistcoat undone, her jerky movements so fierce she threatened to tear the fabric. Not that he'd have cared.

He dragged off his coat, heedless of the fine material and gold buttons, and tossed it away, registering the thunk as it hit the floor but caring nothing for its condition. Then his waistcoat. Instead of unfastening the myriad buttons, he thrust his hand in the opening at the top and dragged it down. Some buttons slid through the holes. Others popped off and scattered over the floor. The waistcoat followed the coat.

Before she could harm herself, Julius drew away far enough to remove the long sapphire pin he'd thrust through his neckcloth. Before he could toss it aside, she took it and turned, laying it on the dressing table with shaking hands.

When she turned back, she stared at him, wide-eyed.

"I'll die if you change your mind now." Desperation filled him to the brim. That part of him that was not filled with desire. No, not desire, but pure, raw need.

He pulled her back against him, beginning to unfasten the front of her gown. The hooks parted easily, and unlike the way he dealt with his own clothes, he took care with hers. At present she did not have many, and they were precious to her. So he went about his task as gently as his excitement would allow, sliding the gown off her shoulders and away and starting on her petticoat. He dotted tiny kisses on her cheeks, her nose, and her mouth, feeling her smile under his lips. A happy kiss. The notion made Julius smile, too.

He had her clothes off in a few minutes. When she was naked, he held her, just held her so he could feel her heat, and then kissed her and lifted her before ripping the covers away from the bed and laying her on the smooth linen sheets.

Eve made no effort to hide herself. Instead, she lay on her side, propping her head on her hand, and watched him strip away his shirt, breeches, hose, and underwear. He'd already kicked off his shoes without undoing the buckles, leaving them where he'd stepped out of them.

Then he joined her. As he fit her naked body to his, he sighed in utter contentment. But they weren't done. To his delight, she laid her fingers on his cock, claiming it for her own. As she should, because he was utterly hers, every part of him. "Mine," she murmured, so softly he hardly heard her, but the silence inside his room was still, the air thrumming with anticipation.

"Yours," he agreed. "Every part of me belongs to you. Do with me what you will."

Her eyes widened, the center growing darker as her pupils opened, an unmistakable indication of her arousal. Her lips were red, plumped by desire and his kisses. He made sure they would stay that way by kissing her again, taking his time, caressing her tongue with his as he pressed against her incredibly soft skin.

Taking her hands in his, he lifted them and pressed them against the pillow as he rolled over her and positioned his shaft to slide against her adorably wet heat. When he broke the kiss, he paused and smiled at her. "You are the most beautiful woman I have ever seen." He stopped her scoffing with a kiss, and instead, she chuckled into his mouth.

He drew back in mock indignation. "You don't believe me?"

Eve shook her head, her curls clinging to the pillow.

A slow smile took over his lips. "Then let me prove it to you, wife."

She sighed when he released her to take his shaft in one hand and guide it home.

He joined them. Eve was ready for him, welcoming him in, her inner walls clinging to him as he slid in and out of her.

"I will never get enough of you. Never. I will arrive in your bedroom with eager anticipation every night. You will never be free of me, even during the day. I will look at you, and you'll know I am saying, 'Eve, come upstairs. Make love with me.'"

"And I will come."

"Oh, yes, sweetheart. You will come."

A sweet flush mantled her cheeks. He kissed each one and then her mouth, all the time moving in a slow, deliberate rhythm. He watched her, marking the rise of her arousal. He changed the angle of entry, keeping his movements gradual until, with one supple twist, she arched her back and pressed against him. She lifted her legs and wound them around his, her heels pressing on the mattress to aid her response to him. Her body clenched, gripped him as if she would never let go, and she sighed, her breath caressing his cheek when he bent to kiss her.

He took her mouth with the same fervor with which he was claiming her body, thrusting his tongue inside in time with the way his cock was delving inside her.

Nothing could ever equal this. He forged inside her as if his life depended on it. Which, in a way, it did. Because if he could not persuade her to stay with him, to be as close to him as she was now, part of him would truly die. This was what he was born for, and this was the woman he was born for.

At last.

His heart stopped as he gazed at her. Then, with one steady thump, it went back into action. A part of his life had died with that pause, but not a part he would ever mourn. He was freshly made because of this woman.

What he felt before—that had not been love. This was love, this all-encompassing joy, this need to care for her, to spend his life by her side.

Smiling at his own foolishness, he drew away so he could watch her face, her reaction when she came. Bringing all the finesse he had learned over the years to the fore, he stroked her, tried to tell her with his body what she meant to him.

Of course that was impossible, but in time he might find a way to do it properly. "I shall practice until I get it right."

A crease appeared between her brows. "Until you get what right?"

"The best way to love you." In case she hadn't understood, he took her face between his hands and met her eyes. "I love you, Eve."

"Oh." The crease melted away. "You do that so well. Surely it's my turn?"

Without warning, except for an extra sparkle in her eyes, she pushed on one side. Taken by surprise, he rolled over, but once he realized what she was at, he let her claim her position on top of him.

He smiled up at her, delighted she was taking the initiative. "You are utterly captivating."

Now she'd won her ploy, she paused, taking her bottom lip between her teeth. "Will you tell me what I should do?"

He laughed, shaking his head. "Oh, no, not a chance. You started this, so you can carry on. Do what you want. Anything. Try something. If it doesn't work, we'll try something else."

"I don't know…"

"Nothing is wrong." He slid his hands up her sides, caressing the swells of her breasts as they pressed against his chest. "We are the only people here. I won't tell anybody. Will you?"

He laughed when she gasped. "Of course not!" she exclaimed.

"Then we're safe. Do whatever you want to. Except for one thing." He moved, enough to remind her he was filling her. "Don't stop."

"Oh!" her eyes went unfocussed for a minute, and then a wicked grin curled her full lips. Flattening her hands either side of him, she levered herself up and brought her legs under her and then either side of him.

Julius groaned. He had never seen such a beautiful sight. Her breasts swayed over him, and her face was animated, full of mischief. He wanted her like this all the time, happy, concentrated on him.

"Did I hurt you?"

He shook his head slightly. "No. I wouldn't care if you did, but you are not. Nor will you, unless you stay there without moving for much longer."

When she laughed, the vibrations travelled right to where he was still deeply embedded inside her.

Still shaken by the effects of her laughter, Julius nearly lost his mind when she rose and then lowered again. She took her lower lip between her teeth and moved again, keeping her attention on his face. He had to do something, or he'd come in an instant, just from taking delight at her initiative. It was true—the mind was the greatest aphrodisiac.

But when she moved, his reason froze. All he was capable of was to respond, to hold his body steady as she lifted and lowered. Julius thrust back, tried to do his part, but she had him helpless. And he loved it. Better than the most skillful courtesan who ever existed, her appeal more potent, her beauty more evident, Eve slid over him, and he gave himself up to her.

He had meant to claim her, but she had turned the tables. Did she know how helpless he was under her ministrations?

Julius grasped her waist, helped her move, but did not try to control her. He kept his eyes open, eager to learn and know what she wanted.

"Is this good?" she asked in a breathless whisper.

"Very good." Telling her everything she did pleased him would not help or encourage her. Would not help her learn, as she evidently wished to do. Changing the angle of his entry, sinking his backside deeper into the mattress, he found her sweet spot. Eve stiffened and gasped, giving a little cry, but she didn't stop moving.

She felt so good, her warmth flowing over him, the sweet and spicy aroma of their lovemaking surrounding them. The sight of her—he needed more. Releasing her waist with one hand, he curved it around the back of her neck and drew her down to taste her.

He didn't linger. He'd yearned for her. Urging her back up, he opened his eyes and gently restored her to her upright position. She laughed when she resumed her actions, before she increased them, using her knees for traction so she raised her body and brought it down again, grinding her sweet rear against his thighs with every stroke. Her actions increased as her confidence grew, driving him further to his release.

Julius set his jaw and gave her everything she needed, giving himself up to her. His wife. He could do nothing else, especially when she cried out and froze above him.

Her inner passage gripped him, clenching his cock in an iron grip, spasms racking her. Her breasts quivered with the impact. Julius wanted more, but he could hold on no longer. She worked on him like the most potent of drugs, the best French brandy, intoxicating him, drawing him in. He went willingly.

Then it was his turn. He cried out, giving her all he could, his seed jetting into her. She had worked for it; the least he could do was give it to her. Not that he had any choice.

When she fell forward, he let her, unable to help himself or hold her off. She collapsed on to him, a hot, damp blanket, her weight surrounding him, the most desired of coverings. Her hair fell over his face, covering them in a swathe of dark, silky beauty. Julius didn't care that he was almost smothered by it. A small price to pay.

She moved her head to one side, resting it on his shoulder. He cupped the back of her head, preventing her from hurting herself or falling awkwardly. Now it was his turn to care for her. She was exhausted, sated, for now at least. Gently, he moved to one side so she slid off him. Keeping her close, he crooned her name, and kissed her forehead.

Eve opened her eyes. Warm velvety brown met his gaze as he smiled. "That was so good, my love. So wonderful."

"I will learn."

"As far as pleasing me is concerned, you don't need to learn. But the next time I want you to come at least twice before I do. I want you limp and happy."

"Oh, I think that is taken care of."

He chuckled and claimed a kiss from her warm, full lips. She opened to him, licking his lips and his tongue, and he gave her the same in return.

"Together now," he murmured as they parted. "Sleep, my love. God knows you deserve it."

* * * *

Eve awoke wrapped in her husband's arms. She opened her eyes and there he was, looking back at her. Close up she could discern the different shades of that blue made up the startling color of his eyes, the gradations from cobalt to sky blue, the subtleties adding up to an intensity that astonished her.

The corners of his eyes were lightly creased, because he was smiling. "I've been waiting for you," he said, and kissed her.

He plunged her right back into ecstasy, one hand around her rib cage, under her breast, the other smoothing her back and teasing her shoulder blades.

He touched his lips to her ear and then her throat, giving her no time to protest. "Did you let me sleep on your shoulder all night?"

"No, love," he answered, between feathering kisses on her collarbone and licking under it. Heavens, was there anywhere she wasn't sensitive to him? "I woke in the early hours, my muscles numb. I nearly woke you when I eased you away and the feeling came back." He urged her to roll on her back and continued with his attentions, talking to her between kisses. He cupped her breast in one hand, stroking his thumb across her nipple until she gasped with renewed sensation.

"I seem to have married a weighty woman," he said thoughtfully as he studied the result of his handiwork. "I can see I have my work cut out with you."

She loved this playful Julius, the flirtatious man who was both the man she had married and something else. But now she had recovered from her shock, she was discovering more and more about him, factors and depths she had previously not known. His air of command never left him, but he had it well in hand, as he did her body.

Yet he had given her complete control over him last night, letting her make love to him until they were both exhausted. She bore some of the results this morning, small pink marks where his kisses had grown more passionate, a slight soreness between her legs. Not that she would have admitted to it for one moment. Otherwise he might stop, the last thing she wanted him to do. This morning she would let him guide her to pleasure.

"Are you seducing me into forgiving you?" She twined her fingers into his hair, tousling it for the pleasure of smoothing it out again. The bright locks had a definite wave to them.

"Am I succeeding?" He lifted his head and met her gaze. He was still smiling.

She smiled back. "You'll have to try harder than that."

"I intend to." With a deep chuckle, he continued his self-imposed task, kissing his way down her body.

She thought he would stop at her waist, but he did not. He nuzzled lower, and lower still. When she tried to flinch away, he placed his hands on her hips, firmly holding her still.

"Open your legs, sweetheart."

"Julius, I—"

"Do as I bid you." The command did not sound in the least demanding, only persuasive, but she did it anyway. He kissed her at the apex of her legs and touched his tongue to the tip of the sensitive bundle of nerves at the top of her feminine crease. "Beautiful," he murmured, but his tones were indistinct, muffled when he dived deeper.

She would have jerked away when he sucked her, except for his hands holding her steady. She had no choice but to accept what he was doing to her. Reacting on instinct as the thrills turned to lightning strikes arcing from her femininity to her head and the tips of her toes, encompassing her completely. She belonged to him, utterly helpless, but she thrilled to the knowledge as she did when she realized he only wished to bring her pleasure. He would not hurt her. He would hurt himself first.

The sounds of his activity brought forbidden delights. Never would she had thought Julius, even in his Julius Vernon guise, would have allowed himself such joyous activity at the expense of personal dignity.

Yet the evidence was here. He made love to her with total intensity and a complete abandonment of his own considerations.

How could she not love that?

His untrammeled enjoyment drove her to do follow his example, to throw herself into the experience. Whatever came after did not matter. How they had got here did not matter. Only this.

Sharp, hard spasms of delight sent her soaring, and she cried out, panting his name. Her mind went blank and her sight blurred over. When she had regained a measure of her senses, he was over her and in her, her legs propped on his shoulders.

The fierce intensity in his eyes reflected the sensations rioting through her body. Clutching the sheet under her, a reminder of reality, but a fleeting one, Eve arched up, pressed against him.

She could not come again, not in the same way she had before. Her sensitivity was like nothing she had experienced before. Every time he touched her, even looked at her, she soared a little higher. This could not be right. Eve fought to regain control.

Without effort, he found the point inside her that sent her crazy. How could this happen again? He slammed his shaft inside her, the wet slaps echoing through the room.

He smiled, bared his teeth. "No, Eve, don't think. Stop trying to reason and go there. I'll join you, I promise."

How did she not think? What was the key?

All at once, the task became shockingly easy. His pace quickened, but he penetrated her as deeply every time he slammed into her. Then he changed the rhythm to something unpredictable, driving deep inside and then, giving a few shallow jabs, barely grazing her, and then deeply.

Eve lost all her sense. She would give him everything she had. "Don't stop."

His answer came in a rough laugh. "As if I could."

She came in a series of hard shots, pulsing around him. Becoming aware of his cries, reactions to his own senses rather than answering hers, she deliberately tightened inside and then released, pulling him in, trying to grip his shaft so hard he couldn't leave her.

They tipped over the edge simultaneously, his seed gushing into her as she jerked uncontrollably like some kind of madwoman. She lost her breath, her mind and her heart, all in the same instant.

If she concentrated she could try to remember this moment. Something profound had happened, but she could process nothing. Not until she went limp, completely spent.

Covered in sweat, his hair clinging to his head in damp strands, his eyes still wild, still fixed on her, Julius stared at her as if nobody else existed. His chest heaving when he gasped for air, he watched her. She still had her legs over his shoulders, but warmth and sense returned to his eyes, and his mouth moved in the smile now so familiar to her. Moving slowly, he withdrew from her. An immediate sense of emptiness, followed by anticipation of the next time crept over her.

He let her slide her legs down, and helped her straighten them, returning to take her in his arms.

He said, "I love you, I do."

She blinked hard several times. "You don't have to say that."

"I know. I misjudged you. I went about everything the wrong way." He went up on one elbow and tenderly smoothed the tousled hair off her cheeks. "Can you forgive me so easily?"

"You call that easy?"

When he joined in her shaky laughter, she swallowed, and the tension that had invaded her ever since her discovery of his true identity relaxed. After all, this was still Julius. That was the heart of him. Everything else came after. That was what he had tried to tell her, but her shock when she discovered whom she had married so blithely had blocked any understanding of that.

Now the clouds had cleared and she saw it. An innate sense told her she would lose that sense or fight to recall it, but she vowed never to let it leave her. If she did, she could lose him, the essential reality of him.

She initiated the kiss, leaning up and touching his chin, his overnight stubble abrading her finger as she urged him closer until their lips met. Their kiss took on the nature of a vow, the oath they should have made to each other on their wedding day.

Instead, they did it now, the personal vow that should have accompanied the public ones. "For richer and poorer?" he said when they parted, a trace of anxiety in his tones.

"Sickness and health." Smiling, she kissed him again, no longer afraid to show him how she felt. If he hurt her, so be it. He would, because couples often did. Julius was not an easy man to know. Although he had given her his heart, he had other concerns, things that might take him away from her.

He startled her with his response. "It won't be easy, will it?"

The sentiment was so close to what she was feeling. "No, but we can do it."

Their marriage would take work, as well as love. Their gazes clung and held. This time he kissed her, a sweet, almost worshipful salute. "We can. We will."

"Tell me about your first wife." She couldn't wait to know everything about him, and that included what he did before they met.

He blinked. "Now?"

"Yes. How did you feel about her?" Noting his uncertainty, she smiled, nothing tentative about her now. "You love me. I believe you. Nothing can change that, can it?"

After gazing at her without speaking for a moment, he nodded. "You're right. We need to understand each other, do we not?" He sighed, but it wasn't for her. "Caroline was pretty and lively, completely enchanting, with an energy that matched mine. In those days I wanted everything now, that moment, an impulsiveness that led me into a multitude of problems. She was impulsive, too. We were completely wrong for each other, but Caro was the most damaged."

Her heart went out to him. He had been young in more than years. Young at heart, probably not ready to marry. Eve remained silent and let him talk. Was this the first time he had told anyone? He would certainly not have confided in his parents, that was for sure.

"We fell in love, or we thought we did. But it had none of the—" He shrugged and gave her a wry smile. "I can't explain fully. With you I feel more than myself. You make me want to work harder, to make myself worthy of you. I felt none of that with Caroline. She was a companion, someone to encourage my excesses. My love, we did indulge in some excesses that make me blush to recall them."

His cheekbones displayed the evidence, a line of darker color making him appear even more effetely aesthetic. Now she understood the real man, those two words did not fit him at all.

"I won't ask," she said, "But you have made me curious now."

"I have the strong urge to keep you to myself," he said, "To hold you and care for you. With Caroline, I wanted to share her."

Shock pierced her but she refused to show it. He needed to tell somebody. He needed to tell her. "You were debauched?"

"That's one word for it. If we heard of something, we indulged ourselves."

"Everything?"

"Naked and clothed. Everything."

She shook her head and closed her eyes tightly, an involuntary reaction, but she forced herself to open her eyes. He was watching her warily. "Should I stop there?"

"No." She wanted to hear it all. His disclosures did not alter how she felt about him, only deepened her understanding of how he had reached this point.

His mouth tightened. "Very well. I did not notice how wild Caroline was becoming until after the birth of our daughter. Caro insisted on calling the baby after herself, and I had no objections. I had two Carolines in my life now. The birth of the baby brought me back to earth. I could not continue in my present life, could not risk our daughter's reputation or her sense of security. I had grown up in the conventional way, surrounded by attendants. I had little contact with my parents. My only friend was Augustus. Lucinda is younger than we are, so we were almost parents to her."

The muscles in his shoulders relaxed. He was not so concerned talking about his early life. "But while I settled down, made sure our daughter was part of our lives, my wife became wilder. She was rarely in the house, and her moods had grown volatile. Eventually I discerned a pattern. A wild period of joy and frantic activity came before a time when she closed her bedroom door and refused to let anyone in. I tried a few times, but she threw things at me, and I seemed to make her worse. She denied me her bed. I thought she would recover, and since we had always gone into adventures together, we would settle down together. It never happened." He paused, his face settling into the stillness she recognized now. He was drawing away. "I will tell you something now that I have never told anyone else. Her last lover was the second son of the Duke of Northwich, William Dankworth."

Her eyes widened in shock. "So that's why you hate them?"

He shook his head, but paused. "Not entirely. Our families have never seen eye to eye. I fear Caroline took him to her bed partly to spite me. To do something to make me react. It was William who issued the challenge to race her new phaeton. Caroline was a good horsewoman and carriage driver, but she was not good enough for my new team of bays. She took them anyway, her phaeton overturned, and she died."

"I'm so sorry."

He swallowed, and his eyes gleamed. "So am I, but now I'm torn. If that had not happened, if I had not been jerked back to earth, I might not have met you and fallen so deeply in love with you." His lips moved into a smile. "Caroline made me afraid of love. I thought I had lost my senses and fallen deeply in love, but the emotion was shallow compared to the feeling I have for you. I imagined that love meant losing yourself in the other, indulging them in every possible way, but it doesn't. After Caroline's death, I vowed never to allow myself to fall in love with anyone again."

He gazed at her, and kissed the tip of her nose. "I was so wrong. The moment I saw you I wanted you, but I was no longer the wild youth who had cut a swath through London or the bitter man who vowed revenge on everyone who drove a sensitive woman to her death. I was a widower with a daughter. That was what I told you. I should have said more to you, but at heart, I have always felt I was that and everything else came second. I was wrong, wasn't I?"

"No." She cupped his cheek. He turned his head and kissed her palm. "I wanted Julius Vernon. Now I want the Earl of Winterton, although he is more than Julius. I'll do my best to become worthy of you." Hearing the inner life of his first marriage gave her an understanding she had not been privy to before. She could go on. She would do it.

"No, you will not. You will be you. I want Eve, not some imitation of her." He gazed down at her. "Of course you must think of other matters, but never become other than you are today, now."

Now she felt sorry for Caroline. "Did you love her when she died?"

His smile was wry. "You're sparing me nothing, aren't you?"

"I need to know." She wouldn't have the courage to ask him again. He might not want to talk about his first marriage, the events that had molded him after this.

He lowered his gaze, thought for a moment, and then lifted his eyes again to meet hers. "I thought I did, but when she died I felt nothing but relief. I adored my daughter. I still do. Caroline did not believe she had to change. Her parents had not, and neither had mine. I did not want that for our daughter, and the trouble that lay ahead for her worried me. The relief filled me with guilt."

Eve understood. Julius had assuaged the guilt at his relief by trying to ensure the country was as stable as his marriage had not been. The wild card had to be eliminated. Eventually that had led him to her, Eve, the daughter of his enemy. "Did you marry me out of guilt?"

He gave a one-sided smile. "No. I came to Appleton to discover you, and I found more than a daughter of the Pretender. Frankly, I don't care whose daughter you are, except as it affects your safety. I only care whose wife you are." Briefly, he tightened his hold on her. "Mine, in case you were wondering."

Laughing, she shook her head. "You've made that perfectly clear. Now I have to learn to become the Countess of Winterton. I meant to make you suffer much longer, Julius. It was too bad of you."

"I know. I can think of more ways of apologizing."

Eve looked forward to that part.

Chapter 14

After they had breakfasted and dressed, Julius left his wife to a bewildering selection of fabrics and styles. Protesting he would look at them when she had narrowed her choices, Julius went downstairs to face his father. He found his parent in the muniments room on the ground floor. The main door of the Abbey opened on to the first floor and the public rooms. Julius went by these and through a door a visitor might easily overlook. Down the cold stone stairs stood a small unprepossessing door. Julius took out his key and unlocked it. When he went through, he relocked it. Only from this site was it apparent the lock was a sturdy one indeed.

Julius strode down the passage to the only open door along the narrow stone-flagged corridor that resembled a closed-in cloister. The searcher of antiquities would find this place interesting. So would the seeker of treasures. This part of the building was all that remained of the ancient abbey. A few humble stone-built cells that would have housed monks devoting their lives to prayer and contemplation, giving it the air of tranquility Julius loved. He'd come here sometimes, in the course of his frantic careening through life, searching for the stillness he found so hard to grasp. Now his soul was at peace, set, for once, on the right course. This place only admitted a few people. Not even Augustus could come here without permission.

Julius's steps echoed on the ancient grey stone. The ridges and ruts had once fascinated him, wondering who had passed along this place before him. These days he took them for granted.

The door at the end lay open, and Julius swung into it. Sun streamed into the room from the high-set barred windows. Two men sat at the large square table, a pile of papers stacked between them.

His father and the estate steward looked up at him, but said nothing. There was no formality here, so Mr. Norris did not get to his feet and bow. Instead, Julius nodded to him and took a seat. The hard wooden chair resisted him uncomfortably. No maids came here, so dust lay on the few surfaces they had not used recently, and the floor was unpolished and gritty. Julius reached into his pocket and drew out the papers he needed to lodge here. He put them down in front of his father. "My marriage certificate."

The duke grunted and adjusted glasses that pinched his nose. "You have always been thorough, Winterton."

Yes, he had. Julius leaned back while his father perused the papers closely and then passed them to Mr. Norris, who studied them with equal meticulousness.

"We need to draw up a formal settlement. Eve has nothing except herself. I want her taken care of."

Julius might as well never have left home, for all the differences he noted here. The glass cabinets and iron safes contained the deeds of property and the titles accumulated by his family over the centuries, mostly in the form of Letters Patent. Mr. Norris had copies in his office for safekeeping, but these were the originals, required by the courts in the event of disputes, and so more valuable than any of the treasures locked in the other rooms in this small section of the Abbey. Medieval documents with the seals of long-dead kings and barely literate letters and wills all added to the family holdings. Julius had seen them all. Read most of them, a task imposed on him as extra work in his youth.

The room smelled of mustiness, nothing else, none of the potpourris or pastilles his mother employed in the grand rooms upstairs. Julius waited patiently until Mr. Norris put the paper on the pile in the center of the table.

"I will draw up a copy and take it with me, sir. It is in order, although your titles are not evident."

The duke snorted inelegantly. "Why did you do it?"

Julius raised one shoulder in a half-shrug. "Why do you think?"

"It's a big step to take merely to thwart your mother's ambitions."

"It wasn't only that." Julius took his time framing his answer. "I resented my mother's machinations, it is true, but I could have said no without too much trouble. Or rather, not said yes. However, I have suspected one of her bosom-bows for some time."

His father cocked a bushy brow. "You intrigue me. Are you saying your mother has missed something? I would be fascinated to discover what she has overlooked."

"She knows already. The McComyns fought for the Stuarts."

"So did many people who have since been forgiven. They did not repeat the offence." Julius's father glanced at his steward and man of business. "Do you know what he's talking about?"

Norris shook his head. "Not a clue."

Julius was not surprised. "It's new information. I've seen Augustus, and yes, he told me to let you know that he would be here in a few days." Not that Augustus enjoyed shooting half-tame birds any more than Julius did, but he had to report to his parents sometime.

The duke waved a paper at him. "You did not show me this one before."

It was the letter from Augustus, informing Julius of Eve's identity. Julius had thoughtfully written the translation of their code under the original.

The duke tossed the note across the table to Norris. "You failed to tell me that she is a Stuart until after you married her."

"It doesn't matter. I would have married her anyway. I have no mind to be parted from Eve or to bring her a moment's unhappiness." A moment more of unhappiness, that was.

"You brought trouble to the heart of the family."

Julius snorted. "And my cousins did not?" Three of his cousins had married Stuarts. They seemed to have an unholy fascination with the family. "The Young Pretender has taken to visiting London clandestinely, parading in front of the authorities. He has a network I would prefer stopped, people who are keeping him safe. Oh, the government is aware of his trips, but with the death of Pelham, sense seems to have left Westminster. The powers-that-be have decided to take Stuart prisoner if he shows his face in town again."

The duke sucked in a sharp breath. "They would not be so foolish."

"Yes they would." Julius had heard from his cousin and had it confirmed in other quarters. "In my opinion, that course would be disastrous. If the Pretender is taken prisoner, he will become a martyr. He will foment exactly the kind of unrest this country would do well to avoid."

"In that, at least, we agree," his father admitted. "To arrest him is to play into his hands. How sure are you of this information?"

"Reasonably sure, otherwise I would not have brought it to you." Julius had gathered the information from a variety of sources. The Pretender was hunting down his father's legitimate children and creating a deal of unrest in certain government circles. His last throw of the dice before he melted into obscurity.

"I won't stay here long. I want to take Eve to Hampshire. We'll call it a honeymoon." He barely refrained from shifting in his seat as the ramifications of having Eve to himself and no need to follow convention occurred forcibly to him. They could stay in bed all day if they wished, or wander around the gardens and perhaps find a bower or grotto to stay in for a while.

Much better than shooting grouse with society's elite.

* * * *

"Do you know your letters?"

The child glared at Eve. "Naturally. I am six years old."

She was also stunningly pretty, precocious, and more than a little spoiled. Add to that, resentful of Eve. Although she was wearing a new gown, the equal in appearance of anyone else in this house, Eve still felt like a governess the moment she'd stepped into the nursery wing, which was situated close to the chambers Eve was sharing with her husband. She had slipped away, bored with the measuring and the styles. On a visit to the powder room, she'd left by the outer door instead of using the inner door to return to the pretty boudoir.

If she didn't do something useful she'd go mad.

She'd found the child on the brink of a tantrum. When the little girl had spun around and demanded, "Who are you?" tilting her head in arrogant disdain, Eve knew she had found Julius's beloved daughter. As the child tapped her foot on the floor, Eve had answered her. "I'm the Countess of Winterton."

Some might consider her approach unguarded and cruel, but Eve had taken this child's measure instantly. Eve needed the upper hand, or the girl would run her ragged. The tilt of the chin, the cool blue eyes, and the miniature gown, an exact copy of a lady's fashionable one, told Eve all she wanted to know. The servants, hanging back, stared at her in horror.

"My mama was the Countess of Winterton," said Caroline, losing not an iota of confidence.

Eve had guessed well. "I did not bear you, but I'll ensure you are taken care of as if you were my own daughter. I'm your father's wife, though I will leave it up to you what to call me." Knowing the power of expectant silence, she waited.

The child flicked a glance over her, one she must have inherited from her father. The first time he'd seen Eve properly dressed he'd given her just such a look.

Prepared for the reaction, she let her lips curve into a gentle smile. "I'm pleased to meet you, Caroline. Very pleased." She knew better than to say something like she hoped they would be friends. That would put the girl in charge. However, bending to her level might help. She bent her knees and crouched in a satisfying susurration of silk. "My name is Eve. I married your father very recently. He did not have time to tell anyone."

"He has to marry someone," the child said. She kept her arms folded but lowered her gaze before flicking it up again. "My grandmother said so."

If Eve had been more sentimental, she might have expected a fulsome welcome, or a tantrum. But this child had control. True, she was not happy with her attendants for some reason, but no screams had emerged from the room as Eve had approached, merely a firm little voice. This would do, for now. "Is there something amiss here?"

"My maid appears to have forgotten my pastels." The chin trembled, just for a second.

Oil-based coloring chalks. "Then we shall find you some. Unless they turn up in your luggage."

"Papa is here. He enjoys drawing with me."

Ah, now she understood. Her time with her father meant more to the child than she wanted to admit to Eve. "I will ensure we find something that will serve. I promise." Eve met Caroline's eyes and inclined her head.

The child studied Eve, her eyes wide, and then she gave one decisive nod. "Thank you."

Eve relaxed a tiny bit. She had expected an indulged sprite, the terror of the nursery, like the ones she had taught when she was a governess, but Caroline was a different kind of child. Strong-willed, but with added control. Where had she learned that? Was Julius's almost terrifying control of himself responsible? Did Caroline wish to please him, and so had emulated him?

Impossible to give an answer yet, but the reaction to her promise gave Eve more clues about the character of Julius's only daughter. Caroline was a child of reason. "Is there anything else you like to do?"

Caroline tilted her head to one side. "I like to read. Papa says I am advanced for my age."

Not to mention beautifully spoken. "Then would you like to read with me? I have been choosing new clothes, and I would appreciate a dish of tea and some quiet time."

The girl nodded to her gown. "Is this one of them?"

"It will be. My maid says it doesn't fit right, but she has taken my measurements and is making herself and some of the housemaids busy on the others."

"Do you not like clothes?"

Eve got to her feet and glanced around, discovering a comfortable sofa set under the window. She made her way to it and disposed her skirts, leaving Caroline to join her, if she wished to.

Caroline wished to. She folded her hands neatly on her lap and turned her attention to Eve.

"I like clothes, especially new ones, but the way the maids were fussing gave me the headache. Who needs twenty gowns?"

"You do," Caroline said. "You will need more next season, too."

Eve nodded to a maid, who left the room, presumably in search of tea. "I'll look at them when the maids have finished their quarrelling." She picked up a book from the side-table, relieved to discover it was not a book of improving sermons. She remembered those from her own childhood. They were all her father had allowed them to read on Sundays, tedious moral tales of children who had done the wrong thing and been damned for it. Eve believed in forgiveness and second chances. "Is this the book you're reading?"

"Yes."

"Do you like animals?" Aesop's fables had been a staple of Eve's own reading, when she was not forced to open the dreaded book of sermons. Although they all had a moral lesson to teach, the stories also had a charm and a lightness absent in the heavier tomes.

"Yes. Papa says I must learn to care for them, but he will not allow me a puppy." The wistfulness in her tones wasn't easy to miss.

Eve did not miss it. "We shall see. Perhaps your papa has a good reason for his decision. Have you asked him?"

"He says I must think about my choice and convince him I need one."

"I see. Then we must do that. If you are set on a puppy?"

"Or a cat."

Eve would ensure Caroline had time to play with both potential pets, but she thought the child might be better off with a small dog to romp with. Perhaps soon there would be a brother or sister for her, and if there was, a pet of her own might help to assuage her realization she was no longer an only child.

They settled to Aesop and to get to know each other. Eve answered Caroline's questions honestly and thought the better of the child when she showed no response to Eve's humble origins. Of course Eve did not mention her connection with the Stuarts.

When the door opened, she did not look up. She didn't need to, for she was now as attuned to her husband's presence as to her own. When she did, he was smiling at them, the kind of intimate smile he rarely shared with others outside his immediate circle.

Eve lost herself smiling back. She had no idea how much time passed with her grinning at him, but he came forward, hands outstretched, and took one of her hands and one of Caroline's. "My two favorite ladies in the world. I cannot tell you what a lovely picture you make."

"She is beautiful, Papa, is she not?" Caroline piped up.

"Indeed she is." He turned an unabashed look of admiration on to Eve. "But that is not why I married her, Caro. There are many reasons for marrying a person, but good looks do not form an adequate one."

"And yet—"

He quelled his daughter with a fulminating glance. "In time you will learn the truth, I hope and pray. Have you had a productive morning?"

"We did not linger on the morals, I have to confess." Eve flipped the book closed, keeping her finger in their place, so Julius could see the title of the book.

"All the better. I loved that book." He nodded. "Meantime, my lady, I came to see how you were doing in your selection of costumes and found you had eluded them. Do you not enjoy the process?"

"To an extent." Eve met his eyes. This close, she detected an edge in his slightly narrowed gaze. "But such fussing over details tries my patience. I told them to narrow all choices down to three each, and I would make the final decision when they had done so. I chose half a dozen gowns they could alter immediately, and they may set to work on the rest."

"A taskmaster." He seemed amused by her response, his mouth curving, but when he glanced from his daughter to herself, the edge returned.

Ah, she understood. Of course, she should have known. "Instead I introduced myself to Caro. We have come to an agreement. She will call me mama, but neither of us will allow her mother's memory to lapse."

He breathed out, the sapphire at his throat glittering in the bright sunlight that streamed through the window behind Caro and Eve. Eve had guessed right. He'd probably planned how to introduce his wife to his daughter. Instead, she'd done it herself with as little fuss as she could contrive, exactly how she preferred to run her life.

She feared there would be much more drama in the future, but she could do her best to eliminate as much as possible. She had a role to play in this marriage, and she was finding her way toward it. She could be of use, could be more than a helpmeet, a vessel for heirs.

Relief swept through Eve, she had for once placed her foot on firm ground. Since she had met Julius and learned her little secret had come to mean much more than she had ever wanted or dreamed of, she had wobbled along her path, taken far beyond the place she knew and felt safe in.

She had a long way to go, but at last she'd begun to regain her footing.

Julius tilted his head slightly, a mere change of position but she was learning him and that, with the slight frown, told her he had noticed and he wanted to know. Smiling, she shook her head. "It's nothing. In a little while I'll return to our rooms and discover what the maids have decided. I daresay they had little time to present me with the options in a coherent way. With any luck, they'll have arranged matters." She shot him a grin. "Of course that might be because what arrived was the contents of a shop or even a warehouse. With so many choices, anyone might be forgiven for going into a mild panic."

He frowned. "Your maids panicked?"

"In an orderly way. They pretended, but on consideration, I don't think they had any better idea than I did. I told them to sort the fabrics into colors and then into the time of day the fabric should be worn. If I give them a few hours, they may have achieved that task."

"My wife is a woman of order," Julius said with that smile.

Caroline made a discovery. "Why, Papa, you are in love!"

Julius did not deny it.

* * * *

Guests continued to arrive for the next few days until the Abbey was filled to bursting. The house party at Edensor was a much coveted invitation and only available to the friends and family of the Duke of Kirkburton. Prince Frederick had attended before his sad demise four years earlier, and now the great and the good crowded into the house. Every room appeared to have someone in it, for as well as the guests, they brought their servants, swelling the considerable staff who customarily attended to the Abbey so they were forced to double up the number in each room.

That meant the duchess had not had time to find her oldest son a more suitable suite, and Eve still shared his bed, much to the delight of both of them. Dressing was less problematic, once Eve had arranged the sitting room as a boudoir and had her maids use that as her dressing room.

On the night of the ball, Eve's maids fussed around her until she thought she would scream. Taylor had an assistant now, and the girl fluttered so much Eve determined to replace her as soon as she could. The girl, thrilled to be serving a countess, would not stop addressing her as "Your ladyship," which was driving Eve mad.

Much of her irritation arose from nervousness. At the ball, she would be presented as Julius's wife. Although the company naturally knew, this was a formal step Eve was not looking forward to with any enthusiasm. That was despite the gown, the finest she had ever worn in her life. The white silk petticoat was heavily embroidered with spring flowers, and the gown itself, ice blue, was of the finest, coolest silk. She shook back the triple ruffles of Brussels lace foaming from her elbows and picked up her fan, a gift from Julius she feared was decorated with diamonds rather than the brilliants she had originally thought them.

When the door opened, she smiled up at his reflection in her mirror. He waited until her maid had carefully inserted the last diamond-headed pin into her hair and then took the woman's place, setting his hands lightly on her shoulders, his fingertips tickling her throat. He wore a coat of deepest ultramarine velvet over an ivory silk striped waistcoat, his clothes complimenting hers but equally magnificent.

"Every inch a countess," he murmured, ignoring the two maids as he bent to feather a kiss on her neck. "You were wrong, my love. You are the epitome of aristocracy. When you are presented at court, they will fall before you."

Eve sucked a breath in deep, despite knowing he said it to accustom her to the idea. Already she had become used to the luxury around her, everything she touched, everything she saw was the best it could be. No skimping on food, furniture, or anything else was allowed at the Abbey.

But court? Royalty? "Will they know who I am?"

"Of course."

He pressed her shoulders in warning, but she needed no reminder. She would not speak in front of any servant. The fewer people who knew her origins, the safer she would be.

"But not everything. That is our secret." He kissed her neck, working up to her ear, and murmured, "You are my princess, always."

She caught his hand where it rested on her shoulder, her eyes filling with tears. Determinedly, she blinked them away. She would not spoil the evening. Tomorrow they would slip away, or so he claimed, but she doubted his family would allow that. They would want to send him off with a great deal of pomp.

Shivers coursed through her as she responded to his caresses, but with a final gentle kiss to her lips, he straightened. "I have something for you."

From the capacious pocket of his coat he produced a velvet box. The air stilled, as did the two maids. Such boxes rarely contained anything but jewelry.

This was no exception. Out of the box, Julius lifted a glittering strand of sky and stars. The sapphires were oval, clear and rich blue, surrounded and linked by diamonds. Simple in design, breathtaking in execution. He draped the necklace around her throat, the cold stones imprinting themselves on her skin. As he fastened the clasp, Eve stared at herself. The stones flashed with a life of their own, drawing her in.

She touched the central pendant, now draped above her breasts. The jewel glinted. "I love it."

He grinned but said nothing, producing the earrings and bracelet that completed the set. When they were in place, he narrowed his eyes and surveyed her reflection. "Perfect. I am glad you decided not to powder your hair. You'll make an impression nobody will ever forget."

Enthralled by the inner life of the stones, Eve hardly heard him. The value of the gems occurred to her, only for her to dismiss it immediately. What did it matter when compared to items as beautiful as this? While she had tolerated the plethora of silks, satins, brocades, tabbies, lustrings, lace, and the paraphernalia that went into the wardrobe of a fashionable lady, her heart went out to the precious stones. These were worth dressing for.

At last, the key. She had to make her appearance worthwhile, to earn the right to wear these beautiful things. She got to her feet and faced her husband. He was as multifaceted as the jewels she now wore, as worthy of study and adornment. In order to appear as Julius Vernon in Appleton, he had hidden a great deal of himself, but now he was in the open. He dazzled her.

How could she not love him? While amazed he loved her, Eve accepted he did. How could she not, when he was gazing at her with that slight smile as if she encompassed his whole world?

She spoke the simple truth, the one thing resting in her heart all the time these days. "I love you."

He raised her hand and kissed it. "And I you. Shall we go down to dinner?"

So all her days she would run with this man, whom she adored.

* * * *

They found Augustus in the drawing-room. Eve had last seen him just before she and Julius had set out to come here. Her mother, gowned fashionably, stood by his side. After she had embraced her mother, Eve turned to Augustus. He greeted her with the same friendly smile he'd used before, bowing over her hand and breathing heat over her knuckles in an audacious near-kiss. When he flicked a glance at her, Eve was hard put not to burst into laughter. Augustus was all life, bursting with energy, where Julius was restrained, at least in public.

Dinner took on more of the nature of a banquet. Eve sat at the duke's right hand. The great dining room was packed, the long table replete with all its leaves, increasing the size so it could accommodate the fifty guests—or was it more? Perhaps sixty. Eve tried to calm her agitated senses, to accept she was part of this distinguished gathering.

She took her cue from Julius, who appeared perfectly at ease, but every gesture, every pose was carefully considered and taken. As many of his kind, Julius had a distinct public character he used to cover the parts of his nature he preferred to keep to himself. When he was in the public eye so often, the habit was vital for anyone who wished for a private life.

Although he should properly have sat next to his mother at the foot of the table, Julius took a seat opposite her, where she could see him easily, bolstering her faltering confidence.

The chatter rose to a positive din, the gentle clink of silver against fine china pervading the air, crystal glasses glinting in the light of the chandelier and wall sconces. Landscapes of this house and others the Vernons owned adorned the walls in a discreet display of wealth, and the fireplace sported an elaborately carved surround. No doubt the carving was beautiful, but all Eve could think was it must be hell to dust. She exchanged a glance with her mother, who was seated halfway down the table. Her mother smiled back and raised a brow.

Lucinda was on Eve's side of the table, next to a handsome young man Eve couldn't remember. In the drawing room, Julius had kept by her side and introduced her to a great number of people who smiled back at her, their eyes sparkling with speculation. Eve did not need a crystal ball to know. To arrive at the house where he was to choose a bride with one in tow had given society plenty to talk about, as had his evident devotion to her. Nobody knew her. One young man had actually blurted out, "Who is she?" to which Julius had told him in frozen tones she was the Countess of Winterton. Eve felt almost sorry for the youth.

Now she had to make polite conversation about people she did not know. Her mother, who read the gossip sheets, was probably getting on better, but Eve did her best.

Sometime during the third course, someone asked her about the Duke of Newcastle. "Of course you know him," the man said, his air so superior Eve instinctively wanted to slap him.

The man was trying to humiliate her. Either that or he wanted to display his own knowledge. So Eve told him the truth. "Until recently I lived quietly. I have heard of the people you speak of, naturally, but I have never met them. Nor did I expect to. I presume the duke is a man, much as you are, or my husband, or anyone else here tonight?" Without waiting for a reply, she continued. "I shall no doubt meet him, but no, I don't know him. So tell me, are you a special friend of his?"

The man reddened, his cheekbones crimsoning. Someone nearby smothered a laugh, not successfully. From the gleam in his eyes Eve suspected Valerian, who was sitting on her side of the table, easily able to hear the conversation.

Someone else spoke in a moderate but easily heard voice. "I knew I'd like her." The lady tilted her glass to Eve in a salute.

Whether she wanted to or not, Eve was making her place in this world.

Then came the ball. The ladies did not stay alone in the drawing room for long. The men joined them in the space of half an hour, and Eve's mother-in-law announced they would go down to the great room.

The state rooms were resplendent. The ball that heralded the start of the hunting season was so grand its purpose was lost in merrymaking and conversation. To her shock, the Duke of Kirkburton gestured for her to take the floor with Julius. "A wedding minuet," he said, loud enough for the guests to hear.

The minuet was the most graceful and formal dance of the whole gathering, and she was to display her skills. Eve's heart sank. How could she do this with everyone watching and criticizing her?

But as Julius led her to the center of the floor and the musicians—a sextet—struck up the first notes, he kept his attention on her. As he bowed over her hand to begin the first figure he murmured, "Only I exist. Everyone else here is an illusion. Dance for me, my love."

His eyes sparkled as they reflected the candlelight. Eve swallowed and watched him, as she curtseyed low. He snared her gaze and kept her fixed on him.

They began the dance. Eve knew the minuet, of course, but she had performed it rarely. Sir Henry had not favored the more courtly measures and had concentrated on country dances. Determined not to let Julius down, Eve mirrored his movements, taking care to hold her hands at the correct angle and dispose her body elegantly. After the first measure, he snared her, and she lost herself in him. He gave her everything, occasionally allowing his mouth to relax in a smile as she sank into a curtsey or swayed gently when she took the mincing steps the dance demanded.

The sound of her skirts, the firmer rustle of his stiffened coat, and the gentle murmur of the guests did not drown out the musicians. Keeping her face clear, her concentration hidden, Eve twirled and paced and made the graceful shapes. Once she stumbled, but she regained her footing, putting her error to the back of her mind, no doubt to wake up sweating in the night when she recalled her blunder

Except she would not be alone. Julius would be there to hold her and soothe her and then make love to her. The recollection brought a spring to her step, an extra push to her glide.

After an interminable time that could not have lasted longer than fifteen minutes, she recognized the music's closing bars and swept into a low curtsey, breathing out in relief. The torture was over. Julius bore her off the floor as other couples swept on to the polished boards and led her straight to his parents. He bowed, and she sank into yet another curtsey.

"You might have warned us," he said, "But my wife is equal to the task."

The duchess lifted one shoulder in an elegant shrug. "I expected no less." She bestowed a frosty smile on to Eve. "However, I will need other evidence of your ability to care for my daughter. A dance means nothing."

"She will be with me, Mama," Julius said smoothly. "Helena has already indicated her preference."

Feeling the family animosity simmering below the surface, Eve interrupted the rising tension. "I would have danced worse had someone warned me. I dance but indifferently."

"I wouldn't say that, my dear," the duke put in. He propped his hand on his hip and swept his highly-polished shoe before him. "I shall undoubtedly claim a dance from you later." His craggy face broke into a broad smile. "Welcome to the family, Eve, such as it is."

And just like that, she was accepted. Her exemplary behavior during the last few days had borne fruit. Either that or his grace had decided to oppose his lady wife. Eve was not foolish enough to imagine the struggle for Helena was over, however. The duchess did not give up easily, and one skirmish did not win a war. But Eve ranged herself firmly on the side of her husband and his sister. The duchess would not have her daughter as an unpaid companion and servant.

Perhaps if Eve found someone to attend the duchess, the lady would not be so insistent for Helena to remain with her? She would think on that.

The duchess did not appear to have any concerns about discussing the matter in public, however. "I have no doubt you will be busy before too long with your own family. I anticipate happy news soon." Her lip curled. "Particularly as you broadcast your devotion to each other by sharing a bedroom."

Eve caught her breath in a sharp gasp. What happened in their bedroom was not for public consumption. There she felt safe. There she could speak her mind and give way to her concerns. "Large as it is, this house is filled to overflowing."

"As my son is the heir to the estate, I cannot conciliate my feelings to his decision to cram into a corner of the place in a room totally unsuited to his dignity." The duchess lifted her chin. Her lack of height did not detract from her self-important air. She seemed to take up far more space than she physically occupied.

"Nevertheless, we will do this." Julius paused and grew perfectly still. "You want me to leave? I shall do so with the greatest pleasure, ma'am. I had already planned to take my wife away for a more secluded time together. You are helping me to my decision, are you not?" This time his smile had nothing pleasant about it. "However, if I go, so do my daughter and my sister."

While that would make a novel kind of honeymoon, Eve was forced to agree with him. His mother had taken another step. She would drive Julius away and retain Helena. This dispute was going beyond the simple concern of whom Helena would live with. It was turning into a full-scale battle between mother and son.

"Helena must do as she pleases," Eve murmured.

"And so she will."

Without anyone noticing, Helena had crossed the room to join them. A full-scale family argument threatened. Augustus was heading their way. Would they stand in the ballroom and shout their disagreement for the world to hear? An army of ants crawled over Eve's skin. She took a step back and then another. This threat militated against everything she had worked for. Was she to be known as a wedge, a weapon the participants could use against each other?

Revulsion filled her soul. While mother and son glared at each other, Eve stepped back.

Her triumph had come before a potential scandal. How ironic. How typical of her life, which followed the one step forward, two steps back pattern so closely it could have been invented for her.

Augustus's voice pursued her. "Would you appreciate a drink?"

She turned to see him advancing on her, two chilled glasses of white wine in his hands. Condensation ran down the glittering surfaces, softening the sharp cuts and the hard-edged shine. Although she did not want any more to drink, she recognized salvation when she saw it.

As she accepted the glass he offered, he touched his against hers in a quiet toast. "Welcome to the family."

"Is that why you live in Rome?"

He smiled wryly. Although he and Julius barely resembled each other, that quirk reminded Eve of her husband, a reminiscent echo.

"Partly. I am a scholar, and I have found my work there absorbing. I would not stay away merely because of that." He gestured dismissively to the small group garnering everyone's attention. "They do this all the time. You must not allow it to upset you."

"But everyone is looking!"

"With resigned acceptance." He took a sip of his wine. "The dispute between mother and son is well-known and ongoing. The rest of us steer as clear of it as possible. For the most part, they agree to disagree, but while Helena remains at large, they're at loggerheads. Wait until she marries. I promise it will settle down."

Eve cast a glance at the fiercely disputing mother and son, their faces tight and the duchess's flushed. "So I have a job to do."

"Don't interfere. Truly, let it run its course."

She took a swallow of wine. It made its cool way down her throat, bringing some order to her confused mind. "I thought they were private people?"

"Our mother is the one person who can make Julius lose his temper in public."

Why did that make Eve want to prove Augustus wrong? She wanted to be the person to drive Julius mad in public—and in private, come to that. Her possessive streak had never reared up before, but she could not deny it now.

She refused to look. Augustus was facing them, but Eve was trying desperately to prove she didn't care, it was something she was used to. Across the room, she caught her mother's horrified stare.

Her moment of triumph had not lasted long.

The scent of his cologne told Eve her husband had come up behind her. "Eve," he said softly.

She would not give the crowd any more fodder for gossip. Fixing a bright smile to her face, she turned around, her skirts swinging. "You've finished your discussion, then?"

"Completely. Totally." Julius closed his eyes and then opened them again. They were clear, as if he'd wiped the scene from his mind.

Augustus lowered his voice and gazed past Julius's head, as if he were saying something of no consequence. "I need a private word with you as soon as possible."

Julius's smile revealed nothing. "You've learned something?"

"Yes. At least I think so."

"Tomorrow morning." Julius turned a particularly charming smile on to Eve. "The country dances are beginning. Would you care to dance?"

"Dear me, Julius, you are turning into a provincial before my eyes!" Augustus grinned when Julius turned his astonished blue glare on to him. "Brother, don't you know it's bad form to dance with your wife all evening? Some would say at all, but you are newly married, and so you may be allowed a certain leeway." He offered his arm. "Would you care to accompany me on to the dance floor, ma'am?"

Time for some revenge. However petty, the notion warmed Eve's heart. "I would love to, sir."

As Augustus swept her on to the floor, Julius's chuckle echoed behind them.

* * * *

Once in their bedroom, Julius swung off his coat and tossed it on to a nearby chair, ignoring Lamaire's irritated tut as he swept up the garment and draped it carefully over one arm. He left the room on Julius's curt nod.

Julius turned his whole attention to Eve. She stood in the center of the room, uncertain, an edge of fear touching her. What had she married into? Her resolves of the morning were proving fugitive. How could she make a success of this world?

He crossed the room and stood before her, but did not touch her. "Don't look like that," he said roughly.

"Like what?"

"As if you don't know what to do. I told you how it was between my mother and me. I'm sorry she chose tonight to create a scene. I think she did it on purpose."

Eve raised a brow. "Does anyone do that?"

"Yes. *She* does." Spinning around, Julius took a turn of the room. When he returned, she was waiting, arms folded. "My mother is a user, a manipulator. When I was a child, she separated me from my brother." He grimaced. "At least she tried to, though both of us became adept at climbing the walls of the Abbey so we could see each other. I was the heir, Augustus the mere spare. When he showed an aptitude for study, she procured an excellent tutor and gave him his head. It was only a few years later I realized the behavior was typical of her. She has read her Machiavelli. She was separating us to control us both."

Eve still had her doubts. "Are you sure that was what she was doing?"

"Yes," he said firmly. "She has repeated such behavior over the years. She works toward what she wants with little regard to anyone's feelings or what she does to their lives. That is why I do not live at home.

As soon as I finished university and the Grand Tour, I set up my own establishment. My tour was curtailed because Augustus was with me. He chose to remain abroad. If we were not so strong-willed, we would have become everything she wanted."

Eve had a choice. She could believe him without limits, but that would not be good for him or for the relationship they were carefully building. "If I accept your word without asking for evidence, I will not be the kind of wife you need, will I?"

He bit his lip. Even now, despite her distress, Eve yearned to taste it, to lick the sore spot. She desired him, always. These emotions, so new to her, threatened to overwhelm her.

Eventually he spoke. "You're right. I want my Eve, a partner, someone to take equal decisions with. Come." With a brush of her elbow, he guided her to the day bed. Disposing her skirts, wishing she had the forethought to take off the pinching stays or the tickling lace tickling, she nevertheless waited for him to talk to her.

He took her hand, but made no effort to draw her into his arms. "Let me tell you about some of the times Augustus can corroborate. When I was barely sixteen and Augustus was younger, two maids entered our lives. One each. And yes, I lost my virginity to one. Alice was sweet, demanding, and much older than I had thought her. In her mid-twenties, as a matter of fact." He continued steadily, but his eyes revealed a glassy bleakness Eve had rarely seen before. "My mother had sent to London for the pair. Augustus discovered his woman's true identity and purpose first. He found a letter and payment. Mother had employed them to keep us busy. She wished to control our intimate life." With an uncharacteristic jerk, he moved his head away to stare at an unremarkable corner of the room. He was avoiding looking at her.

Her shock and disgust was all for the duchess, the woman who had worked to control her sons at all cost.

"When you found me...?" She let her supposition tail off into space.

He turned his attention back to her, and this time his eyes were blazing. "I came to Appleton to investigate the existence of another of the children of the Pretender. Instead, I found you." His grip on her hand firmed. "I knew my mother had invited her candidates here. I was furious but determined not to accept any of her choices. Maybe a touch of petulance drove my decision to investigate you in person. You see, I am being completely honest." A touch of a smile touched his lips. Eve was glad to see it. "But when I saw you, everything changed. You may recall my state of tumescence and how long it lasted."

Now she smiled. "I remember. I didn't know whether to move away or if you would know I knew if I did that."

A laugh escaped him. "I cannot say if I fell in love or lust with you at first sight. I forced myself to stay and learn more about you, rather than fall on you like a starving wolf. You did not disappoint me. You could never do that."

"You weren't to know." If she doubted he loved her, she doubted herself. That part was her bedrock, the foundation on which she would build. She refused to contemplate anything else.

"I knew. I wanted you so badly I shocked myself. Believe me, Eve, I thought of nothing else. I should have crowed at the notion of thwarting my mother. I should have rushed you here to throw you in her face. But I was worried for you. I do not want you involved in my mother's sordid schemes. I won't use you in any way. Whatever you wish to do, I will do it. If my mother had employed you, I would have been lost."

God help her, she believed him. How could she not, when she loved him so dearly?

She leaned forward and kissed him. He sat passively, letting her taste him, smooth her lips over his, and caress him. Until, with a fierce growl, he grabbed her waist and hauled her close.

Nothing of the elegant man of fashion remained under the onslaught of this complex warrior. For Julius had fought, Eve had no doubt about that now. He was far from the pampered, privileged son of the elite. He had been used, worked on. After the story of the maid, Eve did not want to hear any more, but she would have to. She had to do justice to him and at least listen.

But she loved him with the same madness that he loved her. They were together, and they would remain so. That certainty sank into her, invaded her, and grew tendrils, binding her to him.

Willingly, she gave herself. When their lips parted, she gasped against his cheek. "Love me, Julius."

"I do. I will." His words held a promise every bit as deep as the promises they'd made on their wedding day. Already he was working at the hooks that held her gown firmly on her bodice and then the laces beneath. His fingers worked frantically as she set to work on his waistcoat buttons. They undressed each other in haste, kissing when they could, only pausing to remove another item of clothing and toss it out of the way.

She stood to rid herself of her hooped petticoat, and while she did so, he was at her feet, unfastening her garters and dragging off the stockings. Her shoes came next, after he'd loosened the buckles for her. Then it was his turn, and she sank to her knees, undoing his diamond-studded shoe buckles so he could rid himself of his breeches and undergarments.

He dragged his shirt over his head and spun her around to tackle her stay laces. He had it undone in a trice and Eve felt the familiar sense of relief as she breathed deep, stretching her compressed flesh, reclaiming her natural shape. The brocaded stiffly boned fabric fell away, disregarded, and Julius drew her close. Wearing only her fine shift, Eve felt his flesh, firm against hers, heating her all the way through.

His erection prodded her stomach insistently, but his voice was gentle. "If you say no now, if you wish me to leave you alone, I will. I will do it if it kills me because I love you. Your well-being is far more important than mine, your needs paramount. Say you understand."

She swallowed. "Yes." Because she felt the same way. She would do anything for him. She was lost.

Swinging her up into his arms, Julius waded through the layers of discarded silk to the bed, holding her with one arm while he swept the covers back and placed her gently down. He came over her, his gaze never leaving hers, not for a second.

Taking his erection in his hand, he guided it to her. Eve opened her legs and lifted her knees, curling them around his waist as he joined their bodies, binding him to her.

"You may have noticed I did not say no."

The tension on his face was different to that of half an hour ago, when they'd first come into this room. The corners of his mouth creased as he smiled, revealing indents, dimples. "I do believe you are my salvation, my love." He thrust into her and held himself there, filling her up.

Sighing, she tried to draw him closer. "I don't care what you call me. I want you, Julius. So badly I can taste my need."

Framing her face with his hands, he kissed her, drawing away to say, "So can I. Or maybe it is mine," before he began to pump into her.

She had needed no preparation. Her wetness bathed him, eased around their thighs, as he drove into her. Desperation left them, all but the need to bring each other pleasure. Her fingers curled into claws, and she dug her nails into his back.

He gasped, a light "Ah!" escaping him, but he was still smiling.

Fierce need flashed from him to her as she moved in synchrony with him, inner thrills moving from where they met along her veins, the fibers of her being, until desire and passion swamped her.

She cried out, only his name remaining in her mind and her heart, the only coherent word left to her. His face bore the stark evidence of his need for her, his gaze passing over her with a possessiveness that thrilled her, his grip on her enough to cause bruises. He slammed into her, every stroke driving her higher, but she responded, arching her back, pushing her groin against him with every deep thrust.

Heat and light grew, expanded, and burst, becoming the divine moment when the world fell away. She savored and bathed in the moment, before he rolled them over, so she could lift up and finish.

He let her see his greatest moment of vulnerability, exposed shamelessly for her to use any way she wanted. She had given herself to him, and he had taken her offering, absorbed it and given it back to her.

She fell on to him, gasping for breath. His chest heaved. They lay still for a while, relishing each other and their complete rapture.

* * * *

Eventually Eve fell asleep and Julius stayed awake, merely for the pleasure of holding her. He did not deserve Eve. He was fully aware of that, but he had her, and he'd be damned if he was letting her go. She lay, breathing softly in deep slumber, her head resting on his shoulder as he held her close, his arm wrapped around her waist. She'd tucked her leg between his, an easy motion that filled him with delight.

Julius would have tumbled into sleep as fast as his wife had he not wanted to enjoy this time, the peaceful hours before day broke and he did what he had decided upon. He would take her away tomorrow, the day after at the latest, and leave the house party from hell to disport itself however it chose.

He would tell Eve more, the ways his mother had used and manipulated him, or tried to, and his father's indifference or lack of knowledge. He had not succumbed to her wiles, which was why she had turned to her children. His mother needed someone to control. Julius had no idea why, nor did he wish to discover the reason, because any interest would merely help her to ensnare him all over again.

Tonight he'd told Eve his greatest shame, the story of the woman his mother had used to control him. She was not the first, either, and the names of the girls drawn here on this visit meant the duchess intended to continue it. She cared nothing for human happiness or contentment. She subsumed everything to the family, or rather, the family's influence and reach.

Julius had removed all his investments from the family pot. In time he would return them, but on his own terms. His causes belonged to him alone. Eve was his reward. After years of striving to keep his country stable, the way he could not with his family, Julius had met the one woman he knew without doubt he would love until his dying day.

That was what he wanted to enjoy. But in the knowledge he had many more nights to come of such happiness, he let himself drift into sleep.

Finally, he was happy. He had everything he wanted.

Chapter 15

A gun fired, its retort slamming into Julius's consciousness. At the same time, a woman screamed, her mouth uncomfortably close to his ear.

Instantly, he came awake, sitting up and reaching for the pillow to hurl it at whoever had invaded the room. Wetness coated his arm.

Lamaire stood by the bed, a smoking pistol in his hand, a worn serviceable weapon, not something Julius would associate with the valet. But this man wore a look of determination, deep resolve.

Julius rose from the bed in one swift, powerful move and caught the end of the pistol. Heat seared his palm, but he ignored it and twisted his wrist, wrenching the weapon from his manservant.

Lamaire let loose a volley of French, little of which penetrated Julius's confused brain. He swung the butt of the gun at Lamaire's head, but the bastard ducked, and this time spoke in English. "My lord, the other—stop him!"

Despite the warning voices in his head, Julius glanced to one side.

A pool of bright blood stained the sheets where his wife lay. A stranger was slumped over her body. Gore pumped from a gaping hole in his back, the edges fouled with the brown threads from the coat he wore. He still gripped a pistol in one hand. Julius cursed and grabbed it.

He trained the weapon on to the valet, who stepped back from the bed.

"This man was standing over you but he was aiming at your wife." His English was perfectly intelligible, if heavily accented.

"I thought you spoke little English?" Julius was already shoving the body of the stranger off Eve while he spoke. She wasn't moving.

Cold invaded his limbs, sent clamps around his heart so he could barely breathe.

"It was better that nobody knew. I kept my tongue, here and downstairs. I heard something that made me wonder, so I came here."

"Eve!"

Julius took her shoulders in his hands. They were still warm. Blood still pulsed, a sluggish stream, slipping against his fingers.

Then she stirred. When she opened her eyes, she gazed straight into Julius's. "Am I dead?" she murmured.

After a swift examination, Julius nodded to Lamaire, who rounded the bed. He paused at the dressing table to grab the knife Julius used to pare his nails. His intention became obvious when he pulled a sheet out from where it was tucked into the corner of the mattress and sliced a strip away.

"You are far from dead," Julius said to Eve. He kept his voice as steady as he could, relief pouring through him when he saw where she was hurt. Lamaire had saved her life. Julius had no doubt Eve had been the target in the stranger's sights, but thanks to Lamaire's prompt action, the assassin's bullet had grazed her upper arm, instead of plunging into her heart.

With the swiftness of a man born to decision, Julius had assessed the situation and found it as Lamaire claimed. He shifted slightly so his servant could attend to the wound, pressing the makeshift pad over it to staunch the flow of blood. "You have been hurt, and your arm will be devilishly stiff for a while, but nothing else. My love…"

Words choked him. He could not imagine a world without his beautiful wife in it, not his world at any rate.

The sound of thundering feet came from the corridor outside and someone pounded on the door before, with a curse as good as anything Julius could devise, Augustus slammed in to the accompaniment of splintering wood. "What in hell happened here?"

"Someone tried to kill us, but Lamaire discovered him and shot him." Julius glanced up at his valet. "Who sent you?"

Lamaire met his eyes with total candor. Or what looked like candor. "I am a French Protestant, as I told you."

Julius wasn't sure he believed him, but wherever he had come from, his manservant was loyal to him. He would discover more later, but now Eve was his main concern. She was crying now, tears pouring down her cheeks, and her body trembled with shock. Ignoring the blood that stained them both, Julius held her close, refusing to let her go until Lamaire had completed his task.

Augustus examined the room as other guests poured in, no doubt keen to see the damage for themselves. Julius was not at all concerned with his state of undress, but Eve might not want so many people to see her naked, so he grabbed the nearest piece of cloth, which happened to be the silk bedcover, and pulled it up to hide her breasts.

Not all the tears came from Eve.

* * * *

Considering someone had actually shot at her, Eve felt strangely calm. Sitting in one of the many small parlors adorning this side of the house, she contemplated her dish of tea, decided she did not really want it, and patted her husband's hand instead. With her left arm set in a snowy white sling, she could not take his hand in both of hers, but settled for a reassuring smile. She did not truly need the sling, but it seemed to calm Julius, so she tolerated it. Besides, her arm was very sore now.

Once she'd recovered from the shock of finding so many people in her bedroom and realizing the dampness she lay in was not a part of her disordered dream but a pool of blood, she had remained the most steady person in the room. A near shave with death could do that.

The shouting was something else, until Julius had risen from the bed and demanded, through his teeth, that everybody leave except his manservant and his brother. Since he'd given no heed to his nudity or his mother's protestations for him to cover himself, they'd done so in short order.

Now, pampered and cosseted, Eve sat in an indecently luxurious but softly draped gown next to Julius, who seemed to be having difficulty releasing her hand.

"Are you sure the journey will not overset you, my love?" he asked for the umpteenth time.

She shook her head, trying not to show her weariness. He insisted on leaving that very day. They would reach Chatsworth before nightfall, where the duke would give them a bed for the night, and then travel on toward Hampshire in the morning. Julius would not rest until they had shaken the dust of the Abbey from their shoes, so she had smiled and told him she would be glad to. He needed to leave and give her a severe cosseting, so she would put up with any discomfort for his sake. That was what loving couples did.

Lamaire had disappeared, another concern for Julius, who had set queries in train to discover him. The valet had undoubtedly saved Eve's life, but after revealing he had a perfectly functional command of English, he had calmly set out for the kitchens and promptly left the house. Nobody knew when or how, but the household had been in such uproar after he had announced the Countess of Winterton had been shot that nobody could be very surprised at the circumstance.

Downstairs, the servants' hall had erupted into a mass of people rushing about like headless chickens. The Duchess of Kirkburton had been obliged to go downstairs and command order, since her husband told her he was busy elsewhere, namely, supporting his daughter-in-law.

The remainder of the guests had agreed to an informal breakfast and lingered, ears flapping for any juicy gossip. Despite the uproar, Julius remained steady and in control, issuing orders with a cool air of command that reminded anyone who might have forgotten he was the next master of the Abbey and as such, his word was law.

"If you carry me to the carriage, I will object," Eve said. "Strenuously."

Julius favored her with a warm smile. "If you do not lean on me, heavily, I will carry you."

Eve knew when she was beaten. "Very well," and added, with emphasis, "my lord."

Triumph warmed her when he gave a sharp bark of laughter.

Her mother frowned at her. She had decided to remain here, a wise decision in the circumstances. She wanted her husband to herself. Except for Caro, of course, who would accompany them, travelling in her own carriage with her nursemaids and attendants. Caro had pouted at Julius's decision, but despite her pleading, he had remained firm.

Eve had not asked her husband to put her above his daughter, but this tangible reminder of what he told her melted her heart. She could not deny a little peace and quiet spent in her husband's arms would do her more good than any amount of physic. A small child would not increase her comfort.

Augustus entered the room, frowning mightily, and gave the ladies a perfunctory bow. His dark red coat strained over his shoulders, as if his muscles were longing to free him of the constraining cloth. "I'm afraid your errant servant is nowhere to be found, and his horse is missing from the stables."

"I had no notion he had a horse," Julius responded.

"It might be one of yours," Augustus conceded, "But I assumed you did not want him taken up for horse theft, after his service to you."

Julius gave a decisive nod. "Of course. Let it be. But I would like to know where he went."

"As would we all." Augustus glanced around and found a chair. Only Eve's mother and Julius remained in the room now, after the invasion of so many people wanting to see for themselves Eve's injury was minor. The shooting would start later the following day, the duke making the great concession that the house was in too much disturbance for them to commence today. The guests had plenty to occupy them.

Augustus heaved a heavy sigh. "At least there are no potential brides in here."

Julius chuckled. "Setting their sights at you, are they, dear brother?"

"Precisely. Two kinds of hunting are taking place in this house. Game birds and husbands. When I arrived I recalled you telling me they were here for you. Now you're out of the picture, you've put me dead in their sights." He nodded at Mrs. Merton. "Present company excepted, of course."

Eve suppressed a snort as Augustus took on the unmistakable appearance of harried prey. If he'd had long ears, they'd be flattened against his skull. "Thank you, ma'am. Much appreciated. However I fancy I will take my leave before the end of the week. I do not hunt, and I have no desire to become the hunted."

"What will they do?" Julius mused.

"Tear each other to pieces, I imagine," Augustus said. He waved a hand. "In any case, it's no concern of mine. I merely came to assure myself you were on the mend, Eve."

"I'm fine," she said, having repeated the same sentiment many times before during the course of the morning. "I'll do."

"What about Helena?" Julius demanded. "She is refusing to come with us. Will you take charge of her?"

Augustus raised a brow. "I doubt she will need me. She says she'll be fine here, for the time being, and she promises to withstand any blandishments our mother might throw her way. Likewise, commands."

"I have a mind to settle an annuity on her," Julius said. "She has her portion, of course, but that is set aside for her marriage. My only fear is she will choose to live apart from us all and dwindle into spinsterhood. She deserves better."

"She does." Augustus twitched his neckcloth. Although not as well dressed as Julius, Augustus still made a fine show, although he appeared uncomfortable in his formal coat and waistcoat and snowy white linen. Every now and then he fidgeted, as if trying to get comfortable. "But if that is her choice, she should be allowed the freedom to make it."

Julius paused, the silence in the room complete before he spoke. "You're right. I have never considered the matter before. What if she wants to be alone? I will make arrangements for a suitable annuity. She may do as she wishes with it, so long as she doesn't give it to our mother."

"You can make that a condition of the gift," Augustus said. "You underestimate our sister sometimes, Julius. Given the right weapons, Helena is perfectly capable of coping with most obstacles thrown in her way."

Augustus was repeating ideas Eve had, but had not broached with Julius yet. Helena did not appear to her to be the kind of helpless female who needed a man's support every inch of the way. Maybe Julius had grown used to caring for her. She kept still, unwilling to affect Julius's decision. Unless he made the wrong one, of course.

"Do you plan to stay in England this time?" he asked now.

Augustus frowned. "Not if all the hounds of hell were after me. My work is nowhere near done. I came home because every now and then I have to. Now I've done my duty and congratulated you on your nuptials, I'll be on my way."

"In the summer?"

"I've travelled in worse conditions." Augustus shrugged.

Eve recalled something Augustus had said. "You wanted to meet with us, did you not?"

"As I am doing." That crease appeared between her brother-in-law's brows once more. "Ah, there was something else, but I daresay it is nothing. It can wait. A small matter I wanted to clear up before I went on my travels."

"If it's a small matter, we might as well clear it up now," Julius pointed out. He leaned back, crossing his legs at the knee. "Out with it."

"Very well. It was merely a confusion of dates. In the documents I discovered in Rome, there was mention of the children." He glanced at Eve's mother. "I take it you are aware of the whole situation surrounding Eve's birth?"

The lady gave a regal nod. "Naturally." Her jaw tensed, as if she were gritting her teeth.

Augustus spread his hands. "I like everything precise, details in order. The confusion probably lies with the haste with which the events emerged. I have records of two more children. Perhaps, but the document is hand written by one of Maria Rubio's servants and could be forged or mistaken. I will of course furnish you with a copy before I leave. The other children, the ones you have discovered, are listed. Since the letter is damaged, torn in several places and worn with age where the paper was folded, it is difficult to interpret, but the letter seems to list Eve's birth as January and not August."

Mrs. Merton's sharp gasp interrupted him. Muffy, who had behaved impeccably since he came to the Abbey sprang to life, jumping up and placing his paws on his mistress's lap.

Augustus watched her, as did Julius. At times like these, the similarities between the brothers grew more apparent—the perceptive, sharp blue eyes, the inherent power, leashed in Julius's case, carelessly displayed in Augustus.

"You have something to say, ma'am?" Julius said.

Tears gleamed in Eve's mother's eyes. She swallowed heavily before she spoke, then sat up straight. "I decided to let matters lie after my husband died," she said, explaining nothing. "But I needed—oh, I know I have done wrong! I never meant matters to go this far!"

Although tears ran unchecked, nobody rushed to help her. Julius tensed, his hand tightening around Eve's. "From the beginning, if you please, ma'am."

Mrs. Merton turned her attention to Julius and gazed at him. She swallowed once more and groped in her pocket for her handkerchief. After dabbing away the wetness, she closed her eyes, and breathed deeply, her bosom rising and falling rapidly. She opened her eyes and met Julius's gaze directly. "I will tell you the truth, although I do not know what we will do after." She flicked a glance at Eve, her eyes guilty, and then turned her attention back to Julius as if nobody else existed. "You know most of the story now. How we went to Rome and took charge of a baby girl."

"We do," Augustus murmured.

She ignored him as if she had not heard him. "We balanced the sin of lying against the sin of leaving the baby to certain death." She spared Eve another glance. "But I had fallen in love with the mite. I wanted her, could not bear to think of her death. That much you know."

Julius nodded, his mouth tight.

"What you do not know is I was pregnant, but so early in my pregnancy I did not realize it until a month after we had agreed to take the baby girl. I gave birth in July, in France. My baby was robust and healthy but despite our care, the baby we took charge of sickened and died. We gave the baby the same name as the dead child. And when I had recovered, we came home."

"Why did you not record Eve's birth as earlier?" Augustus said.

"I could not bear any more lies." Eve's mother clasped her hands tightly together, the skin turning white under the pressure of her fingers. "I saw the death of the baby as punishment. I wanted to tell them, to send a letter, and to return the money they had given us for the child's care. I had not known it, but Maria Rubio had given my husband a considerable sum when he told them he was nothing short of indigent. I insisted he gave me the money, so I could return it. But instead, I bought an annuity."

She lowered her head. "I wanted it for a dowry for you, Eve. The lawyer drew it up so my husband could not touch the capital. He said that was normal in such settlements. I do not know, but even then I welcomed it, because I had realized my husband's inability to handle money. When he died, he left us penniless. If not for the money from the annuity, we would have all starved." Tears were dripping off her nose, but she made no effort to use the handkerchief crumpled in her lap.

Eve swallowed. "I would not have had you go through this for anything, Mama. You did what was right."

"I did not!" Her mother lifted her tear-ravaged face and confronted her daughter. "I should have told them their baby was dead, instead of passing you off as her for so many years. I did not want to tell you, but you found out, and I let you believe it. I should have told you the truth, but the knowledge you were more than people thought you gave you the confidence you so lacked. Without that, you would never have held your head up in Appleton society. You would have shrunk away. And Eve, you are so beautiful that would have been a crime."

"Another point on which we agree," Julius said.

Although he sounded perfectly steady, Eve detected a note of concern in his voice. Immediately she turned all her attention to him. "Does the news bother you? Does this make our marriage invalid?"

"By no means," he said. "In any case, I will marry you as many times as I need to if there is any doubt. I married Eve Merton. You are still that woman. The date of your birth is accurately recorded. That you had a foster sister you knew nothing about has no effect on the matter."

He was right. Her mother's slip in recording her true birth date instead of the feigned one had put everything right.

"I stole from the Stuarts," her mother moaned now. "I have caused this. I had no idea people would come after you. They gave us a copy of the marriage lines, but what are copies? Anyone could have drawn that up. It was enough for me that you—your sister—was in danger. For the rest, I cared not."

Eve believed her. Her mother had done what she thought was best. "Where is the baby now?"

"Buried in an obscure churchyard in France."

"Under what name?" Augustus rapped out.

Mrs. Merton lifted her chin. "Eve Stuart. The name of her death is accurately recorded. I left a letter and copies of the documents with the priest. We had the baby interred under Catholic law. That seemed appropriate, since she was born into that faith."

"I want details," Augustus said.

Julius sent him a smile. "You see, Augustus is my secret weapon."

"I'll tell Val before I leave," Augustus said. "He can tell the others. I'll pay a visit to the churchyard and get the relevant documents. Then you may let the truth be known." He turned a glare on to his brother. "You, Julius, are no longer directly involved. Your duty is to your wife, the daughter of a country vicar."

"So it is." Julius turned his head and met Eve's gaze. "That will make you safe. Once they know who you truly are, nobody will pursue you. Except me."

A burden had fallen away from him. He seemed lighter, closer to his age instead of appearing bowed with care or covered with a fine veneer, a mask he used to hide behind. The true Julius, the one she had only seen in the privacy of their bedroom emerged to encompass her in love and care. This Julius was the man she loved. This one was the one she wanted.

Julius spoke again, solely to her. "We will go home, and I will take care of you. In the spring, or maybe the autumn, we will go to court and have you presented. You may wish to do some shopping. I will visit my father from time to time, to ensure I am up to date with the affairs of the estate. You'll like the house in Hampshire. It's smaller and more comfortable."

"What about my mother?" she asked. Her mother's distress filled the room, although she had kept her voice soft and her sobs quiet.

"We'll buy her the house recently vacated by Mr. King. She may visit us when she pleases."

"The cause?" she asked, because she had to.

"The Jacobites, you mean?" He hesitated, and she spoke before he could.

"You must continue," she said. "I cannot see you without that purpose. You have invested too much in it."

He stared at her. "Not if it interferes with you. I want to broadcast the details of your birth to anyone who needs to hear it."

"Agreed," said Augustus. "I'll make a stop in France on my way back to Rome and send you the results."

"I'd appreciate that." Julius covered both her hands with his own and smiled into her eyes. "Nothing matters as much as your safety. Nothing matters more than my love for you."

Hearing it spoken so clearly, so sincerely in the presence of others made Eve burst into tears.

* * * *

The summer day blazed into the windows of the morning room. Eve got to her feet and crossed to the window, gazing out in pleasure at the closely cropped grass and the neatly trimmed roses. She had helped to prune them that morning, delighting in the fragrant blooms. They had red roses and white, symbols of the royal houses that had caused such strife in the world, interspersed with pink and apricot blooms.

Julius came up behind her and rested his hands either side of her waist. "I'm glad you like it here."

"How could I not, when you are here?" Turning in his arms, she lifted her head for his kiss, confident her unspoken request would be fulfilled.

When she raised her hands to put them on his shoulders, she flinched, reminded of her rapidly healing wound. At once he broke the kiss and made a soothing sound at the back of his throat. "You should not have stayed in the garden so long."

"Nonsense! A little gentle exercise will do me good."

He raised a brow. "I can provide all the gentle exercise you need."

"That you can, my love. That you can."

Coda

Lamaire met his employer in a small churchyard in an obscure part of London. The man stood, staring at the gravestones, paying no attention until he came up to him.

"It is done?" he asked.

"Yes, my lord. It is done, and the lady is safe. You were right to suspect the man would not give up once his agent was dead. He sent another, who is also dead."

"It appears we were mistaken in the lady. She is not who we thought she was."

Lamaire watched the tall, lean figure moodily gazing at the crooked stones, their legends covered with lichen and moss and completely illegible. "She is not. This means Lord Winterton is no longer involved in the cause."

The man turned to face him, his dark eyes cynical. "Oh, he is, Lamaire, never doubt that. And it is about to get worse."

Keep reading for a special sneak peek of another book in the Emperors of London series!

Dilemma In Yellow Silk

It is up to the Emperors of London to protect the throne—without risking their hearts…

Governess Eve Merton would have fallen into serious trouble on her walk home if a handsome stranger had not stopped to help her. But when Mr. Vernon gives her a lift on his horse, he makes no secret of his attraction. As a well brought-up young lady, Eve does her best not to notice, but when he sets about courting her, she knows she's in trouble. For she has a secret: she is the daughter of a deposed king, which means not only is she without a dowry, but also that her life is in danger…

Little does Eve know that Mr. Vernon has secrets of his own. In truth, his name is Julius, Lord Winterton, and he's well aware that Eve is the offspring of the Old Pretender. In order to save his sister, he must convince Eve to wed—though he wants nothing to do with love. But as the two grow closer and an attempt is made on Eve's life, Julius may realize that fighting his heart's true desire is a battle most pleasurably surrendered…

A Lyrical e-book on sale now!

Learn more about Lynne at
http://www.kensingtonbooks.com/author.aspx/31603

Chapter 1

A cloud of dust puffed out of the window of one of the state apartments at Haxby Hall. It was about time someone shook out the rugs.

Standing at her drawing-room window, Viola Gates had a good vantage point of the great building, the pride of the neighborhood. By her reckoning, the cleaning team had reached the double salon.

She turned around to face the other occupant of the room.

"What are they doing, girl?" her father asked.

"Bottoming," she said succinctly. "Nobody bottoms like Mrs. Lancaster." She cast a backward glance at the hall. "I should go and help, since it's your fault the marquess is coming."

Her father chuckled. "They didn't expect him for another month. More fool they. And do you know why he is coming?"

She turned her attention to his heavily bandaged foot, wondering why he was stating the obvious. "To see you, Papa. You're an old retainer."

He snorted. "I'm a bit more than that, my girl. I'm related."

"In a way." He was a cousin of a cousin of a cousin. Her father had used the nebulous connection many years ago, and the previous marquess had given him the position of land steward here. Well, not land steward immediately, but he'd gained the position, and he wasn't about to give it up any time soon.

Situations like his often ran in families, but since she was the only child, they weren't about to give her the job. "Do you think they'll use your broken ankle as an excuse to force you into retirement?"

Her father shook his head. "Not a chance." He fidgeted, wincing when his foot shifted on the padded footstool. Mrs. Lancaster had brought it from the house for his use while he recovered. She'd always been a bit sweet on Viola's papa, but he wasn't buying her careful solicitude. Not yet, at any rate. She wouldn't surrender her position at Haxby yet. If she married him, she would probably have to retire, and she was queen of the hall, except when the marchioness was in residence.

"His lordship is sick and tired of London. Any excuse will serve to get him back. He's probably made out I'm at death's door. That's the actual reason he's coming."

The Gates household had heard the marquess was coming yesterday. From what she knew of the current incumbent of the Strenshall title, that information meant he'd arrive soon.

Her father was right. The family had lingered in London this year. His lordship was probably aching to get back to the country. Viola should really go to the hall to help.

The drawing room she currently stood in was beautifully neat and tidy, its comfortable furnishings inviting guests to take their ease. They did not want for visitors, especially since her father's recent fall. Nobody expected George Gates, who was perfectly at ease on a horse, to fall, much less suffer a tumble bad enough to cause his horse distress. However, he had, and now both participants were recovering in their respective residences. The land would hardly go to rack and ruin in the two months it would take her father to fully recover.

The great hall drew her. Mrs. Lancaster would need all the help she could get. Her father was comfortably ensconced in his favorite armchair with the newspapers that had been brought to the hall fresh off the mail. After tomorrow, the staff would keep them at the hall for the use of his lordship. Her father would only receive them in the afternoon.

Apart from that small hitch, estate managers at Haxby tended to live well. They even had the use of this house for the duration of her father's tenure, though he owned a perfectly good one in nearby Scarborough. Too far to travel when his impatient lordship required his presence.

George Gates hated fuss and bother. The fewer people who disturbed him, the better he liked it. And while he was off his feet, he said, he could concentrate on going through the books. He had the overview of not just Haxby Hall, but all his lordship's properties. That made for a lot of paperwork.

"Perhaps you should open one of those books, Papa," Viola said.

He scowled at the stack of account books on the side table awaiting his attention, as they had for the last week. "Perhaps. Account books have never held much appeal for me, but the sooner I start, the sooner I'm done. Your dear mother always proved of signal help there."

"She was more dutiful than I am, I fear," Viola confessed. "But if you wish it, I'll take half." She heaved a heartfelt sigh, letting her shoulders rise and fall.

Her father chuckled. "You could never abide adding up, but be warned; I'll make use of you later." He made a scooting motion with his hand. "Go, girl. Make the housekeeper happy."

Laughing, Viola hurried from the room, making her way to the front door before her father could change his mind.

Had she been in the city, she'd have had to don gloves, shawl, cloak, bonnet, fan, all the accoutrements of required outdoor wear, even on this glorious summer day. Instead, she crammed on her old straw hat to protect her complexion from the sun, shoved her feet into her sturdy leather shoes, and set off. Her small hooped petticoat kept the fabric of her gown away from her body. When she ran, holding on to the hoop to keep her skirts from swinging, a comfortable breeze gusted around her legs.

The hall was less than half a mile away, a distance she accomplished in very little time, around ten minutes by her reckoning. The side door to the hall was never locked, except when the marchioness took it into her head to have every door and window secured. Viola went in and grinned at the footman standing inside.

Tranmere was in full uniform, the blue-and-silver livery blinding in the sun.

"That must be hot," she commented.

"Don't want his lordship to catch me out," Tranmere said, his deep voice booming across the spacious hall.

"You could always take the coat off and then put it back on when you hear he's arrived. He won't come in this way."

Tranmere grimaced. "I can't. Mrs. Lancaster's orders. She wanted to inspect us all, although it's not her place."

"Don't let her hear you say that."

He grinned, the expression revealing the severe lack of teeth on his lower jaw. In his chequered past, Tranmere had engaged in prize fighting and had, so he claimed, won a trophy and a purse for each tooth. "She's all right, as long as you do what she says."

While they spoke, Viola was unbuckling her heavy outdoor shoes and putting on the light slippers she used inside the hall. Haxby had too many treasures to risk damaging the floors or the rugs. Mrs. Lancaster would have her hide if she caught Viola indoors with outdoor shoes on.

With a cheeky wave to the footman, who had taken her advice and slipped off the heavy coat, she ran up the wrought-iron staircase. It was built on a cantilevered spiral, one of the wonders of the house, based on the Tulip Stairs at Greenwich. Not that Viola had seen the Tulip Stairs, but she'd accompanied Mrs. Lancaster on so many guided tours she knew the words by heart. Almost without thinking about them.

Along the corridor, she opened a jib door and scampered up the servants' staircase. The only stair she was forbidden to use was the grand staircase in the main hall. She rarely went that way, and in any case, she had no desire to use it. If anyone asked, she'd touch an imaginary forelock and tell them it was too good for a servant girl like her. But in reality, the estate manager was more than a servant.

If Viola had insisted on her consequence, she'd have found herself very lonely indeed. She preferred to let everyone forget she was a daughter of a cousin of a cousin. There might even be another cousin in the way there.

Upstairs she opened the door at the top and entered the great state rooms. These were the absolute pinnacle of the house's grandeur and wealth. Public openings centered here, and when the family were in residence, they would hold balls and gatherings here. Viola had attended a few, but always standing at the back, not drawing attention to herself.

In the first room, she paused. The covers were off here, the glass, furniture, and china buffed to a fine dustless sheen. From the Meissen figures on the elaborately carved marble fireplace to the glittering crystal drops on the chandelier, the room looked pristinely perfect.

The rooms were set in a line—enfilade people called it—and when all the doors were open, a person could see right to the end. At the moment, the staff were opening the doors as they moved to the next room in the sequence.

The second chamber was the huge double room, so called because it could be split into two spacious rooms by using the panels embedded into the walls on each side. The current marquess preferred to keep it open. He only used it for large gatherings and when he wanted to impress people. A couple of maids were dusting, holding each ornament carefully while plying the feather dusters. Both greeted Viola with smiles, and she nodded back before moving on. The cleaning army had finished with the music room, too, so she passed on.

Mrs. Lancaster and most of her cohorts carried out their duties in the library. The family only kept precious books here, the ones they rarely read. Between each bookcase was a marquetry wooden panel depicting a literary figure. Mrs. Lancaster was applying a liberal amount of honey and lavender polish to Chaucer's nose. "Ah," she said, looking over the tops of her spectacles at Viola. "I wondered when you'd get here." Since she was standing at the top of a stepladder, she could look down at Viola. The rest of her staff, half a dozen maids, all sweeping, buffing and dusting. "Could you go into the music room and check the instruments? The tuner came last week, but nobody else can try them."

Viola had undergone torturous music lessons because one of the marquess's daughters, Lady Claudia, had hated learning, and Viola had to help her. Claudia still avoided musical instruments when possible, although her twin, Lady Livia, could hammer out a piece if forced to it.

Viola had hated the lessons, but once she could pick out a tune, she changed her mind. Not that she would ever make a professional musician, but she was at the level of a decent amateur. None of the maids could play.

Delighted she was spared the dirtier work, she went into the music room.

The instruments here were precious. A gold-encrusted harp stood in the center of the Aubusson carpet. She padded over to it and tested the strings. They sounded all right to her, but she didn't play the harp. Such a lovely instrument, with nobody to play it.

The room also contained an old set of virginals dating back to the time of James the First. Viola knew better than to touch that. It was a relic, not a real instrument. The king had presented it to one of his gentlemen as a token of his thanks for some favor long forgotten. A case contained wind instruments, but they would be fine. A mandolin stood in one corner.

Viola turned to the harpsichord. The inner lid bore a painting of a woman dressed as the Muse of music, Euterpe. Viola lifted it carefully and put the prop under it. The strings gleamed, daring her to touch them.

She dared.

Sitting on the broad padded bench-like seat, she ran her hands over the white-and-black keys. They trilled. She did some scales, up and down, the automatic movement of her hands lulling her into a state where she could link with the keys. Each note sank into her. She absorbed them and made them hers. She could have stopped there. It sounded fine.

The piece of sheet music propped on the stand was a two-hander. She could always play one part of it, but mischief led her into doing something else. The locals had a wonderful collection of music, some of it scurrilous, some quaint. She started with a few quaint ones, and when she sang the verses, a few voices rose in song from the next room.

How far could she take them? An urge took her to hear the ditties in this beautiful treasure-chest of a state room.

Viola began with a few more local songs, the innocent kind about lovers losing their ladies, ladies losing their soldier lovers and running away with the gypsies. Moving closer to her goal, she played a tune about a poacher and his boy.

The song described poaching from a more innocent age, when peasants snared creatures for the pot instead of gangs of organized ruffians stealing animals by the dozen. It bled innocence. Except in the last verses, when the song revealed the uncomfortable punishment demanded in those days—the stocks, where a man could die if the crowd took a dislike to him.

She grew a little bawdier in her choice. Not all the way, or Mrs. Lancaster would call a halt to her playing, but the maids would work well for a little entertainment. Mrs. Lancaster would not have been the superb housekeeper she was if she had not understood that.

They sang. She joined in, singing of maids lying in the fields, tossing up their skirts for their swains and paying for their sins, or simply marrying. The keys, cool to the touch, warmed, the ivory taking on the heat from her fingers as she progressed.

She'd played with the notion of finding someone who could help her assuage the need she occasionally felt, but then dismissed the notion as foolish. At her age, she would probably never marry. The prospect didn't worry her as it might another. In fact, she had agreed with her father that she was probably better remaining a spinster. She would inherit a comfortable income and a house, the one her father owned in Scarborough, so she would not want. But sometimes, when she allowed herself to think about it, her body heated and the memory of kisses seared her.

Several people next door joined in, so she continued on to a local song she'd found in a gossip paper recently. At first she played just the tune, a folk tune from another part of the country. Many people hereabouts considered Yorkshire the only part of the country that mattered. Although loyal to the county where she lived, Viola was aware of what was going on elsewhere. She had to be. Her father and she shared more knowledge than most, and they had to maintain a certain level of vigilance.

This tune spoke of the King, and the other king—the one in Rome—and the confusion between the two together with the futility of choosing one side or the other. The cheerful jig-like tune belied the underlying cynicism in the words.

This one took some concentration, for she had only just learned it. She failed to notice the silence that had fallen until too late.

* * * *

Marcus loved coming home. He always regarded Haxby as his home, not the London mansion his family occupied during the season. This time he'd come with his father alone, a fast journey to see Gates and arrange affairs for the estate manager's period of infirmity.

The gatekeepers barely got the huge iron gates open in time, but the coachman was stopping for no one and he swept through. Any faster and he'd be taking the corner on two wheels.

The impetus pressed Marcus against the side of the coach. "You need to tell Harrison not to travel so fast," he said to his father.

"Ah, but his thoughts of seeing his sweetheart engross him," the marquess said, smiling. "He left her behind to take us to London. We'll find someone else to take us back."

Marcus groaned. "Do I have to return? It's the end of the season. Surely there is no need to have me there."

"Your sister is marrying, and your mother is on the verge of betrothing two of your sisters. What do you think?"

The curse of being the eldest of a large family. They expected Marcus to wish them well and substitute for his father, if necessary, when he'd prefer to stay here. He'd had enough of London and its intrigues. With the season nearly over, he'd hoped to remain at home, one of the main reasons for accompanying his father.

"Could they not marry from home?"

"If they marry at all." He cleared his throat. "Besides, I have something particular to discuss with Gates. It seemed an opportune moment to do so."

Another sweep of the drive and the house came into view. As always, Marcus feasted his eyes on the place. The central structure boasted a tower in the middle capped by a lantern dome. It was not the largest of the great houses in the county, but to his mind it was the most beautiful. The central block rose a story above the side wings, the huge pilasters fronting the façade creating a grand display.

When his father died—may that be many years hence—Marcus would inherit this and all the responsibilities that went with it. The notion of becoming the marquess had always shocked him, an emotion he kept to himself, as not worthy of the heir to the marquisate. Hundreds of people would depend on him for their livelihood.

They swept up the elm-lined drive, the spaces between the trees affording glimpses of the parkland beyond. The occasional sheep, kept here to keep the grass down between scything, lifted its head to watch the coach going past. The sight warmed him. This—not the house in London—was home for Marcus.

"Your mother says she will look out for a likely bride for you," his father said.

Marcus sighed. "I would like nothing better than to select my own bride. I swear I will choose someone suitable."

"She has eyes and ears that penetrate further than ours. She knows the most promising young women about to make their debut in society." Lord Strenshall shifted in his seat. "Devil take it, these seats are damnably uncomfortable. I'll have this carriage reupholstered when we return to town."

"There are people perfectly capable of doing the job locally," Marcus pointed out. "Then you won't have to pay London prices."

"But we need to get back in it." His father sighed. "Perhaps I can wait until the summer."

Considering this was June, Marcus considered summer well under way. The day was fine, and they had come home. It had taken three days, since they could move faster without the ladies to cater for. Both Marcus and his father preferred to travel for longer and eat quickly rather than linger on the road.

"We'll have a shooting party, come August," his father said.

That gave Marcus a clear eight weeks until he needed to concern himself with entertaining guests, including the ones who wanted to marry him. He didn't fool himself. They wanted his title and his family name as much, if not more, than his person. While not exactly unprepossessing, he wasn't the kind of person who enjoyed dallying with ladies when there was work waiting for him.

There was always work. Mostly Marcus told himself he didn't mind, but sometimes he fretted at the bit. When he dreamed, he soared free, but he rarely remembered his dreams. Just the sensation of flying remained for a few moments after he woke.

While here he'd talk to the gamekeeper, and ensure the coverts were well stocked. "If Gates is—" He couldn't finish the sentence. He'd known Gates all his life—and his daughter, although they had drawn apart recently. Necessary, because they lives were destined to take different paths. His duty took him somewhere she couldn't join him. Much to his regret. But he would not burden the free spirit he remembered with the duties that belonged to him.

She didn't deserve that.

The carriage drew up outside the front door and the efficient machine that ran Haxby Hall clicked into action, its cogs running to the inevitable conclusion. When the liveried footman unfolded the steps of the carriage, Marcus got out and stood before the magnificence of his house with his hat in his hand. The butler stood at the top of the stone staircase. As his father climbed down to join him, Marcus took his first step, and then hesitated. The spirit of rebellion stirred within him, as if it had remained dormant until now.

"I'll go around the side way," he said.

"Trying to catch out the servants?" his father said with a grin.

Marcus returned the smile. "Something of that nature."

He would avoid going through the "Good afternoon, my lord" ritual the footman, and then the butler, and then the maids would go through. His father enjoyed it as little as he did, but Marcus didn't have to endure it yet.

He strode off to the side of the house. That in itself was a fair walk, but one he enjoyed, as he reacquainted himself with the place. He'd been in London too long. In November he would refuse to rush to town at the start of the Parliamentary season. What was the point? They never got anything done.

Scents assailed him as his feet crunched on the gravel path. Flowers, mostly, the kind women enjoyed, but they made a fine show in the beds at the front of the house. His mother had decided to remodel, and they were looking into replacing the formal Tudor gardens with a more informal stretch of parkland.

While the house would appear more à la mode, Marcus would miss the bright displays. Perhaps they could keep something. He wanted the flowers.

The stone walls were not entirely even, partly from design and partly because the Palladian façade covered a much older house. Parts of the central block dated from Tudor times, when a courtier of Elizabeth won the land for singular service to his queen. Marcus's grandfather had extended the house, making the E shape into a closed double quadrangle and adding to the wings on either side. He'd created the grand enfilade of state rooms from a hodgepodge of salons, creating the house Marcus had grown up in.

Marcus descended a staircase, opened a door, and entered the servants' quarters. He looked to neither right nor left as he took the well-remembered shortcut to the side door. That cut out traversing the wings. He wasn't in the passage long enough to create a commotion; in fact, nobody saw him as far as he knew. He was into the inner courtyard before anyone could register his presence.

A short walk along the stone paved path took him to the side entrance, and the shortcut to his rooms. His valet had set off early that morning, so he could arrive early and have everything ready for his master. Marcus prayed that included a decanter of burgundy and something to eat. Freshly baked bread and local cheese would not come amiss.

Then, fortified, he'd return to being the Earl of Malton and join his father for whatever duties awaited him.

Entering the side door without ceremony, Marcus enjoyed the sight of a large footman scrambling into his silver-laced coat. "My lord!"

"Good afternoon, Tranmere. How is Gates?"

Tranmere stared at him and then found his voice. "Broken ankle, my lord. He's resting at his house."

"Ah." Well. That was one concern dealt with. Gates had fallen from his horse and hurt himself, but the messenger had left in such haste they had not ascertained precisely what was the matter. Marcus had been glad to use the excuse, but worry for the estate manager had also driven him to discover for himself.

Leaving the man stammering, Marcus climbed the stairs two at a time, not giving the poor footman a chance to sort himself out. His childish amusement was not worthy of him, he knew that. But the welcome had suited him in his present mood more than the ceremonial one awaiting his father.

Pausing at the state rooms, he decided to go through them. His rooms were equidistant if he took the corridor with guest rooms or the state rooms.

He opened the first door. He recognized the sign that maids were about. The door at the end was closed, but the others were open. That meant they'd finished up to the closed door.

Marcus grinned. Mrs. Lancaster would be furious he'd caught them working. She preferred the family to think that fairies dealt with their needs, invisible ones preferably.

Notes of music drifted to him, so delicate his fanciful notion of fairies became real. Through the first salon, the anteroom, and then the main salon, the huge space that never got warm in winter unless they packed it with people. Then the third. The music room.

He paused. The maids chattered in the library. Some sang along with the music. Smiling, he tiptoed across the parquet floor to the connecting door and closed it as silently as he could.

Meet the Author

Lynne Connolly was born in Leicester, England, and lived in her family's cobbler's shop with her parents and sister. She loves all periods of history, but her favorites are the Tudor and Georgian eras. She loves doing research and creating a credible story with people who lived in past ages. In addition to her Emperors of London series she writes several historical, contemporary and paranormal romance series. Visit her on the web at lynneconnolly.com, read her blog at lynneconnolly.blogspot.co.uk, find her on Facebook, and follow her on Twitter @lynneconnolly.

CPSIA information can be obtained
at www.ICGtesting.com
Printed in the USA
BVOW08s2349251016
465986BV00001B/26/P